HOLDING

THE ICED SERIES

KRISTINE ALLEN

Holding: When a player grabs another player's body, sweater, or stick, to prevent them from getting to the puck.

I'm Jordan Beck, goaltender for the Austin Amurs. Holding is my penalty. In my defense, if they get in my crease, they're fair game.

Hockey runs in my blood—literally. Four generations of NHL goaltender greats gives me damn near royalty status, but it's not all it's cracked up to be. Living up to legends can be exhausting. It can also make it difficult to trust women and their motives.

Until Blair.

She had no idea who I was and adamantly refused a relationship—it was perfect.

What sounded good in the beginning quickly got muddled, and before I knew it, we had crossed more lines than an iced puck. Then it all went to sh*t when my ex showed up with my baby on the way. Thinking I was doing the right thing, I ended things with Blair.

Worst mistake ever—I'm miserable. My game is suffering, my team is pissed at me, and I'm on the chopping block if I can't pull out of it. If I can find a way to get her back, I'm holding onto her with both hands.

To Jake Oettinger, Adam Scheel, Matt Jurusik, and Matthew Murray. Some of the most badass goalies to grace the Texas Stars ice. I'm proud to say I watched you get your start in professional hockey. May your careers continue grow by leaps and bounds. Go Stars!

HOLDING

ONE

Jordan

"MOVING ON"—ASKING ALEXANDRIA

"Y ou guys are all assholes," I muttered to my teammates as I stood there in my towel. There was a bunch of chuckles and laughter as everyone enjoyed making a joke out of my emotional upheaval. Fuckers.

"Aww, come on, Beck. You look cute," Alex said as he gripped my shoulder and looked around me at all the photoshopped images taped up in my locker. They'd damn near wallpapered the space. Alex Kosinski and I had become friends shortly after he was traded to us from Montreal.

"Fuck. You."

His grin was contagious, and despite myself, I laughed.

"See? This is why I don't date. You dickheads might've gotten lucky, but I'm no longer willing to gamble like that—and this is why." I wildly gestured at the stupid pics lining my locker. There were bride and groom images with my head and Zena's head photoshopped on them titled "Mr. and Mrs. Jordan Beck." My favorites were the ones with my head photoshopped onto a baby held in parents' arms that also had mine and Zena's heads photoshopped.

Zena had turned out to be a psycho. Don't get me wrong, she is beautiful, successful as a swimsuit model, but absolutely, undeniably, batshit crazy. I made the mistake of going out with her for several months after a bunch of the other single guys started pairing off.

We'd met one of the nights that the guys bailed on me to be with their women. Instead of going home like I should have, I went out to an upscale bar in downtown Austin. I'd had too much to drink, she was hot, and I was horny. Then we'd run into each other at a fundraiser. One thing led to another, and we began seeing each other more and more. Before I knew it, she had her shit on my bathroom counter and tampons under the sink.

I remember I had rationalized that it's normal for a guy to see people around him starting relationships and thinking maybe that's what he wanted too. It didn't hurt that she looked good on my arm.

Until Zena proved me wrong. Boy, did she prove me wrong.

"Hey, I think Beck Junior is cute," Cameron McGregor, smartass extraordinaire and one of our centers with the Austin Amurs, piped in as he pointed at the baby with my face on it. I swung out and back to nut-punch him, but he jerked to the side just in time to miss my fist that would definitely have taken him to his knees. Still, the fucker laughed, but all I could do was shake my head.

"I still can't believe she had the balls to do that shit. I also don't know why you didn't press charges against her," Kristoffer, our team captain, added as he sat on the bench in his towel and briskly scrubbed a second towel over his hair.

"For what? Lying about me proposing? Photoshopping me into a proposal pic?" I muttered with a shake of my head. "My attorney got her to retract everything."

"That's still gotta be defamation of character or slander or something against the law, surely." Alex frowned as he dressed.

"Not worth the ugly press a legal battle would be," I explained.

Jericho Baranov and Dmitry Kalashnik, cousins that were both defensemen, ambled in from the showers, clad the way the rest of us were. Jericho backhanded Dmitry in the ribs and pointed at my display.

"What the fuck?" Dmitry asked through wide-eyed laughter.

"Ask these yahoos." I thumbed over my shoulder to the rest of my teammates that I knew were all involved in my new decorations. Several snickers popped off around the locker room.

Kristoffer ducked his head and dried his feet as he sat on the bench. Being the team captain, he was attempting to hide the fact that he was laughing. Trying to be diplomatic and all.

Dick.

The chuckles continued, but the majority of the ribbing died down as I ripped each image down and wadded them up. With a perfect arc, I shot the wadded-up ball into the nearest trash can.

"He shoots, he scores!" Cameron announced and made crowd noises and cheering. A cheesy grin split his face. "Too bad we don't play basketball."

While I dressed, I ignored all the shit talking and instead finished getting ready.

"What are you doing tonight?" I asked Mikko, one of our left wings, as I dug out my keys and slung my bag over my shoulder. I didn't bother asking Alex, Cameron, or Kristoffer. They were going to be up their girlfriends' asses. Isak Bergström had his wife and two little kids. Everyone else was chilling with family before we flew out for a four-game road trip tomorrow.

"Not a damn thing," Mikko replied, his accent heavier in his fatigue. Though his mother was American, his dad had been from Finland and that was where he was raised. His English was impeccable, but the accent was still there.

In complete agreement, I nodded. All I wanted to do was go home, fall into bed, and sleep.

After saying my goodbyes, I left the practice arena. As I was pulling out of the parking lot, my phone rang, and I smiled before hitting answer. "Hey, Mom."

"Hi honey! What time do you fly out?"

"Too damn early," I grumbled.

"Well, I can't wait to see you!" Mom had moved to Toronto after her and my dad finally divorced. I loved them both, but they were two people not meant to be married.

My father had been an NHL great in his time as his father was before him and his grandfather before that. Dad had met Mom early in his career, but they hadn't had me and my sister until the end of it. Sometimes I wondered if we were the reason their marriage fell apart. I'd rarely seen them truly happy together over the years.

Then again, I think the end to his hockey career had caused a lot of problems with them. Despite the years he played, he'd never really come to terms with it being over—especially considering our family's legacy in the hockey world. In a way, he kind of lost his identity. Beck became a name synonymous with professional hockey. It was what his family was known for and what he believed defined him.

After my parents' divorce, he'd gone through what seemed like a midlife crisis. He married a woman significantly younger than him and started a second family. At first, it pissed me off because his priorities shifted from me and my sister. But I couldn't imagine my life without my youngest siblings. My sister and I survived and we are closer than ever now.

"Me too."

"How are you doing?" Mom knew about the bullshit with Zena. Hell, everyone knew about that shit thanks to social media.

I sighed as I changed lanes. The last thing I wanted to do was rehash my shitshow of a life while driving in lunchtime traffic.

"I'm fine, Mom. Honest." The jury was still out on that one. Feeling betrayed was one thing, but what Zena had done left me feeling violated, despite how relatively minor of an act it had been. "Who are you bringing to the game?"

It was time to change the subject.

"Well, besides your sister, which you already know, I invited my new friend Gillian. We work together, and she's a huge hockey fan. She about had a heart attack when I asked her to go to the game with me. Still, I'm sure she's nowhere near the fan I am." She laughed, and I shook my head with a goofy grin.

"That's cool, I'm glad you're excited to go. And you'll always be my biggest fan."

"Damn straight! And thank you for the tickets. You're so good to me and your sister."

I scoffed. "You're my mother. If I'm playing in your town, you and Everly are getting tickets. Anything for my two favorite women."

She sputtered a laugh. "Don't lay it on too thick."

"Well, I'm hoping if I butter you up enough you'll make me one of your berry pies."

"Ahh, now the truth comes out!"

"You got me," I mock confessed as my mother laughed.

"Okay, well, I need to get back to work. Just wanted to hear my boy's voice and figure out how much time I have to get that berry pie done," she teased.

"Love you, Mom. Tell Everly I said hi and I love her, too," I told her before we ended the call. By the time we hung up, I was entering my neighborhood. It was the same neighborhood where a shit ton of my teammates lived. As soon as a house went on the market, we passed the word and one of the guys snagged it.

I hit the button, and the garage door was rolling up when I approached my home. Slowly, I drove inside. Not gonna lie, it freaked me out a little each time I went in because it seemed like the top of my truck would scrape going in. Thankfully, it never did. Trust me, I'd measured it at least twenty times before I tried the first time.

It was almost November, but central Texas was experiencing what felt like a rebounded summer. In other words, it was hotter than hell. It kind of made me miss my home in the Yukon. No, I really missed it, but there was nothing left for me there. On the other hand, I loved being in Texas because it meant I was an Amur.

"Honey, I'm home," I called out into the empty house, for no reason other than because I had a sick sense of humor. Then again, at one time I truly thought I'd have someone I'd be coming home to. "Did you miss me?" I asked the little succulent my mom had bought me as a housewarming present. She had said they were hard to kill, and I'll be damned if I hadn't kept the little bastard alive for over a year. I named him Herman.

Thirsty, I opened the fridge and stared into it like I had no idea what was there. Wanting a beer but settling for a bottle of water, I closed the door. After cracking the lid off, I guzzled half the bottle. Drinking before a game left me feeling sluggish, and that was something I couldn't afford.

"Alexa, shuffle my favorites," I called out. When she told me she was doing as I asked, I muttered back "Alexa, you're the best girlfriend."

"Hmm, I don't know that one," she replied, and I rolled my eyes. I instructed her to play throughout the house.

I finished the water and tossed the empty bottle in the recycle bin before heading to the bedroom. After I kicked off my shoes, I lined them up on the shelf with the rest. Then I reached up to the top shelf and grabbed my suitcase. Meticulously, I folded each item and arranged it to suit the perfectionist in me. Once everything was packed, I zipped it closed and set it by my bedroom door.

As I made my way through my house, I realized how massive it felt. I bought it with foolish dreams—ones that involved a family being here with me. Instead, all I heard were the sound of my own footsteps. I ignored the pang that hit. Shaking it off, I refolded the blanket on the couch. Bored and hungry, I went back to the kitchen.

An early dinner sounded good. In the freezer were several meals that had been professionally prepped. They sounded as good as anything. A stir fry caught my attention, and I reheated it and sat at the island to eat.

"Alexa, stop," I instructed, and the music stopped. "I have more of a relationship with you than I'll probably ever have with a real woman."

As I chewed, the silence was almost deafening. I should've left the music playing. The last bite was hard to swallow, and I had to grab my second water to wash it down. My shoulders slumped, and I scanned the room.

"I should've gone out with Dmitry after all," I mumbled to the quiet room. Then I glanced at Herman. "You're not much for conversation, are you?"

The puck hit my gloved hand with a resounding *thwack*, and the crowd moaned and booed. Mikko gripped the top of my helmet and shook it with a huge smile. I tossed the puck to the ref. Just as quickly, we were back in play.

One of Toronto's forwards, Slovecky, kept backing up and crowding me into my crease. Tired of his shit, I gave him a shove. When he spun around and tried to come at me, I stood to my full height. At six foot six, I was one of the tallest goaltenders in the league. With skates, I was damn near seven feet of massively padded, pissed-off goalie.

"What? You wanna do this here? I will wipe the ice with your fucking face," I taunted with a sneer.

"Back the fuck up," Dmitry told Davidson, the Toronto player that was puffed up like a goddamn peacock.

"Fuck you!" Davidson turned on him and shoved him with both fists.

Bad move.

Dmitry's satisfied grin exposed his mouthguard with sharp teeth printed on the front, and he was on the other player in a flash. My bulky friend dropped mitts and prepared to have the other guy spitting Chiclets. The refs watched closely, and once the helmets came off and the players hit the ice, they were breaking it up.

As the refs escorted Dmitry and Davidson to the sin bin, number four for Toronto, Jakovich, started running his mouth.

"What's that?" Alex asked. "Your mom said I was good last night? Yeah, she's meeting me after the game!"

Jakovich started toward Alex and tossed his gloves to the ice as Alex and Jericho laughed. Jakovich's teammates shot in front of him and held him back, knowing that an instigated secondary fight would catch them a major. As they skated back to their bench with him, I rolled my eyes.

"Fucker," Alex muttered.

"Tsk, tsk," Cameron interjected. "What would Sydney say if she knew you were meeting up with moms?"

Alex snorted a laugh, and they skated to the bench to change the line before the puck dropped.

For the remainder of the game, I held onto our one-point lead. They didn't call me "The Wall" for nothing. It was well-earned and part of a family tradition. My boys bombarded me in celebration as we all laughed, then headed for the locker room.

We had a few brief interviews by the media as we left the ice. Then it was our coach's turn. With the celly done, Coach left us to clean our rank asses.

I hurried through my shower and dressed so I could meet up with my mom for a couple of hours. When we were on the road, we had a strict curfew, but I'd gotten permission to stay out later because I would be with my family.

"Catch you later! Make sure you hang the DND if you're not alone!" I called out to Mikko who was my roomie. Laughter followed me as I hurried out, tucking in my shirt.

"There's my boy!" I heard my mom before I looked up. I'd asked security to let them into the back hall where our locker room was to wait. My mom's tiny ass was standing with my willowy sister and a chick that looked more my sister's age than my mom's. Suspicion hit me immediately, but I brushed it off.

"Mom!" I said as I scooped her up and swung her around like she was a feather.

"God, no matter how old you get, you're always gonna be a momma's boy," my sister teased. Looking her way, my grin went wicked, and I set Mom down. "No!" Everly said backing away and holding her hands out.

"Too late!" I announced as I scooped her up over my shoulder. She squealed and beat on my back.

"Put me down, you asshole!" Everly demanded, but I ignored her as I turned to our mom.

"And this is my son, Jordan," Mom introduced as she motioned to me. "Jordan, this is my friend Gillian."

"Ma'am," I greeted with a nod. The entire time my sister tried to overpower me, but we both knew it wasn't going to do anything. I chuckled at her attempts.

"Oh please, you're making me feel old. It's Gillian," she corrected with a coy lift of her lips and a slow blink.

Goddamn it, Mom.

"Excuse me, is this man bothering you?" I heard Jericho pipe in behind me and realized several of my teammates were exiting the locker room and heading past us to the door where the bus waited.

"Oh! Hello there. As a matter of fact, he is, but I'm sure you could help me out. Maybe you could take me off his hands," my sister replied in a flirty tone, and I looked over my shoulder to see Jericho leaning

10

down with his hands resting on his thighs. My sister was pushing her blonde hair out of her face as she grinned at him.

I spun to face him, Isak, and Dmitry.

"No!" I practically growled.

"Ohhh sorry, didn't realize you called dibs on this beautiful creature that has poor taste in players," Jericho came back with as he motioned to my jersey that Everly wore.

"This is my sister," I gritted out. I was distracted enough that my sister wiggled loose and to her feet.

"Everly," she clarified as she held her hand out with a brilliant white grin.

I smacked her hand down, but not before Jericho had slipped her a piece of paper. "No!" I repeated to her, then pointed a finger in warning at Jericho.

When the fuck had he had time to write his number down?

"Asshole!" I told him as I made like I was going to go after him, and he took off for the exit with a laugh. Then I turned to glare at my impish sister. "You will *not* call that number!"

Thick black lashes fluttered as she gazed at me coyly. "Why, big brother dear, I would never!"

"I don't think they'll ever change," my mom explained to Gillian who was giggling at the entire exchange.

"Are we ready?" I asked, anxious to get my sister out of there before more of my horny teammates came out.

"I'm parked in the VIP parking." Mom pointed to the doors the opposite direction of the team's exit.

"Lead the way," I said, motioning for the women to go first.

Mom and Gillian started walking but not before Gillian cast me a flirty glance over her shoulder.

Everly fell into step next to me as we followed. "She's cute. And she seems really nice."

"Are you serious? Hell, no. For one, I live in another fucking country now. For two, she's Mom's coworker slash friend. After I banged her and blew her off, I'd never hear the end of it," I adamantly whispered to my shit-stirring sister.

"Well, you can't blame her for wanting to give you another reason to come home." She shot me a cheeky grin as she looped her arm through mine. I couldn't help it, I smiled affectionately down at my little sister.

"Home was the Yukon, but now it's Texas." We'd lived in the Yukon since Dad had retired from the league when I was about five and Everly was three. We considered it home since it was all we remembered.

"Ugh!" She rolled her eyes and hip checked me. "Don't remind me."

As we stepped out in the frigid cold, Everly and I huddled together. While we walked to the car, I leaned down to her ear. "I mean it, don't you dare call Jericho."

Her laughter was downright devious.

TWO

Blair

"SHE'S SO MEAN"—MATCHBOX TWENTY

CENTRAL TEXAS WEATHER WAS BIPOLAR. WE HAD GONE FROM a late summer that had lasted into late October to windy and cold in the span of about a week. Though it had nothing on Midwest winters, I'd grown acclimated to warmer weather since moving to Texas. Freezing, I rushed from my car into the diner.

Exhausted both mentally and physically, I dropped into the seat across from Tori, my best friend since second grade. Shrugging my bag off my shoulder, I tossed it in the booth before I pulled off my beanie, slid down, and rested my head on the back of the cracked seat repaired with duct tape.

"Well, hello to you too, Blair. Coffee?" Tori asked me with a smirk she tried to hide behind her cup.

"A gallon, please," I replied, closing my eyes. Cracking one open, I stared at my friend. "Do I have to go in to work?"

"Well, you could call in sick," my best friend offered with a shrug.

"I should."

"You won't."

"I could."

"You won't."

She was right, I wouldn't.

"Why do you look so put together? It's not fair that you look like that. And how did you get here before me again?" I glared at her for appearing all nice and pretty while I was hanging on by a messy, fraying thread. We both lived equal distance from the diner we met at for breakfast—okay, technically dinner to the daywalker world. It was right across the street from the hospital where we worked nights in the ER. Thanks to self-scheduling, we even made sure we were on the same shifts.

"Well, for one, you took on two extra shifts this week. So, while I've been off the last two nights, you've been working. And I'm certainly not put together, I'm the same hot mess I always am. Hell, this morning I forgot to wash the conditioner out of my hair."

I hated her logic. Also, she was a liar—she was definition of cute and adorable with her curly light brown hair and bright blue eyes.

"Well, if I didn't have three big, fat, stupid credit cards to pay off, I wouldn't have to take on extra hours," I grumbled.

"That's because Hen—"

With a grunt, I held up a hand before she could finish. "Don't say it."

"Okay, then 'he who shall not be named' was a douche and ran up all your cards before—"

"Oh my God," I interrupted. "Can we not talk about him?"

Though she tried her damnedest to hide it—no she really didn't—she chortled.

"Were you two ready to order?" Nettie, our usual before-shift waitress, asked as she set a saucer with an upside-down coffee cup on it in front of me.

"A gallon of coffee and the bacon and cheese omelet. Extra bacon," I rattled off.

"And you?" She turned her attention to Tori who had her mouth twisted as she looked over the menu we probably knew by heart. Finally, she looked up.

"Egg white omelet with all the veggies for me, please," Tori replied.

"You disgust me," I told her as Nettie took the menus and walked off giggling. Tori rolled her eyes at me. Ever since she and Owen had moved in together, she'd gone all health nut on me.

"Back to what I was saying… He's a piece of shit," she said, then gave a definitive nod.

"Ugh. Who are you telling? And you know what was the worst? Even worse than the bills he left me with?"

Yeah, I'd been the one who said I didn't want to talk about my ex, Henry. *Doctor* Henry. The asshole who had run up my credit cards. He was a fucking doctor. He was supposed to be making decent money, not needing my nurse's pay. Too bad his ex-wife got the majority of it, so he'd used me—and I wasn't the only one.

"Do tell," she prompted.

Nettie came back with a carafe of coffee and set it down, then left again.

"The sex sucked," I muttered with a huff.

"What? You were with him for a year and a half, girl! So, you're telling me you had a year and a half of shitty sex and stayed in the relationship? Why didn't I ever know this?" Her eyes bugged, and her mouth hung open.

"Because it was embarrassing. You had Mr. Bang-You-Through-The-Walls-Owen, and I had Mr. You-Do-All-The-Work-Henry. Unless we were missionary, of course. I guess I kept thinking sex was not the entirety of a relationship. I'd convinced myself it was just me. Then, I rationalized not everyone can be good at it, so I shouldn't be so critical." Defeated, I dropped my head and huffed out a sigh. In all honesty, I'd been flattered that a handsome doctor had been interested in me. I'd been shallow and willing to forgive a lot of signs that should've been red flags.

"You cannot be serious right now. While there might be some chick out there that is happy with mediocre sex and thinks it's the bomb-diggity, we both know that ain't us. You should've cut your losses. Hell, you should've known with a name like Henry that something would be off with that." She shrugged and refilled her coffee from the carafe.

"First of all, hello… Henry Cavill. And obviously there were plenty of women that were happy with that," I muttered, earning me a sympathetic wince that I hated. "Ugh! Tori! Why are we saying his name? You know when you say their names they show up!" I demanded with bugged eyes. It was a joke with us—if you talked about a former problematic patient, they seemed to pop back in. We both laughed, but mine morphed into a groan.

"Honest to God, he seemed so awesome at the beginning. He was a good-looking, successful doctor, and he was interested in *me*. Now I realize I was likely just desperate, and he was a manipulative asshole. And he sure thought he was a sex god. Just because a guy has a big dick doesn't mean shit if they don't know what to do with it. You think maybe he watched too much crappy porn? I mean for God's sake, his idea of talking dirty sounded like he was reading from a fucking cookbook."

Tori's eyes went wide.

"I know, right? If I had to hear another 'sit on my face and suck my penis,' I was gonna lose my damn mind. First of all, never in the history of ever has it been sexy to say penis while having sex. Then it was 'While you're there, I want you to come on my face.' Like I can multitask like that. Obviously, my brain only focuses on one or the other. Either I'm working my ass off so I can come, or I'm trying to get him off. Both ain't happening, so invariably, he gets his, and I finish myself off as he snores." When I spoke Henry's words, I said them in an exaggerated low voice like I was talking about Papa Bear from *Goldilocks and the Three Bears*. Tori shook her head slightly, and her mouth fell open again.

"You see what I'm saying? Or he whined for me to be on top, but he wanted it like that *the entire time* like I'm a fucking show pony. Don't guys think we get tired? I'm out of shape. I reach muscle failure early. For fuck's sake, my hips hurt after too long. Why can't a guy just yank my pants down, bend me over the back of my couch, swipe a finger to make sure I'm ready, then grab my hips and fuck. The. Shit. Out. Of. Me?" The last I said through gritted teeth, and each word was punctuated with my hand grabbing the edge of the table as I made wild thrusting motions with my hips.

My coffee cup rattled with my actions, reminding me I hadn't filled it yet. Tori kept looking over my shoulder and giving me this tiny shake of her head.

"Fucking Henry could bang interns in the supply closet bent over the linen cart, but did I get that? Hell no. For once, I would really like a guy who knew what he was doing. Is that too much to ask for? I want a guy that can pick me up, put me where he wants me, tell me what he's gonna do to me, and *just do it*. Yep, like a goddamn Nike commercial. 'Babe, as soon as we get home, I'm gonna spread you out on the bed and have dessert, then I'm gonna fuck you from behind while I wrap your hair in my fist.' BAM! BAM! BAM!" I again had to act out my sex scenario.

"Um...." Tori choked before clearing her throat.

My shoulders sagged, and I sighed.

"I know. That was probably a bit much for over coffee, huh? Fuck it, maybe I'll just enter into a common law marriage with B.O.B. after I buy stock in Duracell. Better yet, I think I'll order one of those rechargeable ones I saw people talking about on social media—you know, the ones that made a girl see Jesus. Yeah, those." As I spoke, I filled my cup and grabbed two sugars. "Maybe masturbation is better anyway. I can get off without wearing myself out and being all sweaty."

Before I could rip the pack open, Tori interrupted me.

"Blair!" she whispered as she shook her head again and tried to surreptitiously point over my shoulder as I dumped in the sugar. At the same time, I heard a slight rustle behind me.

Still, it took long enough for me to stir in the sugar and lift the cup before my brain caught up.

The lightbulb finally went off, and I literally froze—coffee lifted halfway to my open mouth. Slowly, I set my cup demurely on the saucer as my lips were pressed together and I rapidly blinked. "Someone sat down behind us, didn't they?" I asked with no emotion and attempting to swallow my mortification.

Wide-eyed, Tori nodded, her curly ponytail bouncing.

For a moment, I pressed my lips flat, closed my eyes, and prayed for the floor to open and swallow me. A shudder ripped through me. Then I pasted a smile on my face to apologize to the person behind me as my face burned.

God, don't let it be kids.

Thankfully, it was two adults. Not that it was truly that much better. Guy number one was trying to hold in his laughter and not make eye contact. Guy number two, the big oaf directly behind me, wasn't so discreet. He was sideways in his seat, back to the window, with a huge-ass grin on his face. Fuck. My. Life.

"If you need help with that issue, I'm available," he offered. While he certainly wasn't hard on the eyes with his big muscly body, sexy smile, and brilliant blue eyes, that slight accent I couldn't place with the tone of his voice was panty-melting. Tattoos stretched up his arm that rested on the back of the booth. Those didn't hurt his overall image either.

Jesus, he was gorgeous.

Shit, they both were.

All I could do was blink. Especially since I knew I looked like, as Tori would say, a hot mess. My scrubs were wrinkled because I'd forgotten to take them out of the dryer, and my hair was haphazardly thrown up in some semblance of a bun, but there were a few—okay a lot—of pieces that were falling out. I'd planned to redo it in the locker room before report. I hadn't worn makeup because I'd overslept.

My hand went to my hair as if I could fix the mess with that useless motion.

"Uhh, sorry about that," I mumbled as my face heated.

"No, by all means, continue. We men would love to know what we're doing wrong." His stupidly straight white teeth gleamed, and his smile grew as he leaned closer to me. I wasn't sure why I expected him to say he was the Big Bad Wolf, but honestly, I didn't know if I would've complained. "Though, I can assure you, you wouldn't have any issues with *my* performance."

The last part he said quietly enough that I was pretty sure I was the only one who heard him.

Still… I. Was. Mortified. With a tight smile, I turned around to face Tori.

"Jesus, can I get my food to go?" I whispered furiously.

She had pulled her lips between her teeth, and I knew she was holding back her outburst of laughter.

Biting my tongue, I glared at her while I tried to pretend the two guys weren't still sitting there. My face burned as I tried to forget everything they'd overheard.

Why did the passing seconds seem like hours?

The waitress interrupted our stare-off when she brought our food. A quick glance at my watch showed we thankfully didn't have a lot of time. Ignoring the people behind us, I asked Nettie for a to-go container.

"Sure thing, hon," she replied and went to grab it.

I yanked my beanie down over my head so at least it covered my hair and straightened the pom-pom to center it. Then I regally gathered my things and stood. The entire time, I ignored the two hot guys at the neighboring table.

Nettie came back, slid my plate of food into the container, and handed it to me with a smile. "Here you go. Have a good night, hon."

"Thanks, Nettie." I gave a pointed look at Tori who continued eating as she tried not to smile.

"I'll see you at work," I muttered. She waved at me with her fork as she chewed.

As I tried to ignore the guys, the biggest one got up and followed me out the door. I whirled on him as a gust of cold air blew my strangling strands over my nose.

"Why are you following me?" I demanded as I pushed the hair out of my face.

"I wanted to give you something," he whispered with a cocky smirk.

"I just bet you do," I muttered.

He laughed, and of course it was as sexy as everything else about him. Incredibly so. But regardless of how good-looking he was, I wasn't in the market for a hookup in the shopping center across the street from where I worked. Not to mention the whole descriptive sexual conversation he'd overheard was so fucking embarrassing.

"Well, I'm flattered, but I think you may have gotten the wrong idea about me." My cheeks flamed. "That was… uh… well… it…," I stammered.

"Oh, I'm pretty sure I know exactly what that conversation was about, and I'm just trying to help you out." He dropped a folded napkin in my bag. "In case you change your mind."

That ass.

I shamelessly stared at the way he filled out his jeans as he returned to sit with his friend. When he got inside and glanced back, he caught me. The entire time he slid into the booth, he held my gaze through the window.

Thoroughly flustered, I shook off the slight stupor the giant man had left me in and tromped through the parking lot and drove across the street to work. Busting into the locker room, I dropped my shit on the bench and dug through my bag so I could attempt to fix my hair. The crumpled-up napkin mocked me from the jumbled mess. I ignored it, knowing I should throw it away.

"Argh!" I practically growled in embarrassed frustration. Of course, I'd forgotten a damn brush. Add that to the awful start of my day.

What a shitshow it had turned out to be. Man, I prayed it wasn't indicative of what our night was going to be like.

I should've known better. It was, after all, a full moon.

THREE

Jordan

"I LOVE ROCK 'N ROLL"—JOAN JETT & THE BLACKHEARTS

"I CAN'T BELIEVE YOU GAVE THAT CHICK YOUR NUMBER," MIKKO said as we dressed for our game three nights later.

Honestly, I couldn't either. Not only did I not hand out my number after Zena's bullshit, but I had really shied away from women period. But something about the cute nurse and her animated conversation with her friend had made me laugh my ass off and turned me on at the same time.

"Well, she hasn't called so I'm pretty sure she threw it out." I shrugged as if it didn't matter. Which it didn't. Really. I shouldn't have given it to her to begin with. So, it was cool.

I was lying to myself, and Mikko knew it. He shook his head as he chuckled.

Coach Soderberg gave us a last-minute pep talk once we were all dressed and ready to hit the ice. He ended with "let's go win this thing!"

Every single one of us shouted in agreement. We were pumped and prepared to play. I pulled on my bucket, dropped my face mask down, and tapped the floor twice with my stick. I was ready. One by one, we left the locker room.

The second I walked out of the door, I could hear the roar of the crowd. Each step toward the ice in my bulky gear had my heart slamming against my ribs. By the time my first skate hit the frozen surface, adrenaline raced through my veins.

The first thing I did was circle the net a few times. On one rotation, I noticed a poster pressed to the glass.

I grinned at the young kid who held up the hand-drawn poster with my jersey number on it. He wore a little goalie mask, and his freckled face beamed as he waved at me. After giving him a fist bump through the glass, I skated back to the net.

After marking up the ice with my skates, I warmed up by shuffling and crouching in each direction from the net. Once I had gone through my usual movements, I stretched. It was insane the flexibility needed to be a goaltender, but my mom had insisted that I knew how to condition myself. She had been a gymnastics coach, and on the off-season she drilled stretches to the point I could do the splits without thinking twice.

"Show off!" Cameron called out as he skated past me. Laughing, I rolled my eyes. The fucker had no room to talk, considering he'd taken figure skating lessons until he started playing in the juniors.

I got to my feet and squatted. Kristoffer approached, and I stood upright. He grabbed my cage and rested his helmet on mine as he stared me in the eye. "You got this."

He did it every game I started.

When he let go, I nodded, and he skated off.

By the time the game was underway, I was in the zone. Heart racing, I took a deep breath and slowly released it. I was an Austin Amur. We didn't accept defeat. Shutting out the chirping of the crowd, I focused on the puck. The Nashville Falcons were relentless though. They had so many shots on goal, I couldn't keep up. It was like they had a million biscuits on the ice that they were shooting at me nonstop. My defense tried to help, but the Nashville players were aggressive as fuck.

Time after time, they were on me. Sliding from post to post, I was able to hold them off until the end of the second period when the first puck slipped by. It was okay though because we were still up by two.

It didn't help that it seemed like the refs had it in for us and nailed us for shit they let slide for Nashville. I wouldn't be surprised if this game went down in history as our worst for penalties.

"Fuck you!" Jericho shouted at the Nashville player he'd beaten the crap out of, but the guy was still talking shit. The ref escorted Jericho to the sin bin, knowing he would go after the guy again if he didn't. Dmitry used his stick to scoop up the glove his cousin left behind. He skated it over to drop it off with Jericho before returning to the bench where he was relieved by Xavier Westergaard in the line change.

The last period was a clusterfuck of epic proportions. Almost the entire time we were down a man because one of our players was in the penalty box. At one point, both Halvorson and Kosinski were in the box. Two more pucks made it past me, and we were tied.

Eight seconds left in the game and Washburn from Nashville got one through the crease and to the back of the net. I missed it by a hair. They played out the last few seconds, and the buzzer sounded, signaling the end of the game. I was pissed.

I'd lost us the game.

My heart plummeted, and my stomach churned. Disappointment burned in my throat.

"Fuck!" I roared. Not that it did a bit of good. The scoreboard still read the same numbers as before.

Sweat poured down my back as I skated off the ice with my teeth clenched.

"Hey, it happens, man," Dmitry said to me as we walked down the hall. All I could do was shake my head. My entire body trembled with the need to lash out.

The fact that I'd let four pucks past ticked me off so bad I broke my stick as we poured into the locker room. That last one was what cost us the game with mere seconds of play left on the clock. If I could've stopped it, we would've gone into overtime and had a chance to win it.

The mood in the locker room was solemn after the slam of the door reverberated through us. Coach was pissed, and for good reason. We had definitely not been on our A game. While we knew we had an ass chewing coming, it still sucked.

Food had been catered in, but with nausea swirling in my guts, I didn't have an appetite.

"Hey, Beck! You wanna go grab a beer?" Dmitry solemnly asked me as I shoved my shit in my bag.

"No." Ordinarily, I would've been up for it. Maybe on a normal night, I would've found someone warm and willing to hook up with. Someone to drown my sorrows in, but I wasn't feeling it.

Mikko shot a glance my way, but he didn't say a word. Everyone parted as I passed through and shoved the door open with enough force it banged on the wall. Irritation simmered in my blood the entire way to the parking lot. As I tossed my bag in the passenger seat of my truck, I wanted to roar in frustration.

I wanted to fight or fuck. For a second, I reconsidered going out with the boys.

Instead, I climbed in the driver's seat, started the vehicle, and tore out of the parking lot. If coach saw me or heard about it, I'd likely get an ass chewing for that too. Except in the moment, I couldn't have cared less.

Initially, I had every intention of going home to sulk. The problem with that idea was I knew I'd sit up all night watching replays of the game, and it would only infuriate me more. Avoiding home, I drove around aimlessly until I found myself approaching the little restaurant where I'd met the nurse.

Without giving it too much thought, I pulled into the small parking lot off to the side of the building, found a space in the back row, and shut off my truck. For several minutes, I strummed my fingers on my console as I stared blankly into space. Finally, I decided to go in and drown my feelings in pecan pie and ice cream. Maybe it wasn't my mom's berry pie, but it was close. It had become a guilty pleasure that would mean extra time in the gym but was so worth it.

The bell on the door jingled as I walked inside and found a table.

"What can I get you to drink?" the waitress asked as she set a menu in front of me. I wouldn't need it, but she didn't know that.

A quick glance at the table *she'd* been sitting at revealed an older couple. Not that I expected her to be there, but I'd be lying if I said I hadn't hoped. Sighing, I returned my attention to the waitress. "Water, please."

Though something much stronger would've been preferable, I was driving and in a family restaurant so that wasn't gonna happen.

"And I'll take the pecan pie à la mode," I added, then handed her the menu.

With a flirty smile and a wink, she took it, and I watched as she pulled the pie from the case, heated it, and dropped a heaping scoop of vanilla on it. She returned with my glass of water and the pie. As she set it down, I read her name tag. "Anything else, handsome?"

"This will be all. Thanks, Cat," I replied with a smile I didn't really feel and started to dig in.

Halfway through, the bell rang, and I looked up. Chestnut hair up in a ponytail and scrubs hugging a perfectly curved ass, my nurse walked in.

Though I tried, I couldn't deny the immediate hard-on I sported looking at her ass in those navy-blue scrubs. She didn't notice me sitting at the booth in the back as she trudged to the counter on my end of the restaurant and dropped her bag to the floor next to the last stool.

"Hey, Blair. You're running late," the waitress said as she stopped in front of the woman inadvertently giving me my nurse's name. As I stared at her profile, I took a bite of my pie. Slowly chewing, I listened to their conversation.

"No, I just got off. I got called in to work the swing shift because we were shorthanded on both days and nights. Worst. Shift. Ever." She sighed as she rummaged through her bag.

"I feel you. I've pulled that shift a time or two here. It's exhausting but probably not as bad as you have it," the waitress commiserated as she set a glass of water on the counter in front of Blair.

"I'm just glad I'm off. I didn't get a chance to eat all day. Can you ask Ray if he can make me a cheddar grilled cheese with bacon?" How did she make ordering food look sexy? I couldn't take my eyes off her.

"You got it," Cat told her before turning to talk to the cook through the window.

Blair was swiping through something on her phone when she froze. Then she slowly turned her head to look my direction, as if she could feel my gaze on her. Recognition had her eyes widening, her cheeks flushing, and her perfect pink lips parted in surprise.

"You," she murmured, and I swallowed hard, almost choking on my bite of pie. Hoping to see her again and being caught staring were two different things.

"Hey," I shot back, trying to sound cool, but the crack in my voice from swallowing a bite whole kind of ruined that.

Lips pursed, she studied me for a moment before she shocked the shit out of me and grabbed her bag and her water to join me at my booth. She slid into the bench across from mine, set her things down, and rested on her crossed arms.

"Are you stalking me?" she asked, face red before she squinted and pursed her lips.

"Are you kidding?" I responded. Her cocked brow told me she wasn't. "No, I'm not. This place just has the best pecan pie for miles."

"Hmm," she hummed in contemplation. Her sweeping gaze took me in. "You're awfully dressed up for this place."

"I just got off work," I evasively replied.

"Same," she admitted.

"Rough shift?" I asked, then wanted to kick myself for sounding like a dumbass, but for the first time in forever, I was tongue-tied with a chick. A chick who hadn't called me. It was a little bruising to my ego.

"Why did you give me your number?" She cut right to the chase, ignoring my pointless question. Her hazel eyes stared boldly at me.

The waitress brought her a thick, gooey-looking grilled cheese cut in two triangles with bacon protruding from the edges. The smile she gave Cat was breathtaking, and I had to force myself to breathe. "Thanks, Cat."

"You got it, hon," Cat told her, then gave me a knowing grin before she walked off to clean the recently vacated tables.

Blair peeled the sandwich open, and steam billowed out. Once it didn't seem like it would burn the skin off the roof of her mouth, she stuck it back together and took a big bite. The entire time she ate, she stared at me.

Each time she licked her lips, I watched the movement of her tongue and mine wanted to mimic the motion. Like if I did, I could taste her. When she lifted her glass to drink, I wanted to be her glass— to have her lips on me. A drop of water started to run down the glass when she pulled it away. She slowly caught it with the tip of her tongue, and I had to adjust myself.

There was no way she didn't know what she was doing to me.

After the last bite entered her lips and she swallowed, she sucked the butter and crumbs from her fingers, and I wanted to groan.

"You didn't answer me." The corner of her mouth kicked up slightly.

"I wasn't sure if you really wanted the answer."

"Hit me," she boldly demanded.

"I'd like to show you that you were wrong. Not all guys are selfish in bed, and I was willing to prove it."

"Was?" she questioned as her gaze bounced from my eyes to my mouth.

"Well, you never called," I explained with a shrug, trying my best to appear unaffected.

That fucking tongue swept over her lips, leaving them glistening. "And if I was calling now, Jordan?" her voice took on a husky quality as it dropped to a whisper. Hearing my name spoken in that sexy tone made my dick wake up. The fact that she remembered it told me she'd at least read my scrawl on the napkin that day.

"I'd still want to."

"Then let's go." She stood and was digging through her bag again. Not wanting to wait for her to change her mind, I reached into my pocket and grabbed my money clip. I tossed a couple of bills that more than covered both of our tabs and gripped her hand. With my other one, I snagged her bag, then practically dragged her out of the restaurant.

It was pretty quiet as we made our way back to where I was parked. I paused. "Did you drive?"

She nodded and pointed to a beat-up Nissan sitting in the front row closest to the entrance.

"I'll give you a ride back afterward," I boldly announced and started walking again. Without protest, she followed. As we approached my truck, I hit the unlock button and opened the rear door to toss her bag in. But when I turned to face her, she pushed me up against the bed and stood on her tiptoes to slam her lips to mine.

A groan escaped my throat as I reflexively grabbed her hips and pulled her against my raging hard-on. At her moan, I opened my mouth to sweep my tongue along the seam of her lips. She surrendered by parting them, and I swooped in. Like a man starving, I devoured her. All thoughts of the shitty game disappeared, and I was consumed by her bold assault.

Reluctantly, I broke free and bent down to press my forehead to hers. "My place or yours?" I asked as I panted.

"Neither. Right here." She motioned to my truck, and my eyes bugged. Holy shit, I didn't think I could be turned on more, but my dick pulsed, and I realized she might be the perfect woman. Heart on the verge of exploding, I wondered if I'd heard her correctly. "Now or never," she prompted, taking my stunned silence for hesitation.

Without waiting another second, I hopped in the backseat and reached down to tug her up. No way was I waiting for her to change her mind. She straddled my lap, and I jerked the door shut. I had half a second to realize how roomy my backseat actually was before any everyday thoughts scattered.

As she resumed our kiss without pause, I smoothed my hands up her thighs and clutched her ass tightly, pulling her against my length. It was as if I couldn't get close enough to her.

"Damn," she murmured after she gasped. The second roll of her hips caused her to whimper. Her teeth sank into my lower lip, and I thrust up into the heat I could feel through the layers of our clothing. Need clawed at my insides as my dick pulsed. Then she speared her fingers in my hair and started grinding her pussy until I was afraid I'd embarrass myself. That familiar tingle started at the base of my spine, and I groaned.

Panting, I broke away and cradled her head in my massive hands. "Just so you know, I can't bend you over the couch like this. Oh, and you're on top, but I promise you aren't going to be disappointed."

She smirked. "Words are cheap, Jordan."

"Pants off," I demanded and narrowed my gaze.

With a wicked grin, she moved to sit next to me where she kicked off her shoes and divested herself of her scrub pants and panties. Damn, she looked good in those scrubs, but they disguised a banging body. Softly curved hips connected to legs a man would kill to get lost between.

While I watched her, I unbuttoned the bottom of my shirt to move it out of the way. I couldn't be bothered to take it off. Then I leaned forward and reached through the seats to get a condom from my center console. As she put her hand between her legs, I made quick work of wrapping my dick. I'd barely gotten it rolled to the base before she was climbing over me.

"Birth control?" I asked, wanting to minimize complications if a fucking condom failed.

"Yes," she affirmed.

Between the two of us, we lined ourselves up, and I drove up into her as she dropped.

"Holy fuck!" she cried out as she dropped her head to my shoulder.

"No shit," I replied as I waited for her impossibly tight sheath to adjust to my invasion. My eyes wanted to roll back at how fucking amazing she felt as she wiggled to get me in all the way. Snug and pulsing, she fit like a glove as she worked herself lower. Inch by inch, she took me inside her hot wet core.

Once I was fully seated, we both locked gazes and let out a breathless laugh.

"I wasn't exactly expecting all this," she admitted. "You're really damn big."

"Well, I'm probably just proportionate, but I'm not a small man," I rationalized. Then I swallowed hard as I stared into her amber-and-green eyes. "Can I move?"

"God, please," she moaned, and I swear I lost my mind.

With a bruising grip, I held her hips and guided her until she rode me the way I wanted. I loved that she had curves for me to grab onto. Needing more, I shoved up her shirt and lifted her breasts from the lacy cups of her bra. The second my lips wrapped around a dusky-pink nipple, she ripped her top over her head and tossed it to the side. Arching her back, she held my head to her chest as I took turns with each one.

"Oh God," she gasped when I nipped one, then soothed it with my tongue. Then, sucking deeply, I glanced up to see her reaction.

She was absolutely stunning. Dark lashes fanned her flushed cheeks, her plush lips parted, and her head was thrown back. I released her nipple with a pop and caught a single bead of perspiration that ran down between her perfect tits. It left me wanting to taste every inch of her.

We were starting to sweat, and the windows had steamed over, but I didn't care if anyone outside of the confines of the cab knew what we were doing. I no longer gave two shits about losing the game that night. All that mattered was how good she felt. Buried deep inside her, I was free of worries, self-doubt, and anger.

Clutching her close, I held the back of her neck and splayed a hand on her back. Licking up her throat, I bit the sensitive area beneath her ear and was rewarded with a stuttered gasp. Then I thrust hard up into her and slid my hand between us to circle her clit with my thumb.

"Jesus, Jordan!" As she said my name, her pussy tightened around me, and I hoped she was close—because I was about to blow.

"Fuck, Blair, you need to come or I'm going to make a liar out of myself," I ground out, trying to hold off my release with each drive of my hard cock up into her tight, wet core.

Relishing in the saltiness of her skin, I sucked on her neck where it met the slope of her shoulder. Desperate to mark her as mine, I savagely pulled her soft flesh between my lips, though I knew this could only be a one and done.

"Jordan," she whispered in wonder as the first flutter of her impending orgasm rippled over my cock. Doubling my efforts, I put more pressure on her clit and bit the tender area I'd marked. "Yessssss! Oh God, Jordan, yes!"

Her climax was so powerful I was momentarily breathless as she squeezed me like a motherfucking vise. She dug her short nails into my back through my dress shirt and that was all it took.

Wrapping her in a crushing hold, I drove up one last time, and a roar burst from my previously mute mouth. I exploded in the condom, wishing I was bare because to see myself dripping out of her when we were done would've been a sight to behold.

As we came down from our unbelievable high, I sagged against the seat but brought her with me. Her breath feathered over my neck, and I tried to gather my thoughts because they were scattered to the four winds.

"Holy fucking shit," I choked out as she continued to sporadically pulse around me.

I wasn't sure what had just happened, but I'd never had a sexual encounter like the one I'd just had in the backseat of my goddamn truck. It both stunned me and scared the shit out of me.

FOUR

Blair

"THUNDER"—IMAGINE DRAGONS

"I HONESTLY CANNOT BELIEVE I JUST DID THIS. I BLAME A SHITTY shift and very little sleep on my poor decisions," I muttered into his neck—that smelled absolutely to die for. Rich and spicy, he reminded me of leather jackets and bonfires. His chuckle shook me.

"Well, then I blame it on a shitty day too."

"Bad day at the office?" I asked him, my face still pressed to his neck. I felt him swallow.

"You could say that." His tone was depressed, and I lifted my head.

"Wanna talk about it?"

"Nah. It's water under the bridge now."

Searching his eyes, I didn't believe him, but considering we were nothing but a hookup, I kept my mouth shut.

"Umm, so, this was… nice," I mumbled, feeling suddenly embarrassed as shit for what we'd done. The reality of it had my cheeks burning all the way to my chest. For fuck's sake, we were right across the road from my place of employment. In the parking lot next to the diner I frequently ate at. In a truck. That we had sex in. Like teenagers. What the fuck was wrong with me?

He laughed, and it caused his softening cock to start to come out.

"Shit," I whispered, reaching between us to grab the condom so it didn't slip off as I got up. When I squeezed the base of his shaft to hold it on, he sucked in a hissed breath. Then he groaned when I climbed from his lap.

"I'll, uh, just get dressed and um… go."

The brave vixen who knew exactly what she wanted had dissipated with my orgasm. But what an orgasm it was.

Le sigh.

Insanely, it was probably the best sex I'd had in my life.

Fumbling around, I tried to dress, but it proved to be much more difficult to put my clothes back on in a vehicle than it was to take them off. Jesus, I was buck-ass naked and he'd only undone his slacks, pushed them down, and gotten his shirt out of the way.

One thing I could say was this experience would sure give me memories to hang onto for years. The delicious ache that was already forming between my legs told me that my vibrators would likely be a disappointment from now on, but that was okay.

"Hey," he softly called out as I fought to get my long-sleeve T-shirt on with my scrub top over it. I should've separated them.

"Yeah?" I asked, muffled inside my shirts. Tingles shot down my sides when his fingertips brushed my skin as he reached over and helped me find my way out of the shirt maze. Reluctantly, I met his gaze and tried to appear confident and like this was no big deal.

While I'd been fighting my way through my clothing, he had disposed of the condom and fastened his pants. Part of me was so sorry to see his dick was put away.

"It's okay. We're adults. No expectations. It seemed like we both needed to blow off some steam." He shrugged and gave me a small, slightly crooked grin. Relief allowed my shoulders to slump. He was trying to keep this from being awkward, and I appreciated it.

"Thank you, you're not wrong."

"Though I'm really sorry we didn't make it out of the parking lot because I was looking forward to the back of the couch, I hope I was better than ol' limp dick Henry," he comically whispered.

Again, he knew what to say because I started to laugh. "You were, uh, impressive," I admitted before I pulled my lips between my teeth to hold back my smile. I failed, and the corner of my mouth lifted.

His answering grin was blinding and lit up his face. It also brought out a dimple I hadn't noticed before and made him appear younger and carefree. It was a good look for him. Especially paired with that massive, muscular body. Damn, he was really gorgeous.

"Well, I guess I'll be going," I announced before I could suggest a second round.

"Thanks for coming over to my place," he joked, causing me to snort in amusement.

Before I could say anything further, he had opened the door and climbed out. He held out a hand to help me down. Once my feet hit the ground, he grabbed my bag. I reached for it, but he held it away.

"I've got it. Let me walk you to your car."

My brow furrowed in confusion at the manners and kindness after the raw and gritty romp in his backseat. If he was like this after that, what was he like after a real date? Not that it mattered. It was unlikely someone like him would be interested in long term with someone like me. I mean that was if I'd been looking for a relationship—which I wasn't. If his truck and his suit were indicators, the man made money. Not that I was poor, but he definitely seemed a little above my pay grade. I guessed he was a corporate guy at some fancy company in Austin. Hell, maybe he owned his own business. It was hard to say around this area.

He waited patiently while I unlocked my car, then set my bag in the passenger seat. Surprisingly, he followed me to the driver's seat. "Be careful on the way home."

"Thanks. You too," I replied with a grin. Before I could second guess myself, I stood on my tiptoes and kissed his cheek. Then I got in my car, shut the door, and turned the key. Thankfully, it actually started, saving me from the embarrassment of needing to get a jump. It wouldn't have been the first time. My poor car was on its last leg, but I prayed it would last another year or two.

As I drove off, I risked a glance in my rearview. With his hands in his pockets, he stood watching my taillights. Somehow, I knew that would be the last time I saw him again. I'd be a liar if I denied that a little part of my heart ached at the thought.

"You look… different," Tori mused as she stared at me, tapping a pen on her lip.

Not making eye contact, I continued charting. "I have no idea what you're talking about. I got new lashes. Is that it?" I fluttered them at her, and she gave me a smirk.

"Smartass. No, but something has definitely changed with you. You didn't color your hair. Those aren't new scrubs," she continued.

I gave a snort. "Like I would blow money on new scrubs," I muttered.

"You seem like you're glowing." Her eyes narrowed, and she studied me. "New foundation? Highlighter?"

Unable to stop myself, I rolled my eyes. "Really? Maybe I just got decent sleep for a change."

"Hmm, maybe," she murmured as she tilted her head. Then one of her patients used their call light.

Saved by the bell.

Literally.

The last thing I wanted to tell her was that after two weeks, I was still glowing from the amazing sex in the back of Jordan's truck. Nor did I want to admit that I'd saved his number in my phone, and every freaking day I pulled it up and considered calling him for a repeat. Thankfully, the rest of the night we were hopping, leaving little time for conversation. It was a full moon, and the ER was nonstop all night. People could say that was a myth all they wanted, but medical personnel knew the truth.

I'd never been so happy to see day shift come in to relieve us in my life.

"Maddox, I think I love you," I told him as I handed off my patients to him.

He chuckled. "Don't tell Gwyn that. You might have a fight on your hands."

"Pssh! She knows I don't love you like that," I shot back before sticking my tongue out at him. Then I quickly went to retrieve my bag from the locker room.

By the time Tori and I trudged out into the blinding sunlight, I doubted either of us looked like we were glowing. Pretty sure my mascara was down to my cheeks and my eyes were bloodshot as fuck. I'd been afraid to take so much as a glance in the mirror.

"Oh my God. I can't wait to switch to days," Tori groaned as we reached our cars.

"Wait. What? You're going back to days?" I asked, suddenly alert.

"Yeah, while the money has been nice, I feel like I never see Owen anymore."

Stocking out my lower lip, I pouted. "But I thought you loved me more anyway."

She chortled. "Girl, you know damn well I love you, but unfortunately, you don't give me wall-banging orgasms like Owen."

It was my turn to choke. "Jesus. Well, I would hope not."

The little minx snickered, thinking she was so funny. In all honesty, she really was because in the past I would've never heard something like that come out of her mouth.

"What are you doing tonight?" I asked, though I was pretty sure I knew the answer.

"Owen and I are going out to eat, then there's a party at the clubhouse. I wish you'd come," she whined.

"I don't know. Last time I went there, I ended up staying in Slice's room and had no idea where my damn underwear was," I grumbled.

"That was forever ago! Shit, I think Owen was still prospecting!"

"Don't care," I told her with a shake of my head. Those guys partied hard, and while the sex had been amazing, I was a little embarrassed the next day when I couldn't find all my clothes. Especially when I remembered I had started to strip for him out in the common area. Then having to face Maddox at work after I'd behaved like that and slept with his friend? Ugh. Mortifying. That was the last time I drank tequila.

"Well, if you change your mind, let me know," she said with a sigh.

"I won't, but sure."

We got in our cars and headed our separate ways.

Once I was home, I stripped out of my scrubs, showered, and put on my pajamas. As I puttered around my apartment waiting for my laundry to finish, I scrolled absently through social media. After a whole lot of nothing, I dropped on the couch and propped my feet up on the coffee table.

Again, I pulled up Jordan's number. I considered calling him or sending a text. It may have been two weeks, but my desire for the man hadn't waned. Not one iota. Except I truly didn't have the mental energy to devote to a relationship. Not that I thought he would want that, but I wasn't usually the aggressor.

Not true. You were that night you slept with him in his truck.

The little devil on my shoulder grinned.

Before I could do something foolish, I put my phone on silent, took some melatonin, and made sure my blackout curtains didn't let any light in, then climbed in bed. My head hit the pillow, and I was out.

Unfortunately, my dreams were filled with hot, passionate, panty-melting sex with a big, sexy, dimpled man.

FIVE

Jordan

"DRIFT AWAY"—SEETHER

THREE WEEKS AFTER THE EXPLOSIVE NIGHT IN MY TRUCK, I still couldn't get Blair out of my fucking head. My teammates and I were supposed to be celebrating, and there were women aplenty all around me, but none of them caught my attention for long.

None of them were a sassy nurse with chestnut hair, kaleidoscope eyes, and curves for days.

Alex's brother, Cooper, was a member of the Demented Sons MC. Of course, they all called him by his road name, which was Truth. I didn't even want to know how he got it. There were some things with his club you left alone, but all in all, they were a cool bunch of guys.

Mikhail came up to me, breaking me out of my musing. He hooked an arm around my neck and planted a kiss on my cheek. The big Russian was the only one close to my height. He'd obviously been drinking because he was rarely like that. "Ah! The hero of the game! Jordan-The-Wall-Beck!"

Shaking my head, I couldn't help but grin at his antics. It made me want to video him for blackmail later. That thought caused me to snicker.

"Hell, yeah! Complete shut out with thirty-five shots on goal! He's a motherfuckin' badass!" Dmitry plowed into me, wrapping his arms around my waist and lifting me off my feet. Truth and a few of his club brothers held their drinks up and cheered.

"Jesus, you're gonna give yourself a hernia," Jericho teased. The two cousins were often inseparable, and if rumor was true, they shared a lot of things—including women. The other rumor was that Bleu's sister had found out about one such night during an away game and shitcanned Dmitry's ass for it. I couldn't say one way or another and I didn't care. At that time, I'd been dealing with my own shit.

"What-the-fuck-ever. I bench more than him!" Dmitry boasted. Ribbing ensued as everyone called bullshit on his claim, though he wasn't lying. He often benched my 215 and then some. Hell, he squatted far more than I weighed and deadlifted heavier weight than that.

As they bullshitted back and forth, my mind wandered to Blair again. I wondered if she was on shift. I knew she worked at the hospital near the diner that was nestled in the shopping complex in Cedar Park. I remembered her badge from the night in my truck.

I mean, no way was I sitting in the diner, drinking enough coffee to keep me awake for a week, just on the off chance she'd come in.

Every night that I'd been in town.

That would be…stalker-ish. I just liked their pie.

Okay, maybe it wasn't just the pie, but I really did like it. But in my defense, I still didn't have her number. I meant to ask for it before she left that night, but my brain was so rattled from the incredible sex that I hadn't been thinking straight.

Anyway, I'd considered trying to find her at the hospital, but that seemed a bit much after I'd already camped out at the diner after practice each day for the week after we'd hooked up. I'd paid for it too. I hadn't been worth a shit at practice in the mornings because I'd been up all night. Coach had my ass for it, so I reluctantly stopped going.

"You want another beer?" Alex asked me over the thumping bass of the music at his brother's clubhouse. At his question, I realized the rest of the guys had deserted me for willing dance partners. Dmitry, Jericho, Mikko, and Landon were having a ball. Landon Shomo was our fairly new backup goaltender after Johnson had retired, and the kid was in heaven with two chicks fawning all over him. I chuckled at him because he reminded me of someone I knew a few years ago.

"Hell yeah, he does," Alex's brother Cooper said as he came up behind him and looped an arm over Alex's shoulder. "You guys are celebrating, aren't you?"

The corner of my lips kicked up, and I shook my head, then lifted my mostly full bottle. "Nah, I'm good, but thanks."

"Suit yourself," Cooper said before he shook his younger brother and laughed. "Proud of you, little brother."

Alex laughed at his brother's sappy behavior, but Cooper couldn't have cared less. He happily moved on to some chick that had on tight-as-fuck jeans and a low-cut shirt.

"What gives?" Alex asked me, motioning to my bottle.

"What do you mean?" I pretended I didn't know what he was talking about and lifted my lukewarm beer to my lips.

"You've been nursing that beer since we got here. It's Saturday, we won our second game of the weekend, and we're off tomorrow. I already lined up transportation so we can leave our vehicles here and have a good time. I'll even work out with you this next week to burn off the excess calories," Alex teased. Leave it to him to notice everything in detail. Sydney, Alex's girl, walked up and ducked under the arm he held up for her. The adoring expression in her ice-blue eyes as she gazed at him made me a little sick. Not really, it actually made me envious because deep in my heart I wanted that too. Except the whole once burned twice shy saying was a real thing.

"You find the bathroom okay?" he asked her before he pressed a kiss to her temple. She nodded, and I took another drink as I glanced away from their display. Several of the other guys were doing a terrible job of dancing with some of the women that showed up for a Demented Sons MC party. It was impossible not to laugh at them.

"Hey. I hear you're the star goalie," I heard a sultry voice say before the light scent of a woman hit me.

I turned to the sound of her voice and pasted on a smile. It was the same one I used when I was forced to do shit for PR that I hated. Like posing for pictures. I'd never really liked my picture taken, but after that shit with Zena, I abhorred it.

"Yeah, I am. Do you watch hockey?" I kind of doubted she did, but who knew? Long red hair that caught the firelight and shimmered brushed lightly freckled shoulders that had to have been cold in the early December air. She wasn't dressed for winter, even by Texas standards. Big blue eyes blinked up at me, and pouty lips tipped up as her gaze raked over me. Ordinarily, she would've been right up my alley. But not tonight. Instead, all I could do was compare her lean build to the perfect curves I'd held onto in the backseat of my truck.

"Not really, but I'd love to go to a game," she hinted. "My name's Bambi."

Of course it was.

Manicured nails traced up my shirt and circled a button. Then she cast a coy look up at me. In my peripheral, I noticed Alex and Sydney sneaking off to leave me alone with the chick. Little did they know, I wasn't interested.

My phone vibrated in my pocket, and I used it as an excuse to step away. "I'm sorry, I've been expecting this," I apologized as I pulled it out and held it up.

She bit her lip and gave me a seductive smirk as she nodded. I turned away and walked off a bit. No, I wasn't expecting shit, but I wasn't digging Bambi in any way, shape, or form. There was only one chick I couldn't get out of my head. But I was more than digging her, I was *craving* her, and that should scare the bejesus out of me.

And holy shit. No way. It couldn't be.

Unknown: Out of curiosity, was your number for a one-time use only, or is it good for repeat performances?

Me: Depends on who's asking

Unknown: Backseat of your truck in the diner parking lot ring a bell?

The corner of my mouth kicked up in satisfaction.

Me: Vaguely. Maybe I need another performance to jog my memory

Unknown: Vaguely? Yikes. Blow to the ego

Me: Sorry, I was only teasing

Unknown: Bahaha. I figured. I was just messing with you. But you didn't really answer me

Me: When and where?

Her reply was her "pin" with her GPS location coming through the text messages. My heart started to jackhammer against my ribs.

Me: On my way

Without so much as a backward glance, I made my way through the partygoers. As I passed a trashcan, I dropped my piss-warm beer in it. Before I got through the edge of the small crowd, a hand gripped my arm.

"Where you goin'?" Mikko asked with a furrowed brow.

For a moment, I debated what I should say. As Dmitry and Jericho approached, I decided to tell Mikko so I could get the hell out of there before they reached us and asked to tag along. "I'm gonna meet up with the nurse from the diner."

"No shit?" He looked stunned. "I didn't know she ever contacted you."

"She didn't exactly, until tonight. Look, I gotta get moving," I told him as I cast a glance at the rapidly approaching duo.

"Sure you're okay to drive?"

"Yeah man, I didn't even finish my first beer."

"Okay, then have fun and don't do anything I wouldn't," he said as he saluted me with his beer.

As I backed away, Jericho called out. "Where you off to? The party is just warming up!"

Before I could reply, Mikko grinned and bumped Jericho's shoulder. "Beck has a booty call."

"Shit, there's plenty of that right here and you don't have to drive," Dmitry argued with a smirk.

Flipping them off, I left—laughing the whole way.

Not wasting time putting the address into my truck's GPS, I stuck my phone in the holder and clicked on the pin, pulling up the directions on my phone. According to the route, she was only about twenty minutes away if I hopped on the toll road.

Thanks to traffic after I exited, it took me about twenty-five before I entered the gate code she texted me and drove through the parking areas, following the pin to the right building. Before I got out of the truck, I grabbed a few condoms from the console and shoved them in my pocket.

"Hey sexy," I heard called down from above as I climbed out of my vehicle.

I looked up to see Blair resting her arms on the balcony of her second-floor apartment. A blanket was wrapped around her, and I wondered what she had on under there. Her easy smile lit up her face, and I couldn't keep the answering one off mine. "You gonna let me in, or am I gonna have to climb up to you, Rapunzel?"

"My hair isn't that long, and it's not blonde. I think Rapunzel was a blonde. Plus, I don't know if this railing could handle that. How about if you use the stairs?" She smirked as she motioned toward the entrance.

"So boring and basic, but I guess," I joked. Then, taking the stairs two at a time, I hauled ass to where she waited with the door open.

"Hey," I breathed out.

"Hi," she replied, giving me a once-over.

"It's a little chilly out here," I teased.

"Oh! Sorry." Her cheeks flushed a pretty shade of pink, and she stepped back to allow me to pass.

My gaze swept the apartment after she closed the door and led me inside. It was small but seemed nice.

"Do you, uh, want anything to drink?" she questioned, as she appeared to float into the kitchen because of the big blanket dragging behind her.

"Water would be good," I told her, suddenly nervous.

That had me blinking in confusion because it wasn't like I'd never done this. It was a simple booty call. There wasn't a single reason to be nervous. Unless she turned out to be a psycho and poisoned me or drugged me to keep me prisoner in her room. Not that I'd complain if she tied me to her bed.

"Here you go," she murmured, pulling me out of my head. Our fingers brushed when I took the glass, and the shockwave it sent through me made my breath catch.

Her wide eyes told me she'd noticed it too. Our breathing grew ragged, and I gulped half the glass of water trying to get myself to chill out.

Playing it cool, I took another drink and set the glass on the counter that separated the galley kitchen from the living room. When I turned back to her, I almost choked before I could swallow.

Standing completely nude, blanket in hand, she ran her tongue along her lower lip and tugged it between her teeth. Holy shit on a shingle, she was stunning. Her dark hair hung in soft waves over her shoulders, teasing the taut nipples peeking between the strands. Curves to die for, perfect fucking tits, and lips that I wanted to see do dirty things to me. She was no girl—she was an honest-to-God woman. The kind of woman men waged wars over. My cock was immediately at attention and tenting my slacks.

"Working on a Saturday?" She motioned to my dress clothes I hadn't bothered to change out of after the game.

"Yeah." It seemed I could only get out the one word.

Head cocked, she eyed me. "You have too many clothes on," she whispered in her sultry tone.

Like someone flipped a switch, I fished one of the packets out and quickly lost my clothes. Then all I could do was stare at her with a fucking condom in my hand. She held me absolutely spellbound. I couldn't stop looking at her. The things I wanted to do to her body. Fuck. Truthfully, I wanted to take my time with her. I wanted to worship her from head to toe. Wanted to memorize every little detail. Wanted to mark each inch of her with my tongue. She wasn't simply sexy—she was downright sinful. Greed—she made me feel greed when I looked at her. I needed all of her and never wanted to stop. Which I guess made me gluttonous. See? Sinful.

Glancing around her, I took in the couch and chair. Remembering what I'd overheard, I reached for her hand to lead her to the end of the couch. The second our fingertips connected, a buzzing hit my brain, and my mouth went dry.

Without another word, I pressed on her back to get her to bend over. "Like this?" I whispered, ensuring my lips brushed the shell of her ear as I spoke. She shuddered and tiny goose bumps broke out over the surface of her skin. Through it all, my heart was pounding, and my dick jumped in time to each beat. Inhaling shakily, I trailed a hand down the dip in her spine as I opened the foil wrapper with my teeth. When I reached the small of her back, she moaned and arched, bringing her pussy closer to me. Allowing my one hand to explore, I deftly rolled the condom down my length.

"Need any help?" she queried with an arch of her brow.

"Hell no," I insisted. Then I placed my hand between her legs and swiped through her slit. A groan escaped me when my hand was drenched from the motion. As she'd so colorfully described in the restaurant that day, I gripped her hips tightly, relishing in the fact that she had something for me to grab onto. Fuck, she had a great body.

"Hurry," she urged.

Slipping the head of my cock through the wetness she had in abundance, I took several shallow strokes, then pulled her ass back as I drove forward.

"Oh God," she gasped.

My head bowed, and my shoulders tensed as I fought for control. My memories hadn't done her justice, because I swear to Christ her pussy was tighter than it had been last time. Once I figured I was safe and could hold myself together, I slid slowly in and out a few times.

Fuck.

She was absolute heaven. Unable to fight it any longer, I picked up the pace until I was ramming into her. Harsh breaths and the slap of skin on skin echoed throughout the apartment. As I fucked the hell out of her, I leaned forward to press my lips to her shoulder. That instantly moved to my teeth gripping the sexy slope of her traps.

"Jor-dan," she stuttered, and her hot, wet cunt tightened, damn near making my eyes cross.

Knowing I wouldn't be able to hold off much longer, I released her shoulder, rested my forehead on her back, and reached around to rapidly circle her swollen little clit. It didn't take long before she screamed my name and her walls violently spasmed around my shaft. With each pulse, she damn near pushed me out, and I had to keep driving myself back in.

I should've gotten a fucking medal for self-control because

somehow I managed to hold off. When her orgasm faded to little flutters, I stood back up, gathered her hair in my fist, and pulled until her back arched.

"Baby, I'm gonna fuck you so hard you're never going to forget the way I feel," I ground out between my clenched teeth. Then I proceeded to do just that.

Like a machine, I thrust into her over and over. Though this had been what she described, I wanted to see her face when she came. Because she was damn sure fucking coming again. She whimpered when I pulled out, but it morphed to a sigh when I tugged her hair to stand her up and kissed the bruised spot I'd left on her porcelain-like skin.

With a wiggle of my hips, I nestled my cock in the crack of her ass while I licked, kissed, and sucked along her neck. Letting her hair go, I cupped her luscious tits in my hands and gently squeezed as I plucked at her perky nipples.

A soft whimper fell from her lips. "Please," she panted.

"Please what?" I asked as I continued. Her skin was like satin under my fingers.

"Please fuck me," she breathlessly instructed. "I need you to come."

Fuck, I loved a woman that wasn't afraid to tell me what she wanted. I spun her around and pressed her back to the white wall. In one motion, I lifted her legs, lined up, and thrust into the Nirvana that was her pussy.

"God fucking damn, you feel good." I groaned through it all. "Hang on."

"Wait!"

I grunted, and my head dropped before I froze and reluctantly looked her in the eyes. My heart was about to explode, and my balls ached for release. If she told me to stop, I would, but goddamn, I didn't want to.

"Yeah?" I croaked.

"This doesn't mean we're in a relationship. The repeat, I mean," she explained between ragged breaths.

"Not a problem. I just got out of a bad relationship—not looking to do it again."

"Same."

"Thank fuck," I muttered before gripping her thighs and plunging balls deep in the best pussy I'd ever had my cock in.

Like a madman, I chased my release in her willing body. Stroke after stroke, I plugged deep and hard. That familiar tingle hit my spine, and my balls tightened in preparation for the explosion.

Heavy-lidded, she stared at me as her fingers dug into my shoulders. Each time I bottomed out, she gasped an inhale.

"Come," I rasped in a bold demand, my control slowly unraveling.

"I can't," she whispered.

My eyes narrowed, and I wrapped my fingers around her throat and braced her jaw on my thumb and forefinger. I gripped the sweat-slicked column of her neck tightly but not enough to bruise her. I leaned in until my lips brushed hers. "You can. And you sure as hell fucking will."

Ensuring the base of my cock ground on her clit with each stroke, I relentlessly took her. Like I knew she would, she detonated. Fucking hell, she was a sight to behold as bliss overtook her. Unable to hold back any longer, I buried myself deep in her core, and my cock pulsed what seemed like gallons of cum into the fucking rubber.

Panting like we'd finished a marathon, we slowly came down from the high of our climax. Once we'd caught our breath, we went for round two.

It was like we were animals that couldn't get enough. By the time the sun began to peek through her blinds, we'd used every condom I brought up. That wasn't including her getting down on her knees and sucking my cock until I couldn't stand it and I tossed her on her bed. My face between her legs, I was unrelenting. When she finally came on my face, I licked her clean, then kissed my way up her body to collapse next to her.

I pulled her back into my front and held her tightly. The last thing I remembered before falling asleep was how perfectly she fit against me.

SIX

Blair

"POCKETFUL OF SUNSHINE"—NATASHA BEDINGFIELD

THE SILENCE IN MY APARTMENT TOLD ME I WAS ALONE.

A sweep of my hand to the cold sheets on his side confirmed he'd been gone a while. I wondered when he'd left. Aching in the most delicious of ways, I stretched under my linens, and a satisfied curve settled on my lips. The night before had easily been the best sex I'd ever had.

My phone rang, and I answered without checking the screen.

"Hello," I practically purred, assuming it was Jordan calling me.

"Damn." The familiar voice had me sitting upright and clutching the comforter to my chest as I frowned. Definitely not the caller I hoped for.

"What do you want? Unless you're calling to tell me you have a check for me, I have nothing to say to you," I practically growled. Teeth grinding, I clutched the phone so tightly I was surprised it didn't crack.

"Blair, I wish you'd let me explain," Henry pleaded.

"What's to explain? I caught you in the supply room fucking one of the residents! I think that's pretty self-explanatory. Oh, and shall we discuss the money you owe me?" By then I was fuming. If I was a cartoon, steam would be coming out of my ears. Talking about it brought back the visual I wished I could bleach from my brain.

"I told you I'd pay you back. I just don't have it right now because I had to quit my job. Remember?" The last came out as a sneer that I couldn't believe he had the balls to do.

"Gee, I wonder why?"

He sighed. "I'm sorry, Blair. I fucked up. I wish you'd give me a chance to show you I've changed—that you're the only one that I actually loved."

"What a crock of shit. In the year plus that we were together, you were fucking around behind my back the entire time! You used my credit cards without my permission. You lied to me. You stole from me. But you expect me to believe that was *love?* You are a truly sick individual." By then, my blood was boiling. Not only did he have balls for calling me, but he was ruining my post-coital euphoria and that pissed me off.

"I only did it because the feelings I had for you scared me. Please, let me come over so we can talk," he begged, his tone bordering on desperation.

"Fuck. Off. And lose my number," I spat before ending the call. I should've blocked him, but I didn't in case he actually did try to contact me to pay me back. That, however, was wishful thinking.

Mood shot, I got up, pulled on a pair of sleeping pants and an old T-shirt, and started to gather my laundry together. Then I went in my closet where the washer and dryer were to start a load. It was the weirdest thing I'd ever seen when I toured the apartment, but I was just happy to have a washer/dryer hookup.

I sent a message to Tori to see if she wanted to come over for lunch.

Tori: Can't, babe. Owen's parents are in town, and they're leaving in the morning. We're showing them around Austin today

Me: No worries

Tori: Everything okay?

Me: Totally! Just haven't seen you in a few days. I need my Tori fix!

Tori: LOL. Well, we work together tomorrow night.

Me: EW! Work. Bleh. Okay, be that way. Later! Have fun today!

Tori: Will do. MUAH!

Me: MUAH!

Well, hell. I had completely forgotten she said they were in town. I pulled up the conversation with Jordan and debated reaching out to him, but I didn't want to be that girl. What we had was sex. Nothing more, nothing less. I didn't know him. We weren't friends.

With a sigh, I tossed my phone on the bed, turned on some music, and started cleaning my apartment. Three loads of laundry, a sink full of dishes from our midnight munchies, and a good sweep from corner to corner later, and I was still fighting sending Jordan another message.

He had my number now. And he'd left without so much as a note. It was pretty obvious where we stood.

For the twentieth time, I checked my phone to see if he'd called or texted while I was cleaning. Maybe I hadn't heard my phone, I rationalized. Disappointment had my shoulders drooping when there was nothing from him. Shuffling dejectedly into the kitchen, I made myself some chicken noodle soup from a can and tried to push the giant of a man from my thoughts.

Each day after that was much of the same.

Four days later and I hadn't heard a word.

Until I did.

Sexy Giant: You busy?

Me: Night off

Sexy Giant: Can I come over?

I debated telling him to fuck off but then I pursed my lips. We never made any promises. At my request, we had fucked in his truck, then I'd called him over for a booty call. It was idiotic for me to have any feelings about this one way or the other. Before I could change my mind, I sent the text.

Me: Yes

The man must've been around the corner because ten minutes later and there was a knock on my door. I peeked through the peep-hole and couldn't help the skipping thump of my heart. A yearning shot through me at the sight of the tall, handsome man standing outside my door and with it came a warning bell. One that I ignored, reminding myself it was only sex, I wouldn't let myself develop an addiction to his magic dick.

"Hey," I said as I opened the door. Planning to remain detached and in control, I casually looked him over.

"Hi." He grinned. "Why do I get this déjà vu feeling? Except you're not wearing a blanket."

With an answering lift of my lips, I motioned him in.

"I can't stay the night," he started off with. "I have a flight to catch early in the morning."

It was on the tip of my tongue to ask where he was going, but it really wasn't my business. We didn't have that kind of relationship. After the one I'd gotten out of, I was kind of okay with that, though I did feel like we needed to set some ground rules.

"No problem. But there are a few things I'd like to know."

He cocked a single brow before he crossed his arms and waited.

"I'm fine with this being casual, but are we exclusive? Or are we free to sleep with other people?"

His gaze narrowed, and his nostrils flared, slightly telling me something in my questions ticked him off. "I haven't been with anyone else since that first night with you."

"That didn't answer the question, though," I pressed.

"I'm okay with staying exclusive, but I don't have time for a relationship. So, if that's what you're hoping for, then I should leave now," he finally replied, his expression becoming closed off.

I breathed a sigh of relief. "No, that works for me. My schedule is pretty crazy so I'm perfectly happy with hookups when we have time."

Relief blossomed on his face, and a wicked grin lifted his lips as he closed in on me. With each step he took, it became harder to breathe, but I stood my ground until we were toe to toe. "Then let's get naked."

"Sounds like a plan to me," I murmured before I slid my hands up under his long-sleeve compression shirt. It was the first time I'd seen him not dressed up since the embarrassing first meeting. The shirt fit him like a glove, and my mouth watered. My fingers dancing over the hard planes of his abdomen might've contributed to that as well.

The bright blue of his eyes was absolutely mesmerizing. As I stared, I noticed a light sprinkling of freckles over the top of his cheeks that gave him a boyish quality. Without thought, I raised my fingers to trace over them.

He lowered his head, and our lips clashed as I clutched his hair. Frenzied and needy, we ripped each other's clothes off, and before I knew it, he was sliding inside me, and my eyes were rolling in my head.

"Fucking hell," he muttered into my neck.

"God, this is some of the best sex of my life," I admitted through my gasps. With the cold granite of the counter-height breakfast bar at my back, I locked my legs around him. Each time we were together was as good as the first—no, it was better.

"Yes. Fuck yes," he agreed, each word punctuated with a thrust of those powerful hips. A clatter signified I'd knocked something into the sink next to me, but I ignored it. Shivers racked me as his teeth found every sensitive spot on my upper body.

Like he was trying to trace and memorize every inch of my body, his hands roamed over the surface of my skin. One hand slapped to the counter as a brace, and the other continued its exploration. Each movement elicited a whimper of pleasure that I couldn't hold in if I wanted.

Then he slipped that hand between us. I moaned when the rough skin of his thumb dragged over my clit.

"You like that, don't you?" he asked into my chest where he was raining adoration down upon the girls. It was sloppy due to the motions of his hips, but I didn't care. I gripped his head, threading my fingers into his cropped hair and holding him to my nipple. The scrape of his scruff on my delicate skin was another of the sensations driving me over the edge. The rapid circles on my clit finished the job.

For a moment, I stiffened in preparation, breath frozen, then the tsunami hit and rocked my goddamn world.

"Jordan! Oh fuck! Jordan!" I cried out as the power of my orgasm crashed into me. The contractions of my walls around his thick shaft were hitting one after the other like waves in a storm. Relentless, they shook me to the core and left me panting, desperate to suck enough oxygen into my lungs.

"Holyfuckingshit!" he mumbled as his rhythm stuttered, and he forcefully drove his cock to the hilt. Forehead pressed to my chest, he savagely roared, and I reveled in the pulsing that told me his release was as powerful as mine.

Heart pounding, I reeled. I lost track of the time as we clutched at each other's sweaty skin and fought to catch our breath.

"What the fuck was that?" I marveled, staring at the ceiling.

His breath huffed over the damp skin of my chest where his head still nestled between my tits. "I don't know, but fuck, I wish we could bottle it. We'd make a mint."

"No shit," I agreed, willing my pulse to slow down. Neither of us made any effort to move.

Finally, he lifted his head and pressed several kisses up my neck. He ended with one on my lips. It was so soft and searching that it confused my heart. Then he moved to stand upright, and his softening cock slipped out a little.

I pouted and used my legs to pull him back in. Fuck, the man was gorgeous. I didn't want him to go. I'd rather use my tongue to trace the tattoos that covered his chest.

He laughed breathlessly and held my hips. His gaze darted to the clock on the stove. "I gotta get cleaned up."

"Ugh! Fine," I muttered, but the smile slipped through my mock pout.

One last kiss and he stepped away, leaving me empty and bereft in more than only the physical sense. That should've been my first clue that things were shifting in a direction I didn't want them to.

Since I didn't have family to spend the holidays with, I always offered to work over Christmas Eve and Christmas. New Year's I took off because I would hang out with friends. Which meant I was off before and after those days.

Which was why on the night before Christmas Eve, I was hanging out with Tori and Owen. Jordan had to go to the airport to pick up his sister. In a way, it hurt that he hadn't invited me to go with. I made the mistake of telling Tori while Owen stepped out on their porch to take a call.

"Whoa, whoa, whoa. Back that train up. So the guy you've been hooking up with is picking up his sister and you are *upset*?" The gaping mouth and rapidly blinking eyes would've been comical if I hadn't pulled myself up short.

"No! Of course not! That's not what I meant." Turning my back to where Tori sat on her couch with a glass of wine, I pretended I was looking for a movie in the stand under her TV.

"Then what exactly did you mean when you said it 'kind of hurt your feelings that he didn't even seem to consider' asking you to go with him? I thought it wasn't serious. Did something change and you didn't tell me—your mostest bestest friend in the whole wide world?"

"It came out wrong!" I surged to my feet and slapped a movie case to my thigh. Honestly, I had no idea what it was; I snapped the case open in a huff and shoved it in the player. Not believing those words had come out of my mouth because I said I didn't want a relationship. Fuck buddies didn't get attached. I wasn't getting attached!

I was getting attached.

Shit.

I hit play and groaning came from the TV.

"Oh my God!" Tori shrieked and practically flew over the coffee table in a hurdle move and grabbed the remote from me. She repeatedly hit the stop button though it quit playing the first time. Her face was flaming red and her chest heaved like she'd run around the block five times.

For a moment I stood there confused. Then my own problems faded and my jaw dropped. I blinked twice and snapped my mouth shut. Then I blurted out "Please tell me that wasn't a sex tape of you and Owen?"

"It was totally a sex tape of us." Tori squealed and spun toward the patio door where Owen had come back in. He was laughing his ass off.

"Oh. My. God! Who puts sex tapes on discs anymore?" I was a mix between traumatized and wanting to bust out laughing.

"I didn't want it being on the internet!" Tori shouted as she covered her face with both hands.

For the rest of the night, I would periodically turn to Tori and shake my head in disbelief. Owen would crack up laughing, and Tori would cover her head with her lap blanket.

Though I could've lived a lifetime without hearing what my friends sounded like when they had sex, it had been the perfect distraction.

When I hugged them goodbye, I giggled.

"Don't," Tori warned.

I laughed all the way to my car.

When I got home, my deadbolt wasn't locked. Frowning, I tried to remember if I engaged it when I left. I always used both locks. Nervous, I called Tori before going inside. I was a paranoid freak when it came to doors and being able to secure them. But with my past, who wouldn't be?

When I was seven, my mom's drug dealer boyfriend busted into our house drunk or high. She had frantically shoved me in the closet and thrown her dirty laundry over me with a tearful plea to be quiet. She called the police, but they didn't make it in time. He had killed my mom while I hid, trembling and crying silent tears.

They never found him and I had no real information to give them. I was a kid—and a terrified one at that. With no family they could find to claim me, I got a one-way ticket into the foster care system. No one wanted to adopt a seven-year-old girl who refused to talk.

For the first year and a half, I mutely bounced around from home to home. Finally, I ended up in one of the better ones. Not because my foster parents gave two shits about me, but because they lived next door to Tori and her grandmother. That was why Tori and I were best friends for life. Despite the fact that I moved to Texas as soon as I got my nursing license, and I never went back. Tori followed me, eventually.

"Blair, call the police," Tori insisted after I told her what I suspected.

"Why? Because I didn't lock my deadbolt?" Nothing seemed out of place, so I told myself I'd been in a hurry when I left for Tori's.

Except when I went in my bedroom, one dresser drawer wasn't closed completely. I might be a bit frazzled when I'm rushing to and from work, and my car might at times look like I lived in it, but in my home, I'm a neat freak. Obsessively so.

When nothing seemed to be missing, I convinced myself I'd been in too big of a hurry to get to Tori and Owen's. I chastised myself for my foolishness and paranoia and pushed the incident to the back of my mind.

It didn't stop me from wishing Jordan was there.

Over the next few weeks, Jordan and I had a series of hookups. He'd been off most of the week of Christmas, and he'd sneak over to my apartment after his sister had gone to bed. Every free moment I had ended with him fucking me exactly the way I'd been dying to experience. He'd made good on his boast. Several times I messaged or called and he didn't answer right away. He always replied later, though. A sort of friendship with benefits had developed, but with each hookup I worried.

He was becoming an integral part of my life.

And that scared the shit out of me.

"All I'm saying is something seems off about this," Tori said as she refilled my wine glass.

"Like what?" I asked, rolling my eyes in exasperation from the counter across from her where I sat while she made dinner. "We're keeping it casual. Neither of us wants anything to do with a relationship."

"Well, that seems convenient for him."

"Ugh! It's convenient for both of us!" I threw my hands up in frustration. This was all because I'd slipped up that night before Christmas Eve.

"What does he do for a living?" she demanded, crossing her arms and resting a hip on the edge of the counter. Lips pursed and brow cocked, she stared at me.

"Don't know, don't care. It doesn't matter," I shot back. Though I acted unaffected, I was a little afraid that I was trying to convince myself as much as her.

"Well, he goes out of town a lot. You said y'all have never gone to his place. Sometimes he doesn't answer you until late at night." She ticked off each thing she listed. I snickered at her use of "y'all" because she'd become so "Texas" since moving down here. It was cute. It was also a distraction from the thoughts she was putting in my head.

"A lot of people travel for work. Cough, cough, your man is gone right now. The first night he offered to take me to his place, and it was my choice not to go. And maybe he works long hours," I argued before taking a sip of the deep red wine. I didn't want to talk about it anymore.

"I think he's married," she resolutely announced.

My red wine sprayed across the kitchen floor as I choked on my last mouthful.

"Ew! Manners!" she chided as she grabbed the roll of paper towels. She laughed as she wet them and wiped the floor. When she tossed them in the trash, she glanced back at me with a raised brow. "I'm just saying."

The timer went off, and she pulled the hot dish from the oven with her bright pink oven mitts and set it on a burner to cool. Owen was on an out-of-town run and wouldn't be back until tomorrow night. Prime example of people traveling for business and it being nothing insidious.

"No way," I insisted. "He doesn't wear a ring, and there's no indent from one."

"That means nothing. Not everyone who's married wears a ring. He could have a wife and kids stashed somewhere. You see it happen all the time," she countered, taking off the oven mitts and placing them next to the stove.

"I think you're crazy," I chuckled, then lifted my glass to my lips. Except I couldn't meet her gaze. That little voice was back again, and I didn't like that it was agreeing with Tori.

"Blair, what if he's a traveling salesman? Hell, he could have a woman in every city!"

"Don't be so dramatic," I scoffed, then paused and cocked my head. "Do they even have such a thing anymore?"

She shrugged.

"Either way, I don't believe he's married or in a relationship," I confidently reiterated.

But she'd planted the seed.

SEVEN

Jordan

"CRAZY"—FROM ASHES TO NEW

Blair: What are we doing?

Me: Do I need to spell it out or give you an actual list?

Blair: No, I meant is this still casual? Like, booty calls? Or are we… I don't know

Me: Are you trying to give us a label? Because I thought we said we were keeping things casual

Blair: Never mind. It's all good. Are you busy?

Me: I'm out of town

The dots appeared and disappeared several times, causing me to frown. I couldn't help but wonder where she was going with this. Was she hinting that she wanted a relationship now? Or was she worried I was getting too clingy? My heart sped up at the thought of her ending our agreement. I wasn't ready to give her up. That should've set off alarm bells in my head.

Blair: Okay. Let me know when you're back in town

Me: Will do

"Beck! Get off your goddamn phone!" Coach shouted, and I jumped. Realizing he'd been talking, I stuffed it in my bag. Fuck, I was never "that guy."

"Sorry, Coach," I muttered. Alex, Jericho, Cameron, and Kristoffer shot me questioning looks. Mikko shook his head. He was the only one who knew anything about Blair. It wouldn't be hard for him to figure out it was her I was talking to. My mom never messaged me right before a game. She always sent a good luck text early that morning. My dad rarely texted or called. If he did, it was after the game. Not since he remarried and started his second family, anyway.

"Let's get out there and show them this might be their house, but we carry the mortgage!" Coach called out. Everyone laughed and shouted in agreement.

I grabbed my cage and set it on my head. Then I slid my hands in my gloves. Kristoffer, Alex, and the rest of the boys gave me a fist bump as they filed out of the locker room and started the trek down the hall to the ice.

With each step, I questioned what I really wanted with Blair. The thought of waking up to her each morning suddenly had appeal. My stomach flipped and cramped at where my thoughts were going. I broke out in a cold sweat.

"What the fuck?" Mikko asked as we approached the rack where our sticks awaited.

He got a shake of my head before I dropped my mask over my face. It was game time, and everything else went on the back burner. It had to because I couldn't have thoughts of Blair clouding my head.

Stick in hand, I lumbered to the ice. The second my skates hit the frozen surface, my adrenaline shot into overdrive. The worry that I would disappoint my dad's side of the family was something that went through my head every time. My heart sped up, and I had to take a deep breath to quell the initial jitters that always hit me before the first puck drop. Nothing else mattered except keeping an eye on that fucking biscuit and ensuring it didn't make it into my net.

This is my net.

Minnesota wasted no time coming at me. My gaze sharp, I locked on the puck and kept my body loose and prepared to react. The first shot I caught on the arm, and despite my gear, it stung. There was no time to think about it though because they came again, faked left, then passed the puck and tried to backhand it in. I dove down, and it bounced off my glove.

No matter how strong our defense was, we couldn't seem to gain control of the puck, and the whole time, Minnesota was swinging on my nuts like Tarzan. They were playing aggressive as fuck, and I was sweating my ass off less than six minutes into the period.

Tension was high, and the pressure to stop every puck they fired at me was immense. If Minnesota scored, it was ultimately my fault. I couldn't let that happen. It was unrealistic to hope for a shut out every game, but I always breathed a sigh of relief if we scored first.

During a break in play, I skated to the bench with my teammates while the ice was quickly shoveled.

"You're doing great, Beck," Kristoffer encouraged as he came up alongside me. Sweat dripped in my eyes as I worked to slow my heaving breaths.

"They're trying to wear me down. Fucking hell, I need a little more defense guys." I panted. It didn't help that Blair kept creeping into my head at the most inopportune moments.

"We're trying, dude," he replied. "They're playing aggressive and dirty as fuck tonight."

"Oh, trust me, I know," I sarcastically retorted, shooting a glare toward Minnesota's bench.

As I leaned on the boards, I flipped up my cage. One of the trainers handed me a towel to quickly wipe my head and face. Once I was finished, I tossed it back to him.

Coach reiterated what he wanted to see, and we nodded our understanding. As I made my way back to my net, I dropped my cage with determination. They were *not* going to get past me.

That brief respite allowed me to breathe for a second and ground myself. No matter how hard it was, I had to push all thoughts of Blair out of my head. There wasn't room in there for her and the game. Refocused, I found my zen place that they had obliterated at the start of the game.

Everyone got into position, the puck dropped, and we were back in business.

Cam finally got the puck and passed it to Alex as they hauled ass toward Minnesota's net. Alex's shot rebounded off the goalie's pads, and Kristoffer immediately took a snap shot and lit the lamp.

"Fuck yes!" I shouted as the guys congratulated Kristoffer. My smile was huge as a bit of the weight lifted off my shoulders. The first point wasn't against me. Thank Christ.

A quick line change and Sin faced off at center ice against Minnesota's center, Kuznetsov. The puck dropped, and the players crashed the circle as they fought for control. Minnesota came out on top, and they set Tybee up for a perfect slapshot. The thwack his stick made when it made contact with the puck barely registered before it was slamming into my trapper.

"Hell yes!" Sinner and the line cheered me on.

With a grin, I tossed the puck to the ref. But we were only beginning, and I refused to let myself get cocky. Confident, yes. There was a difference.

By the end of the first period, we had three on the board, and Minnesota had none. Not for their lack of trying.

The second period gave us two more goals. Going into the third, we were sitting at five to nothing, but while we were pumped, we knew better than to celebrate too early. A lot could happen in twenty minutes.

I was soaked with sweat by the time we had three minutes left on the clock. The entire period, Minnesota was on their A game, but so was I. The problem was, I was tiring. No matter how hard I tried to keep Blair out of my head, it was almost impossible. Reluctantly, I had to admit my attention suffered each time she slipped into my thoughts.

We ended up with a player in the penalty box almost consistently through the last half of the period. That gave Minnesota the advantage of a power play, and they were on me like nobody's business.

It took everything my teammates had to help me out. Trying for control of the puck wasn't happening. Minnesota was constantly attacking the net as their shots on goal racked up.

Out of breath and darting from side to side in my crease, I did my best to lock on the puck as they passed it at lightning speed. Before I knew what was happening, I lost the puck for a split second. It was enough that Fieldman snuck it in from right outside the top of the crease.

"Fuck!" I grumbled.

"It's okay, big guy. We got this," Westy offered as he gripped my mask and stared into my eyes. Xavier Westergaard was a fellow Canadian and a brute of a defenseman.

I nodded, took a deep breath, and regained my focus.

For that minute of play, nothing entered the net except my ass when one of their players intentionally slammed into me and I hit the ice hard. Pissed, I grabbed him and lifted him until his skates were off the ice. Honestly, I was prepared to toss his dumb ass, but the ref blew his whistle. At the end of the period, I had a penalty for holding.

Fuck it. Totally worth it, because when the clock ran out in the third period, we were the victors.

I couldn't keep the grin off my face.

"Goddamn, Beck! You were on freaking fire tonight!" Dmitry said as he plowed into me and wrapped me in a bear hug.

Yeah, maybe once I got my head on straight and quit letting a certain curvy, dark-haired woman take over my concentration.

"Hell, you guys didn't do half bad yourself. That's what I call motherfucking teamwork," I replied, keeping my admissions to myself.

"Gasp! Such language! Do you kiss your mother with that mouth?" Jericho teased in mock outrage. All the guys laughed, and we ribbed one another the entire time we headed off the ice. Everyone waiting along the hall held out their hands for a fist bump as we passed.

In the locker room, I yanked off my mask and gloves, then set them aside. As everyone laughed and celebrated, I toweled off as much sweat as I could. Spirits were high, and everyone seemed to be talking at once. With a groan, I leaned over to unlace my skates after I'd removed my pads.

"Listen up!" Coach shouted to be heard above the excited chatter in the locker room. Conversations dwindled until you could've heard a pin drop. "Great game, boys! That was some Stanley Cup playing out there tonight. You all should be proud of yourselves. I know you're going to want to celebrate, but I want to remind you that we have an early flight in the morning. You *will not* be late to the bus." He cast a glare Dmitry and Jericho's direction, and they gave him shrugs and had the grace to look properly chastised. We had waited on them in New York, and Coach had been a mad motherfucker.

"Yes, Coach," Dmitry muttered. Jericho wisely nodded.

A snicker sounded from somewhere in the back but was quickly subdued.

"Good job. Thank you. Now go wash your asses." He ended the speech, and a good-natured grin kicked up the corners of his mouth before he gave us a chin lift and left the locker room.

Several of the guys came by and gave me a shoulder bump, knucks, or a straight up hug. I'd lived up to my nickname painted on my throat guard, and I'd been a fucking wall. We'd won the game 5-1. Their goal had been made in the third period when I was getting tired as fuck.

"Party in Isak and Mikhail's room!" Cameron announced. Isak laughed, but Mikhail frowned and huffed. Mikhail had no need to worry. If we were hanging out in one of our rooms, it wasn't really a wild party, it was just us chilling.

"So are you two dating?" Mikko asked when he sat down on the bench next to me.

"No. Absolutely not. We're just having fun. I like hanging out with her. Besides the best sex of my life, she's funny. She so different from the puck bunnies. She's bold but sweet, you know?" I pulled my socks on and stood to tuck my shirt in and do up my pants. What I didn't add was that after tonight's game, I was worried she was becoming too much of a distraction.

"And she has a banging body. Don't forget that part," he added with a chuckle and a devious eyebrow wiggle.

"Hey! Watch it, Heikkinen."

"Oh shit." His eyes were wide as he drawled out the expletive.

"What?"

"You really like her."

"Of course I like her." Not making eye contact, I looped my tie around my neck and cinched it up.

"Man, you just need to be careful."

"It's not like she's an ax murderer, and I'm pretty sure I could over-power her," I snickered, trying to make light of the conversation. If I didn't, we were going to enter territory I wasn't prepared to step into at the moment—if ever.

"That's not what I'm talking about. I'm worried she's after your money or the fame."

"She's not like that," I argued. A frown drew my eyebrows down, and my teeth ground in frustration.

"Yeah, that's what you're saying now, but we›ve seen it before. They all want to latch on to a hockey player, but they say they're okay with casual until it's too late and they're photoshopping us." He pulled the towel from his waist and used it to dry his hair.

"She doesn't know," I muttered quietly as I shrugged.

He stopped mid swipe with the towel, his hands dropped, and he stared at me slack jawed. "Come again? How can she *not know*?"

"It's never come up."

"Where the hell does she think you go all the time?"

"She thinks I work out of town a lot. We don't get personal. It's just fucking," I said the words, but they rang hollow.

Mikko wisely didn't say anything more.

Once everyone had showered and changed, we gathered our shit and headed to the bus that would take us back to the hotel. Mikko and I stopped by our room to drop off our stuff, then I grabbed my bag of snacks and a couple of bottles of water from our fridge.

My grandfather was my first text.

Grandpa: Great job! You were a beast!

I replied with a quick thank you and sent my love to him and my grandmother.

Then a text came through from my dad that had me smiling.

Dad: Good game, son! Proud of you!

While we may not be as close as we once were, I still loved him, and I knew he loved me. He simply had other priorities now. While I was grown and on my own, my siblings were young. It was weird but cool. I just wished I saw them more.

His text was followed by one from my mom and then one from my sister. After replying to them all, I set my phone on my charger. For a second, I considered texting Blair. Instead, I took a deep breath and strengthened my resolve. Though we said we were keeping what we had casual, tonight proved she was taking up too much real estate in my head. I needed to find a way to separate myself better—or maybe I needed to end things with her completely. Ignoring the tightness in my chest at that thought, I went to round up my roommate.

"Let's go! Pinch it off!" I shouted as I pounded on the bathroom door with a grin. It swung open with a scowling Mikko shaking his head.

"I was only pissing. You'd know if I was shitting," he corrected as he grabbed his snacks. We walked down the hall together and were joined by Dmitry and Jericho as we passed their room.

Voices could be heard coming from Isak and Mikhail's room when we knocked. Cameron answered the door and ushered us in.

"Hey!" Several of the guys called out as they held up their bags of trail mix. I snickered at the fact that I'd started a trend. Then I held up my matching bag and grabbed a seat on one of the beds. I tossed one of the bottles to Mikko who gave me a chin lift in thanks.

We sat around discussing the game and whatever other shit came up. What I didn't discuss was Blair, despite Mikko mentioning her when Alex, Cameron, and Kristoffer brought up how their girls had all gotten together to watch the game on TV. Instead, I shrugged the topic off and changed the subject.

"Looks like everyone has your nuts," Mikhail observed as he pointed at the bags sitting around the room. Several of the guys snickered at the double meaning that was lost in translation for Mikhail.

When I'd made my first trip into the local grocery store, I'd had a sweet tooth. Except I tried my damnedest to eat healthy. As I'd gone up and down the aisles, I saw a bag that said "H-E-B Sweet and Sassy Trail Mix" and decided to give it a try. I'd been hooked ever since. Now, so were most of my teammates. I found myself thinking about Blair again when I wondered if she would like them. Then I mentally shook the shit out of myself for thinking about her again.

"Yeah, but they aren't as good as mine." I grinned as I tossed a handful in my mouth, promising myself I wouldn't let her climb in my head again tonight.

"No, I don't suppose they are." Dmitry snickered.

"I have some too!" Mikko piped in as he held his bag up in the air.

Then he frowned as he looked at his, then mine, then Alex's. "Except my sack is smaller."

"That's a damn shame," I mumbled around my mouthful.

"Not everyone can have big sacks," Alex added sagely.

"True. We must be happy with the size of our sacks and be willing to share our nuts with those less fortunate." Jericho's bag rustled as he shoved his meaty paw in and grabbed a handful. Then he held it up to Mikhail. "Want some?"

Mikhail cocked a brow and made no attempt to accept Jericho's nuts.

"Gimme some of your nuts," Kristoffer demanded as he tapped me with the back of his hand.

"You want my sweet and sassy nuts in your mouth, don't you? I knew it," I joked.

Mikhail rolled his eyes. "There is something seriously wrong with you guys."

"He's jealous of my sack," I whispered to Kristoffer who chortled and shot a corn nut onto the carpet.

After about an hour, guys started leaving. Feeling tired to my bones once the adrenaline had worn off, I stood with a stretch. "Okay, I'm out."

Mikko followed my lead, and we shuffled back to our room.

As I stripped down to my boxer briefs, I saw I had several notifications. Telling myself I was only checking them in case it was something from my mom or sister, I picked up my phone. My chest got tight, and I got that anticipatory flutter like I did before a game. Ignoring the alarms that went off when my heart raced at seeing Blair's name and going against the voice in my head telling me not to do it, I opened her messages.

Blair: Hey. I'm sorry if I made things weird.

Blair: I hope you had a good day

Blair: Okay. Talk to you when you get back

Blair: Bye

"I'm betting those aren't messages from your family," Mikko teased with a smirk as he fell into his bed.

My gaze flickered toward him, then back to my phone. Debating, I finally sent her a message.

Me: Can I call you?

Regret assailed me for leaving my phone in the room. If I'd brought it with, I wouldn't have missed her messages. She didn't reply, and I immediately started wondering if she was sleeping or if she'd gone out. I hated the slight burn of jealousy that hit me at the thought of her being out and getting hit on by other guys. Not that I could blame them. She was fucking gorgeous.

And that smile. Imagining it had me throwing all my decisions to cut ties with her out the damn window.

Fucking hell, that smile was worth more than her body.

It was what I fell asleep imagining.

And that's how I knew I was screwed.

EIGHT

Jordan

"DIE WITH ME"—GEMINI SYNDROME

B Y THE TIME I TRUDGED INTO MY HOUSE AFTER THE END OF
our travels, I was wiped. It had been the most exhausting four-
game road trip of my life. I'd taken more pucks to my body than
I had in a long time.

Not bothering with unpacking, I dropped my suitcase by the door
and went to the kitchen for a glass of water. "Hey, Herman. Miss me?"

I poured a little of my water in the dish under his pot.

A sigh left my lips, and I set the glass down to go through the
mail stacked on my counter. My cleaning lady had been checking my
mail and saving it for me. She was freaking amazing. I'd hired her after
Alex spoke so highly of her. When I interviewed her, she had leaned

forward and asked me, "You don't have one of those giant cats like Mr. Kosinski, do you?"

I'd laughed and told her I had Herman.

The doorbell rang, and I wondered which of my neighboring teammates was already trying to crash my few minutes of solitude.

Except it was none of them.

It was one of the guards from the front gate that stood there looking nervous and uncomfortable. When he cleared his throat, I noticed the big basket he was holding.

"Did a fan drop that off?" I wasn't exactly sure how some crazy fans found out exactly where we lived, but it was part of why we either moved into gated communities like this one or in homes with serious security fencing.

"Um, not exactly," he hedged, making me shoot him a questioning stare. I knew that they checked things that were dropped off the best they could. That was when I noticed the fluffy blue blanket and what looked like a baby bottle. Denial ran rampant through me like a freight train.

"Oh no," I immediately argued while shaking my head.

"But Mr. Beck, he's so cute," he asserted with an encouraged, albeit nervous smile.

Heart pounding as my life metaphorically crashed around me, all I could do was stand there with my jaw dragging on the floor. The blanket started to move as the baby underneath began to wiggle. All I could think of was the crazy chick that dropped her baby off with Alex. This could not be happening to me too.

When the blanket was shoved back and a fluffy little creature popped its head up, I grinned in relief. "Beaker!"

The puppy shook the basket in its exuberance, nearly toppling out until I snatched him up. Immediately, he began licking me like a little lunatic. I'd bought the rare black teacup Maltipoo for Zena after she'd begged for the puppy that cost me over five grand. Yeah, for what was essentially a mixed-breed puppy. Crazy, but then again, at the time I thought I was crazy for her and probably would've done anything for her—except propose because I wasn't ready for that.

The bottle turned out to be a squeaky toy. Thank fuck.

"I'm sorry, I didn't know what to do with him when she dropped him off. I tried to get her to stay while I called you, but she took off. Then I tried to call you, but there was no answer. She said there's a note in the basket." The poor guard looked ready to piss his pants. It made me wonder if I was that scary. Maybe I was.

After checking my phone, I winced. "No, I'm sorry. My phone is still on airplane mode."

"So it's okay that I brought him here?"

"Yeah, man. It's all good." I took the proffered basket.

He nodded, and his shoulders relaxed. A smile lit up his face, and he scratched the wiggling puppy, then left.

"What the fuck is your owner up to?" I muttered to the hyperactive ball of fluff. Under the blanket, there was a heavyweight envelope. Breaking the seal, I opened it and slid the folded note card out. It still smelled of the perfume Zena wore.

My stomach cramped and my lip curled at the audacity the woman had to contact me after everything she'd done.

Jordan,

I'm dropping Bubbles off with you because I accepted a modeling job in Singapore. My assistant is going with me, and we can't bring him.

I'll happily take him back when I return, but it will be approximately two months before I fly back.

Kisses,

Zena

"Is she out of her mind? And how could you let her call you Bubbles?" I spoke to the playful but oblivious puppy in my arms. He gave a happy bark. Truth be told, I'd missed the little shit since I'd booted his "mother" the fuck out of my house the day I found out about her insane behavior. The last thing I wanted was for her to have a reason to communicate with me. I didn't want to see her; I didn't want to talk to her. And I really didn't have time for a puppy. I was rarely home.

"Shit. What am I going to do with you?"

He rested his tiny paws on my chest to lick my neck and chin. Then I set him down to go change my clothes. He nipped and yapped at my heels the entire way. It made me laugh, but I was terrified I'd accidentally kick him. Even a light tap from my giant feet could do some damage to him. That was when I found out that I should've taken him straight outside because the little fucker pissed on the rug in my bathroom while I'd changed into a T-shirt and some basketball shorts.

"Goddamn it," I grumbled as I scooped him up and rolled up the soiled rug. Initially, I thought about washing it, but I was afraid he'd still smell the urine and continue to pee on it, so I chucked it. "You're going to be a pain in my ass, aren't you?"

Carrying him outside, I ignored the cold and brought him around the pool to the back of the yard. Crouching, I set him down and watched as he sniffed around in the dead winter grass. He wandered over to the fence and took a shit that would've made a bigger dog proud.

"Damn, buddy," I exclaimed before picking him up again. I worried about him falling in the pool, so I carried him back inside. The accident in the bathroom told me I wouldn't be able to leave him running free, but I sure as hell didn't have a kennel or anything for him other than the basket, the squeaky toy, and the two small cans of food in the bottom of the basket.

Grabbing my phone, I opened up my contacts and dialed Mikko.

"Miss me already?"

"Like a chapped ass," I shot back with a laugh. "But seriously, I need to run to the pet store. Wanna go with?"

"Uhhh, the pet store?"

"It's a long story. I'll explain on the way if you're game."

"Sure thing, because this I have to hear."

"Pick you up in fifteen," I told him before I ended the call and tossed my phone on the bed. Since I needed to go out in the cold, I switched my shorts for jeans. A pair of Vans and a jacket later, I was walking into my garage. With Beaker, I refused to call him Bubbles, I drove to the place Mikko had recently bought on the next block. Who the fuck named a dog Bubbles? Zena, that was who.

I called him Beaker because he reminded me of the goofy little assistant in a Muppet skit I saw on YouTube once as a kid. No clue why, since he sure as hell wasn't orange, but it was something about him—he reminded me of a Beaker.

Mikko must've been watching for me because he came out as soon as I pulled up in front of his place.

"Why are we... Whoa. Where did that come from?" He dropped his chin and raised his brows at me. Beaker hopped out of my arms and attacked Mikko with the fastest tongue in Texas. My friend sat there laughing as we headed to the nearest pet store. On the way, I filled him in.

"So you're telling me she just dropped it off and expects you to dog sit until she decides to come back from a *two-month* job in Singapore?" he clarified.

"Pretty much." Though I was doing my damnedest to remain detached, anger boiled within me, setting my insides on fire. Hatred for the woman's manipulative actions burned through my veins.

"Like you don't have a busy life and out-of-town games?"

"Right." Not to mention, I didn't want any contact with her after what she'd done.

"What are you going to do?" he asked as he pet the now sleeping puppy in his lap.

"I don't know. Figure something out," I muttered.

"Find a home for it," he suggested, but I immediately shook my head. It was probably one of the single most ignorant choices I'd ever made, but I couldn't look in those little brown eyes and do it. Pass him off like Zena essentially did. Truthfully, she didn't have a way to contact me because I'd blocked her on everything. Checking to see how her six-month-old puppy was faring obviously wasn't a concern of hers.

"Why don't you ask your nurse chick if she'd dog sit when we have away games?"

A snort escaped me. "Dude, we don't have that kind of relationship—hell, we don't have a relationship, period. We fuck."

He snorted, and I shot him a glare.

"Right, okay, whatever, but she still might help you out. At least until you can find a reputable dog-sitting company, or person, or whatever they call them."

I shut the truck off and rested my forearm on the steering wheel. My forehead rested on my arm. The thought of asking Blair to do anything for me skated too close to the friendship line. It seemed like she was already questioning our boundaries, and the last thing I wanted to do was lead her on.

"Maybe," I mumbled. "Let's go inside."

Before we got out, I snagged Beaker from Mikko and cradled him in my arms. He initially roused, then dropped back off to sleep.

"I'll get the cart, since you have your hands full," Mikko teased with a snicker. "Dude, I gotta tell you, he's cute, but that is the least masculine dog I've ever seen. Except maybe one of those naked dogs."

I used my free hand to flip him off.

We didn't make it down the first aisle before three different female employees had asked if we needed help finding anything. Mikko ate it up and jumped in before I could say a word. "My buddy got a new puppy. He doesn't have anything for him, and we're kind of lost."

They all gushed over Beaker and shamelessly flirted with both me and Mikko. They went on about how "cool" Mikko's accent was and that I obviously wasn't from Texas either. Exasperation was creeping in because I wasn't at the pet store looking for a hook-up. Especially one that was of questionable age—and not Blair. Mikko was younger than me but still needed to be careful. Any relationship with an underage girl would fuck up his life.

I cleared my throat. "Maybe this would be easier if we just had one person helping us find stuff."

They almost fell over themselves in their attempts to be the one chosen.

"Excuse me, is there a problem over here?" A man had approached where our little crowd was congregated at the end of aisle one. The girls immediately sobered and took on professional demeanors.

"I'm trying to figure out what things I need for him," I replied, pointing to my newly reacquired puppy. A glance at his name tag showed he was a manager. "Tom," I tacked on to my sentence.

"Ladies, please check customer service for returns," he firmly but politely instructed. They all nodded and shuffled off to do as he bid. Then he asked a series of questions that I answered the best I could.

By the time we were leaving the store, I had a cartful of stuff—most of which Tom hadn't recommended but I thought was cool. That made it totally necessary for Beaker. I also had a list of reputable dog sitters.

Mikko and I loaded everything up in the backseat. A smile kicked up the corner of my mouth when I sat the little dog bed where my ass had been as Blair rode me for the first time in my truck.

"Thanks, man," I told Mikko as he was getting out of the truck in front of his house. We'd stopped by my place first to unload everything, then I took him home.

"Anytime," he shot back with an easy grin.

I returned home and stood in my kitchen, staring at the list of dog sitters, then glancing at my phone. The thought of having random people taking care of Beaker didn't sit well with me. No matter how highly recommended they were.

"Herman, you know I value my privacy. I don't want some random ass person in here taking care of Beaker. Too bad you couldn't do it. But I can't even count on you to take out the trash." The little succulent seemed to stare back at me.

"Defiant little fuck," I mumbled.

Heaving a sigh, I found the number I wanted and dialed.

NINE

Blair

"APOCALYPSE"—CIGARETTES AFTER SEX

OSITIVE MY TEXT MESSAGES HAD SCARED JORDAN OFF, I'D prepared myself to never hear from him again. The worst thing I could've done was ask him something like that, especially when he was out of town. It should've been a face-to-face kind of conversation.

Stupid.

It would go down in history as the best sex of my life, ruining me for other men, but I couldn't find it in me to regret a single minute we'd spent together.

Yes, he'd texted me asking if he could call, but I'd been at work and all hell broke loose before I had a chance to reply. Then there was a series of sleep/work cycles that were driving me to an early grave. Add in the random text messages and phone calls from Henry, and I was mentally exhausted. Through it all, I hadn't had the brainpower to think of replying. I simply focused on making it through each day until I could fall into bed, wake up, wash, rinse, and repeat.

My life truly sucked, and I blamed it on my shit choice in men. Henry had put me up to my eyeballs in debt, which was why I had no life other than working now. Then again, it was my fault too for being so trusting. He told me his ex-wife was supposed to take care of their credit cards in the divorce but claimed she didn't and it ruined his credit. Each time he needed me to make a payment on something, he told me he'd pay me back. I'd believed his lies.

Jordan hadn't reached out again after that last request to call. And with each day that passed, I told myself it would be awkward to contact him—that I'd waited too long. I'd resigned myself to accepting it was over.

That's why his call earlier asking me if I could come over had surprised me. Conveniently, it was also my only day off this week.

"I don't know if this is a good idea," I spoke into the car where I had my phone on speaker. The rattletrap was so old it didn't have Bluetooth as an option.

"What are you talking about? This is the perfect opportunity to snoop and see if there's a family in the picture," Tori rationalized.

"Yeah, but what if this is just his bachelor pad?" I asked, staring at the massive house, knowing there was no way. This was a home. One that screamed family. Big family, at that.

"You said the place was huge," Tori shot back. "That doesn't sound like a bachelor pad to me."

She only reiterated what I'd already told myself. I took a deep breath, and my exhale rushed out. "Okay. I'll go in."

"Good. Then call me on the way home. I want deets of the house and the sex," Tori demanded with a giggle.

"You're awful, and I'm not giving you details of my sex life."

"Yes you will. Besides, you heard part of mine. Bye!" With her laughter still ringing out, she ended the call.

"Ew, Tori," I muttered to myself.

My car leaked oil, so I pulled up to the curb, though he'd told me to park on either side of the driveway. The thought of marring his pristine-looking concrete made me cringe.

The hinges creaked loudly as I opened the door, and I winced. My neighbor had offered to spray some stuff in it, but he'd acted like there were strings attached to his minimal aide, so I'd passed. If I ever had a free minute, I'd stop and buy a can of that crap my last foster father had always used. With a heaved sigh, I bumped it closed with finality as I walked up to the covered front porch.

My knock yielded a yapping bark, and I frowned in confusion. Jordan had never mentioned a dog. The voice beyond the door was muted by the thick wood. When it swung open, his tall frame struck me speechless. My heart fluttered, and my breath caught. In that split second, I knew I had messed up. I'd fallen for him.

So stupid.

"Thanks for coming over," he practically burst out in relief. A little black fluff ball darted out between his legs. It growled and tugged at the laces of my hot pink Chucks.

"Whoa there, Killer. What did my shoes ever do to you?" Crouched down, I combed my fingers through his fluffy fur. Immediately, he gripped my hand in his little front legs and licked my hand between pretending to attack me. I took the opportunity to pick him up.

"That's what I called you about. Do you want to come in?" he asked hopefully.

"Sure," I replied, trying my best to act like his proximity wasn't doing crazy things to my body and senses. Yeah, I was already in too deep. How had that happened?

He motioned for me to follow him, and I tried to unobtrusively check out the details of the house as we passed through. The only pictures I saw were sporadically placed and were of him, a woman who looked like she had to be his sister or a cousin, and an older woman that was possibly their mom or aunt. There were pics of him as a young boy with his dad fishing that made me smile. No sign of any kids or what appeared to be significant others. There were several signed and framed images of hockey players, leading me to believe he was a devoted hockey fan, but not much else to go by.

We went into a casual living room, tastefully decorated with leather furniture and dark wood. The floors were tiled in a driftwood pattern and color. It was masculine, but random touches here and there softened it. Bright light washed over the furnishings from the massive windows that faced a sparkling pool in the backyard. In the corner of the room was a little kennel that still had the tags on it. So maybe the puppy was new.

"I need to ask a favor of you," he began.

Suspicion narrowed my gaze as I dragged my attention from the framed hockey jersey on the wall. "For?"

He leaned forward, resting his forearms on his knees, and then pressed his fingertips together. "Would you consider dog sitting on the days I'm out of town?"

"Excuse me?" I was floored. He went from stressing over the thought of labeling whatever we were doing to asking me to dog sit?

He blew me off and sent me through so many ups and downs that my head was spinning. Now he wanted me to watch his dog that I didn't even know he had. Was he nuts?

"Beaker was unexpected." At the sound of his name, the puppy stopped trying to eat my hand and stared excitedly over at the big man who had said it. His tail was wagging like mad. "My ex dumped him here because he became inconvenient. She says she's coming back for him. If I was a dick, I'd rehome him, but I kind of love the little shit—I liked him when I bought him."

Laughter bubbled up within my chest. "This is the least likely dog I could imagine for you."

"No shit. But he's mine just the same."

"Look, Jordan, I'd love to help you out, but I can't have dogs in my apartment, and…."

"You can watch him here," he inserted without letting me finish. The hopeful, eager look made me feel awful that I couldn't step up to the plate.

"I work almost every night," I explained. A helpless shrug lifted my shoulders while I snuggled the tiny dog to my chest. He was adorable.

"What? Why? Surely a nurse shouldn't be scheduled that many hours or days in a row," he sputtered. Not that he was wrong. A few of the nights I pulled were as a contract PRN nurse. I picked up needed shifts at other hospitals after I'd signed up for as much as they'd allow at mine.

"Technically, I shouldn't," I admitted. "But I need the money."

That truth was not something I was proud of, nor liked to admit. Dropping my gaze to little Beaker, I avoided eye contact with the sex god I'd been casually sleeping with—and missed.

"I'll pay you," he immediately offered, and my attention snapped back to him.

"What? No." On the tails of my thoughts of us sleeping together, that sounded like prostitution. Though I knew that wasn't what he was talking about, it still skeezed me out.

"Why not? Whatever you make on your extra shifts, I'll pay. Hell, I'll even add bonuses," he announced, giving me a worse puppy dog face than Beaker.

"Jordan, it wouldn't be right. We've slept together. It would make it weird. Unless we're not going to have sex again," I explained, the thought of never being intimate with him again causing my stomach to bottom out and my heart to ache. Jesus, I was so screwed.

And here I was considering watching his ex's dog. The woman he'd been willing to commit for, who'd then done something awful enough to destroy his faith in relationships. Kind of like Henry had to me. God, we were a mess.

"Is that what you want?" he asked as his chin came up defensively and his expression went blank.

Straightening my spine, I prepared to lie. But no matter how bad I wanted to say yes because the increase in money for less work was so very appealing, I couldn't. My shoulders drooped, and I shook my head. My heart sang at the immediate easing of my budding anxiety.

The relief I experienced was mirrored in him as he expelled his held breath in a huff. Then he raked one perfectly sculpted hand through his hair, leaving it in disarray to smooth over the light growth of beard. The one I'd come to love when it scraped the inside of my thighs.

At the direction of my thoughts, my face burned.

"Please?" he whispered, and I crumbled. The fear hit me that I'd likely do anything for the handsome man staring at me with such hope lighting his bright blue eyes.

"Fine. I'll do it." Though I would've done it for free, I really did need the extra money unless I wanted to end up homeless. Keeping up on my rent I was shackled to because of a lease and keeping up with the credit card payments was slowly killing me.

The smile that caused him to glow also gifted me with a glimpse of that dimple I loved so much. Damn, he was gorgeous.

We worked out the details, then locked Beaker in his new kennel, much to his displeasure. Then we made perfect use of Jordan's massive king-sized bed.

It was weird to be staying at Jordan's home when he wasn't there. Though he told me I could sleep in his bed, that seemed too girl-friend-ish, and I was already having a hard time reminding my fool-ish heart that we weren't a couple and never would be. Instead, I used one of the several guest bedrooms—yes, several—and I stayed as far away from his room as I could.

I was doing the best I could to maintain a business and impersonal relationship. If we got into too much of each other's personal lives it would further blur the already hazy lines.

On the upside, thanks to the money Jordan was paying me, I'd been able to drop back on my hours. A quick glance in my rearview mirror surprised me, like it did each of the last few mornings. The dark circles under my eyes that I'd begun to believe would be permanent had slowly disappeared. It made me look like a totally different person.

"Are you almost here?" he asked, sounding a little nervous.

"It says I'm three minutes away."

It had been two weeks since we agreed to Operation Babysit Beaker as we'd jokingly dubbed it. Beaker had an unexpected vet appointment that morning. Jordan had rushed him in after he ate part of a sock. He had called me in a panic, begging me to go with him, but I'd literally been sitting in my dentist's chair. Jordan took him alone but didn't have time to drive him to the house before he had to leave to go out of town. He'd given me an address that I plugged into my GPS and was blindly following.

"Okay," he breathed out.

Taking the turn my GPS instructed, I frowned. "Jordan, it took me to a parking lot outside the Drago Communications Center."

"Yeah, do you see the bus at the back of the lot. Inside the employee fence?"

"Yes," I acknowledged in confusion.

"Pull in there. It's open right now."

"Um, okay," I replied. The entire time I was passing through the open gate, I was afraid someone was going to chase me down or call security on me. The plain black bus with tinted windows was there as he'd said. His stately form stood outside the bus with another guy, both of them in suits that had to have been tailor-made because they fit like gloves on their large frames.

God, that smile.

And that body.

He approached as I climbed out of my car, and I had to will my heart to stay down in my chest because it was trying to climb up my throat at the way he filled out that suit. A man shouldn't be so breathtaking. It wasn't fair. He was intoxicating, and I was drunk on every scrap of his time I received.

Fucking hell. Kill me and my fickle heart now.

"Thank God. Here he is," he said as he held out my new favorite little canine.

"Beaker-Baby," I crooned in my baby voice I reserved for him as I snuggled him close. "He's okay?"

"Yeah, they were able to remove it with an endoscope. They would've preferred to keep him there for observation, but I didn't want you to have to drive all the way out there to get him. He's still a little groggy from whatever they gave him. Here are the instructions and what to watch for with the number to call if there are issues. I hate that I'm dumping this on you," he apologized as he held out a printout.

Beaker whimpered, then a sigh heaved his entire tiny body.

"Are you going to have to learn all life's lessons the hard way?" I asked the naughty puppy. He lifted his head to look at me with soulful eyes that made me giggle.

"Aww what a cute little family," the guy who'd been by the bus joked with a grin. I hadn't seen him approach because I was so focused on Jordan and Beaker. He seemed familiar, and I cocked my head as I studied him, trying to figure out where I knew him from.

"The diner," he offered, answering my unspoken question. "Mikko."

He held out a hand, and I carefully removed mine from Beaker to shake it. The accent was divine but still had nothing on Jordan's. Though his wasn't really a foreign accent; it was more of a northern one. Either way, I could listen to him talk all day. Mikko's hand wasn't quite as big as Jordan's, but it also wasn't far off.

"That's enough," Jordan muttered when Mikko's handshake lasted longer than was proper. Mikko grinned widely as he turned his attention to his now-broody friend.

Feeling like I was missing something, my gaze darted from one man to the other and back. Mikko put his phone in his back pocket and reached out to scratch Beaker's head and pet his soft fur. "Be good, little buddy."

Of course, Beaker adoringly licked him like he was the love of his life.

"Let's go!" An older man leaned out of the bus door with a scowl.

"Gotta run. Thanks again. I'll call to check on him tonight." For a second, he appeared torn and leaned toward me. Hope beat in my chest that he was going to kiss me goodbye. Except I was disappointed when he spun on his heel and followed after his friend.

Before I could so much as think to ask anything about where he was off to, he was climbing on the bus with his coworker or friend or whatever they were. It made me wonder if they were on their way to a conference or something. Did they work at the stadium, then? I glanced at the imposing structure as the bus pulled away. I'd never attended anything at the facility so I had no idea what someone might do there. Quite frankly, I didn't have the money or free time for anything anymore.

"Well, let's get you home, Trouble," I murmured to Beaker before I kissed his silky head.

I was mopey on the way home to Jordan's place. It shouldn't have left me so unsettled that Jordan hadn't kissed me goodbye. I mean, did I really think he would? Especially in front of his friend?

We fucked like rabbits, but we still weren't anything more than that. Except I really wanted there to be. To myself, I could now openly admit that fact. Saying it out loud might be a different story. Then again, what if the only reason he was holding back was because it was what he thought I wanted?

As I tapped my fingers impatiently on my steering wheel, I cast a glance at Beaker in the passenger seat. He was peacefully snoozing on the blanket I kept in my car for him.

"Maybe I need to have a little talk with your dad when he gets back," I told him. Though one of his ears twitched, he slept on. Of course, he ignored me.

But I came to the conclusion that I couldn't continue to have "meaningless" sex with Jordan. Not when my heart was involved. Because if Jordan didn't have any feelings for me, eventually, my heart would become a casualty.

TEN

Jordan

"THE MASK SLIPS AWAY"—RED

"Jesus, dude. Why would you post that?" I demanded when I saw the pic of me, Blair, and Beaker from when she'd met me to get him the day we flew out. Mikko had captioned it "the happy family."

Not a fan of social media, I hadn't seen it until we were on our way back to Texas, though he'd evidently posted it the day we left. Fucking asshole. Dmitry was actually the one who'd seen it and teased the shit out of me. Of course, I didn't know what the fuck he was talking about until he pulled it up.

"Now you did it. You probably scared away Beck's hot piece of ass," Andreas Papadopoulos chortled. I backhanded him in the guts with a glare. Him calling her a hot piece of ass pissed me off.

Little did they know, I was the one who was scared. I was terrified of the attachment I was developing for Blair. But it was impossible to deny that I'd missed her more than ever during this road trip.

"Nah, she wouldn't see it. She has no idea our boy is a hockey player," Mikko replied with a grin.

"No fucking way," Dmitry stuttered in disbelief.

"How the actual fuck does she not know you play for the Austin Amurs? Jesus, you're one of the number one goaltenders in the NHL. She house sits for you," Jericho blurted out.

"Dog sits," I muttered. Admitting that our relationship was so superficial that she didn't know what I did for a living soured my stomach.

"Still, she's at your fucking place all the time," Jericho countered. "You have hockey related shit everywhere."

"Not everywhere," I argued. Then with a wince, I lamely added, "And I kind of led her to believe I'm a huge fan."

Water shot out of Mikhail's mouth before he could swallow. "A *fan?* And she believes this?"

"She had no reason not to." I dragged a hand down my face. The more the conversation progressed, the shittier I felt about the way I was handling things with Blair.

"I tried to tell him he needed to come clean," Alex piped in.

"Why? If they're only fucking, then what difference does it make?" Sinner questioned.

"What is this, beat up on Beck day?" I muttered.

At least the odds that Blair saw it were slim to none, and she had no idea what I did for a living. At least she hadn't ever mentioned that she did, and we'd never discussed it. She also didn't know

Mikko's last name. There would be no logical explanation for her to see it.

I hoped.

"Oh, come on. It's funny. You have to admit. And it's a great picture."

He wasn't lying, and I'd never admit I took a screenshot of the image. But I valued my privacy—more now than ever. I liked that Blair didn't know what I did and that while she was only with me for the sex, it wasn't for the bragging rights that came with it. Truth be told, she must've been a little oblivious, considering how much hockey memorabilia I had in my place.

Of course, I'd played it off pretty well.

I told her I won the framed jersey in an auction. She didn't watch sports and had no idea it was one of Landon Shomo's dad's original jerseys. His dad had been one of the hockey greats that my dad had played with. Landon was quick on his way to following in his father's footsteps. Landon was one of the goaltenders signed right out of college. He played in the Amurs' AHL team down in San Antonio for about a season and a half before they brought him up to us after Dillon's injury. Kid was good. Really fucking good.

Blair and I were only supposed to be about the sex. Yet, I found I loved our conversations as we chilled in the bed afterward. Or the couch. Or wherever we found ourselves. We were insatiable and combustible. Yet it was more than her beauty. She was witty and free-spirited. She could debate with me for hours about whatever subject came up. Whether it was playful, or serious, she was fascinating and giving. There wasn't a false or selfish bone in her body.

The thought of losing that because of a stupid pic on social media pissed me off. Because I'd basically been a liar to her. I knew almost everything about her, and yet she didn't even know what I did for a living—and she'd honored my requests to keep my private life out of what we had. I'd been the selfish dick.

The problem was, after what Zena had done, I was afraid I always would be.

"Chill out. I didn't tag you in it." He snickered. That was true, but still. Anyone who knew hockey, knew who I was. Anyone who knew him, knew who I was.

"Just delete that shit," I muttered before I climbed in my truck. "I mean it."

Shaking his head, he held his phone up so I could see he was removing it from his social media account. "There. Happy?"

"Yes." My reply was matter-of-fact, and I punctuated it by closing my door in his face. He flipped me off good-naturedly, and I pulled out of the lot.

Anxiety began to churn in my stomach the closer I got to my neighborhood. I prayed that she or someone she knew hadn't seem Mikko's stupid post. I also realized how much I'd missed her while we'd been gone. It had only been for two games, but it had seemed like forever.

Her crappy car was parked out front, but it had me grinning like a fool. It meant she was there. Waiting.

"Luuuuucy, I'm home!" I called out in a mock accent that was really horribly rendered. I pushed my worries away, promising I'd address things with her later. Her laughter rang out from the kitchen right before the rapid click of Beaker's nails on the tiles. The little black blur darted down the hall and slammed into my leg.

It was hard to believe that not that long ago I would've come home to an empty house. Well, and Herman. The difference was night and day. Now when I walked through the door, I was greeted by Beaker—and often, Blair too. While having my puppy there was awesome, it was the woman who made me warm and fuzzy inside.

"Hey, little buddy," I cooed before I knelt to lift him up. He squirmed and wiggled so much I worried he'd fall until I clasped him firmly to my chest. "Aww, did you miss me?"

"Why, yes, crazy enough, I did." The snarky reply drew my attention to the woman who took my breath away. She leaned against the archway to the kitchen with a playful smirk. That long dark hair caught the light, and it brought out the slightly russet tone I loved. My heart immediately picked up its pace at the sight of her.

"Is that right?" I questioned, giving her my most wicked grin. "Maybe I could do something about that?"

My intent clear, I began to advance on her until she had no choice but to run up the stairs as I chased her. Laughter rang out, and I chuckled evilly when she tried to close the bedroom door on me.

"Careful! You'll shut Beaker in the door!" I cried out, and she gasped, flinging the door open with worry on her beautiful face. That was my chance to laugh as I pushed my way in and backed her to the bed until she fell. Her rich chestnut hair fanned around her as I leered down at her.

Fuck, she was gorgeous.

"You're awful," she accused, but her bright smile belied her words.

"And you're beautiful," I murmured as I catalogued each amazing detail.

As I climbed on the bed after her, I set Beaker on the comforter and straddled her legs. He playfully attacked the ends of her silken locks as she gripped my thighs and blinked up at me. Her chest rose and fell rapidly as she waited expectantly. As she wet her lower lip, she watched me, then the corner of her mouth kicked up.

"And you're crazy," she breathed as she gave her head a slight shake.

"Maybe," I conceded before I leaned down and stole a kiss that was the sweetest thing I'd ever tasted. Our sighs echoed contentment as they intermingled. I threaded my fingers with hers, sliding her hands above her head.

The kiss deepened, and I realized I couldn't get enough of her. Not that the feeling was anything new. She drove me crazy on the regular. Her taste was addictive, and I found myself overdosing every fucking time. I was drowning in everything about her—spiraling through murky waters I couldn't traverse and having no clue which end was up.

"I fucking missed you," I whispered against her jaw. Though I hadn't intended on letting the sentiment out, I didn't regret admitting it because they were some of the truest words I'd spoken. My teeth scraped lightly down her neck as she rolled her head to grant me better access.

"Yes," she gasped when I nipped.

"Yes? Yes, what? Did you miss me?" I asked the question, but I didn't wait for her answer. Clasping both of her slender wrists in one of my hands, I used the free one to slowly unbutton her shirt. The rise and fall of her chest brought the top curve of her tit closer, and I licked along the edge of her bra.

"Jordan, Jesus," she blasted out when I caught her nipple through the fabric with my teeth. She arched off the bed and whimpered when I moved to the other.

"No. Jordan Daniel, but you can call me whatever the fuck you want," I told her as I moved down her body.

Suddenly, a fluffy blur was wiggling in between us.

"Cockblocker," I accused Beaker, much to Blair's amusement. Snagging the little brat from the bed, I stared at Blair. "Be naked when I get back."

She snorted in laughter, but I noticed she sat up and finished what I'd started. Satisfied, I grabbed one of Beaker's favorite organic treat sticks and put him in the closet in his little kennel I reserved for our time out. While he was occupied with his prize, I closed the door, leaving the light on.

"Now, where were we?" I asked, removing my own clothing as she kicked her last sock to the floor. In a diving move, I slid my arms under her and slid her up the bed farther. She squealed, and I shushed her. "You'll get him worked up."

She tugged her bottom lip with her teeth as she fondled her perfect tits. Fuck, that turned me on. She was a lush woman, not a stick like most women thought they needed to be. Her curves were some of my favorite parts of her. I nuzzled her hand out of the way and latched onto her peaked nipple.

A shiver rippled through me when her hands skimmed the surface of my shoulders, and she buried her fingers in my hair. The needy tugs only made my cock harder for her, and I pressed it into the bed to gain a modicum of relief. Anything to keep from burying myself in her before I ensured she came.

Leisurely, I worshipped every inch of her chest, her sides, those hips… God, I wanted to devour her. So, I did. Holding her thighs apart, I licked through her wet slit, gathering her wetness on my tongue. "Fuck, you taste good."

Her answering mumble was completely incoherent, so I grinned and did it again, except that time, I pressed the flat of my tongue to her clit and slid a finger into her tight pussy. The way she gripped me through each slow stroke made my dick weep to be inside her. I feasted on her dripping core until she began to writhe under me, and I had three fingers curling against the place inside that drove her crazy. When I sucked on her clit, she exploded, and I lapped up every bit she gave me.

"Oh my God, Jordan!" she shouted through gritted teeth. Grinding against my face, she worked with me to give her every second of that orgasm. After she was spent and panting, I drew one last shudder and an answering pulse of her walls around my fingers.

Making her come was a motherfuckin' rush. Did I love the feel of my dick wrapped in her tight pussy? Of course, I did, but having the power to make her fall apart? Euphoric.

Softly, I kissed her inner thigh. "Can I feel you bare? I'm clean, and I won't come in you. I want to feel you. Just once."

Part of me was shocked at my request. I didn't do that. Ever.

Not even when I'd been in my farce of a relationship.

But this was Blair, and something was different. So different I wanted to mark her in a way that every man she encountered knew she was mine. That thought shook me to the core, but I was too far gone to truly evaluate it. My heart seemed to stop beating while I waited for her reply.

She searched my gaze; I was assuming for the truth of my words. When she appeared to be satisfied with what she saw, she nodded, and my chest ached as my pulse galloped.

Fuck.

Staring her down, I used the cream from my fingers to stroke my cock as I rose above her to one arm and notched myself at her opening. My eyes locked with hers and my shaft pulsed in my grip. Slowly, I fed it in, taking shallow dips as needed to work myself to the base. When I was fully seated, I released the breath I hadn't realized I was holding.

"Fucking hell, Blair," I practically groaned out. The she wrapped her legs around me and made a liar of me, because I went deeper— so deep my eyes crossed and I almost came. I gripped her tit and pinched the nipple in reflex. She was hot and wet as she tightened herself around my shaft. "You feel so goddamned good."

"So do you," she panted before she rolled her hips, and I started to slide out. With a grunt, I drove back inside. Not since I was a dumbass kid had I gone without protection. I'd forgotten how incredible it felt, but then again, it might've been the woman I was with because I didn't think I'd ever been in such heaven.

Being inside Blair had become one of my favorite places to be. But this... this was so overwhelming. With nothing between us, it was like being connected on an elemental level. There wasn't a single thing in the world to compare it to. I'd sell my soul to be able to feel this with her for the rest of my life.

Breathless, I dropped to my elbow, slid my hand under her, gripped the back of her head, and tangled my fingers in her hair. Her lips parted on a gasp, and I sealed my mouth to hers, stealing her breaths and doing battle with her tongue. I brought my hand that had been squeezing her tit down her body until my thumb found her swollen and wet clit.

She moaned and whimpered as I relentlessly fucked her and played her body like a fine-tuned instrument. With every stroke, she met me head-on. Her nails dug into my back as she searched for an anchor in the storm we both knew was coming. Our sweat-slicked bodies moved like a well-oiled machine, though our rhythm grew increasingly wilder.

Desperation hit us both, and we became frantic, needy, primal.

She screamed my name as her body stiffened. While her walls pulsated and contracted around me, I grunted like the beast I'd become.

In that moment, as I thrust in her like a crazed man, I knew I was well and truly fucked. In so many ways.

Because though I pulled out and stroked myself until I came all over her, I wanted to fill her tight cunt with every drop. Wanted to mark her like an animal. Wanted things with her that I had no business wanting.

ELEVEN

Blair

"HYPNOTIC"—ZELLA DAY

"**Y**OU DID WHAT?" TORI ASKED ME AS OUR SHIFT ENDED. IT would be the last week we worked nights together, and I was bummed. I paused and turned to face her where she stopped in the middle of the parking lot. "Please tell me I heard you wrong and you didn't just say you let him stick his dick in you without a condom?"

"Shhh!" I snapped as I gave her a wide-eyed "are you kidding me?" stare.

"Blair. Do the things we see in there not register with you at all?" She motioned wildly back to the ER entrance.

"Yes, Tori. Jesus, I'm not an idiot," I grouched as I glared.

"Really? Because that's not what it sounds like!" she practically shrieked.

"Oh my God, Tori, can you stop? I wish I wouldn't have said anything. So, you're trying to tell me you and Owen still use condoms?" I started walking toward my car again, and she followed. When I unlocked my doors and tossed my bag in the backseat, I spun to face her as I crossed my arms.

She pursed her lips and breathed out slowly. "Blair. First of all, Owen and I are in a committed relationship. We've been together as a couple for over a year and a half. You and Jordan are just hooking up, with a little bit of I don't even know what on the side. I worry about you. You're my best friend. That's what best friends do, remember?"

My shoulders drooped, and I let my arms fall. "Yeah. I'm sorry. I'm just having a really hard time." I inhaled deeply and let it out in a rush. "I think I let myself fall for him."

The way she chewed on her lips and stared at me with such concern wasn't helping, and I had to blink away the tears that suddenly welled up. Everything had me feeling emotional, and I didn't know what to do with myself.

"When you started dog sitting, I knew things were going to change. That freaking little fluffy shit is so damn lovable. There was no way you couldn't fall for him."

Laughter burst from us both, and we hugged.

"I'm sorry," she whispered. "But I think you really need to talk to him. Call him when you get home and ask him how he feels."

"I can't discuss this over the phone," I mumbled. "And between my shifts and covering for Maddox, I work the next three nights. The nights I'm off, Jordan has things going on." I had offered to work for Maddox so he and Gwen could go to a Straight Wicked concert. Jordan was home all week, so he didn't need me to watch Beaker.

"Then reach out to him and ask if you can sit down on your first day off. Make a date or appointment or whatever you have to do." I appreciated she didn't ask "what things" because that was another bone of contention between us—the fact that I knew next to nothing about him other than he worked in some kind of security.

I didn't ask any personal details of Jordan's life, though I'd offered up mine to him. I wasn't going to lie, it kind of hurt that he kept himself walled off. Yes, I remembered him saying he'd had a bad breakup, but we'd been hooking up exclusively and consistently for months. In my mind, that called for a certain level of trust.

"Okay. I will."

"Good."

"I can't believe you're leaving me for the daywalkers," I grumbled.

"You could ask to go to days too," she offered hopefully.

"You know I can't. Not yet," I replied. Though the money Jordan paid me to watch Beaker was insane, I still had one of the credit cards I needed to get taken care of. I was, however, seeing the light at the end of the tunnel.

We were parked next to each other, and we both leaned against our cars to talk.

"I don't know why we can't sneak into Henry's apartment, give him a blanket party, and abscond with his valuables. If we happen to take his family jewels while we're at it, well, then so be it," Tori nonchalantly added.

"You've become such a savage!" I gasped in mock outrage and splayed my hand over my chest.

"Sorry, it's not right. The dickwad stole from you. I hate that."

"So do I, but I was just as guilty for falling for all of his lies. I've never been one to trust easily, but he certainly had me fooled. He sweet-talked my walls down easier than he should've." My brow creased as I turned my head away and chewed on the inside of my cheek.

"I don't want you to take this the wrong way, but I was lonely."

"What?"

I sighed and forced myself to look her in the eyes. "You had Owen. Maddox had Gwen. You were my people, and I was suddenly the third wheel with everyone. When Henry asked me out, I was both flattered and relieved. He was handsome, a doctor, and he was interested in *me*. He wanted to marry *me*."

"Blair—" she began, but I held up a hand.

"Let me finish?"

She nodded, but the sympathy in her gaze hurt my heart. I inhaled deeply and blew it out.

"For as long as I could remember, I was alone. I had you and your grandma, but you also had your own lives. My mom had died, I didn't know who my dad was, and I had no family that I was aware of. All I wanted was to get away from that godforsaken town full of awful memories, even if it meant leaving you. When you finally decided to move down here, I was ecstatic. Then it felt like I lost you all over again when Owen showed up. I'm happy for you, but that little girl inside me was selfish and covetous—because I wanted what you had too. I thought that was Henry. That was another reason his betrayal hurt so bad. I wasn't enough for him—I'm never enough." A tear slipped free.

"Oh honey," she murmured before she dropped her bag carelessly to the ground and embraced me tightly. For the first time in a long time, I gave in to that scared and lonely child and let myself cry as she rubbed circles on my back.

Like the great friend she always was, she let me get it out and remained my quiet, stoic pillar of strength. When I finally got my emotions under control, she gripped my shoulders and leaned back to look me in the eye. I sniffled and tried to smile.

"Honey, I'm going to ask you something and it might be hard for you to think about. But are you sure you're not latching onto Jordan for the same reason?" The concern I read on her expression and body language touched that dark and broken spot on my heart.

"Crazy enough? I can honestly tell you this is different. But I don't know if that's good or bad. I had every intention of keeping my heart out of the agreement I made with Jordan. Hell, it was my idea—and I was adamant about it—not to let things get complicated. Yet, they are so fucking muddied that I can't see the bottom. And instead of strings, I feel like I have ropes attached. Possibly with anchors, because I'm drowning in my feelings for him. Except I can't be sad about that, since things with him are so different from anything I've ever experienced in my life. In the best of ways. I miss him terribly on the days I don't get to be with him. Anytime I see something funny, I want to share it with him. I'm addicted to the talents he has with that body, but the conversations we have about nothing in particular are what I crave," I explained.

"Yet you don't even know what he does for a living?" Tori winced after her question.

"No. I don't. Not that I believe it's been a big secret. I think it simply doesn't really matter to me. Whatever his reasons are for not discussing it, they are his own. I feel like if I asked him straight out, he'd tell me," I confessed with a shrug.

"And if he won't?"

"Then he wasn't who I thought he was, and I'm going to get my heart broken."

TWELVE

Jordan

"SO CALLED LIFE"—THREE DAYS GRACE

A WEEK LATER, I WAS PREPARING TO LEAVE THE PRACTICE ARENA, and I was determined but more nervous than I'd been before my first NHL game.

Today was the day.

Today I was going to tell Blair how I felt and ask her if she would consider making what was already going on with us official. I was tired of pretending we weren't a couple when my heart knew we were. The only thing I prayed was that she did indeed return my feelings like I believed she did.

I wasn't asking her to marry me or anything crazy like that, but I just wanted to know if she wanted to date me. Like really date me, not just fuck. Except, I hoped we could still do that too, because holy hell, sex with her was off-the-charts amazing.

Not wasting time, I hurried out of the locker room because I'd missed Blair like crazy during this past week. Our schedules hadn't been jiving, but she was off today and would be waiting for me at my house with Beaker. The thought of running my hands over her silky soft skin and driving into her welcoming body knowing—hoping— she would be mine left me with a primordial possessiveness.

Lost in the thoughts of what I wanted to do to her the second I got there, I didn't notice anyone had been in the hallway. I heard my name called, and my spine stiffened when recognition of that voice settled in my bones. Instead of stopping, I kept walking toward the rear exit.

"Jordan!" she called out again with more insistence.

Fucking hell, if only I'd been closer to the parking lot and my truck, I could've pretended I didn't know she was talking to me. Eyes closed, I inhaled deeply to fortify myself and hold my anger at bay.

"Zena," I ground out through gritted teeth. "What the fuck do you want?"

The worry in her eyes didn't fool me for a second. She'd already proven she was a calculating and devious woman.

"Well, you have my dog… and I need to talk to you," she softly pleaded with her hand resting atop her stomach.

I froze.

Rephrase—atop her slightly *protruding* stomach.

She caught the direction of my gaze, and her other hand joined the first. "That's what I wanted to talk to you about," she explained in a practiced sultry tone. "I'm pregnant."

"What does that have to do with me?" I asked refusing to believe what I thought she was trying to say. My pulse pounded, and a whooshing sound filled my ears. Denial bubbled up in my throat, choking me.

"It's yours," she whispered, and the world fell out from under me.

"Bullshit," I argued, fighting to catch my breath.

"If we can talk, I'll show you the proof you need." Her words were soft and pleading. She seemed very different, but I still didn't trust her.

"Fine, we can talk," I ground out. "But before we go anywhere, I need to see what you claim you have."

"Okay," she sighed. She dug in her purse and pulled out a small grainy black-and-white image that she handed over. I almost choked when I saw it was a photocopy of an ultrasound. It clearly showed a baby, and the date noted as the conception and due dates were exactly what she had said.

Seeing it in black and white hit me like a gut punch.

"When?" I asked, struggling.

"When what?"

"When did you find out you were pregnant?" I couldn't look away from the paper. My chest hurt so bad I wouldn't have been surprised to look down and find it gaping open.

"When I was in Singapore I started to have trouble with my wardrobe fitting. I'd had no symptoms at all. My manager was furious and accused me of cheating on my diet. As if I'd ever do that," she explained, and I knew she was right because the woman ate like a fucking rabbit, which worried me when it came to the baby's health.

"Instead of losing weight, I kept gaining until he made me go to the doctor. It was like as soon as I got the news my body really started to show. I was fired from the job." She quietly admitted the last, and I could tell it rankled because she worked her jaw as she looked absently out the back windows.

"And you're sure it's mine?"

She shot a wounded stare my way and pressed a perfectly man-icured hand to her augmented chest. That was another thing I began to think about. Would she be able to breastfeed? My mother had al-ways sworn that my sister and I were so healthy growing up because we'd been breastfed. Would she even want to?

Whoa, whoa, whoa. You're getting ahead of yourself.

"Yes, Jordan. I'm positive."

Swallowing the lump in my throat, I nodded. "Let's go talk."

The second I turned off my truck, I dropped my head to the steering wheel. Knowing Zena and I had a lot to discuss and not wanting to air my dirty laundry in public, I'd told her to follow me to my place. I'd called her a liar, but she actually had proof.

My chest seemed to cave in agony at what I'd have to do if the baby was mine. There was still the chance that Zena's lying ass had cheated on me. What kind of man prayed that a woman had been un-faithful? Fucking hell.

Maybe it was for the best that Blair and I had kept up the pre-tense of casual sex. Though I knew we were both lying to ourselves. It had become so much more whether we admitted it or not.

When I raised my head and noticed Zena standing outside my door, the air I'd locked in my lungs rushed out in a heavy sigh. Dread settled in my guts as I climbed out and walked to the front door with-out saying a word to her. For the first time, I understood why my par-ents had stayed together until my sister and I were adults. The sense of responsibility weighed heavy on my shoulders. If it was confirmed that it was my baby, I hated the thought of not being in my child's life as much as I possibly could. With my schedule, it would be bad enough without having to work out a custody and visitation schedule.

Again… *If* the child was mine. Zena wasn't exactly known for her truthfulness. God, how could I even be considering letting her back into my life?

Wisely, Zena kept her trap closed as she followed me into the house. The second the door swung open, yapping commenced, and happiness replaced the dread and disbelief of a moment ago. The click of tiny nails on the floors preceded the little black blur that shot toward me.

The chestnut-haired beauty gracefully breezed out of the family room after him. The brilliant smile that lit her beautiful face fell when she saw the woman with me. Guilt hit me that I was going to ask her to leave for this. Worry settled in my guts as my earlier joy fizzled. A frown marred her brow as she blinked at Zena, then her gaze rose questioningly to mine.

"Bubbles!" Zena exclaimed as she crouched down and picked up the dog that had been jumping on my leg. The stupid name made me cringe.

"His name is Beaker," Blair corrected as she continued to try to gauge the situation.

Zena huffed and shot a glare at me first, then Blair.

Needing to explain as best I could and to get away from Zena, I stepped forward and softly murmured, "Blair? A word?" Then I walked to the kitchen, hoping she'd follow. Thankfully, she did.

"Jordan? Who is that? And why did she call Beaker by that ridiculous name?" Her crossed arms told me she already had some idea but needed me to confirm.

"It's my ex—the one who had Beaker. Blair, I'm sorry, but Zena and I have some things to discuss. I'll call you later," I summarily dismissed her, and the pain in her green-flecked eyes damn near killed me. Except if I allowed myself to soften for her, I didn't know how I'd get through the conversation with Zena. I needed to remain completely resolute until I figured out what was going on.

"So your ex shows up and it's 'get the fuck out Blair?'"

"It's not like that," I argued. "Zena and I just need to discuss a few things."

If only I'd been able to talk to Blair first. I couldn't help but think that if we'd solidified our relationship before all of this, I could've asked her to stand by my side as I spoke with Zena.

It was a lot to expect of her if I had been wrong about my assumptions and she didn't have the same feelings for me as I had for her. What if it was too much for her and it scared her away before I had a chance to get to the bottom of Zena's story?

The thought of losing Blair because of this was shredding my heart to pieces. Anguish sucked my breath from my lungs, and I clenched my fists to keep from reaching out to her. If I touched her, I'd never want to let her go.

I stared at the cup of hot chocolate on the counter next to Herman that she'd obviously abandoned when I came home. I swear to God, Herman was glaring at me. Of course, it could've been my unrelenting remorse.

"I see," she coldly stated, yet I knew there was no way she did because even I had no clue what was happening. The only thing I knew was if Zena was indeed pregnant with my child, my life would change forever and my interludes with Blair were over.

"Blair, please don't be mad, I promise we'll talk about this, I just need a little time to find out what's going on."

"It's fine. I'm not your girlfriend or your wife, right? We're just fucking and I watch your dog." Dry sarcasm underlined every word. Teeth clenched and muscle jumping in her temple, I could tell she was pissed. The last thing I wanted was for her to leave like that, but I was overwhelmed and not thinking clearly.

"We'll get together, and I'll explain everything later," I tried again, raising my pained gaze to her.

She held up a hand, not answering as she stoically gathered her things and put them in the huge tote she carried with her everywhere. My heart cried when she passed by without touching me. Inside, I screamed for her to stop. Silently, I begged her not to leave and needed her to demand I tell her what the fuck was going on.

Instead, I remained mute, and she kept walking.

With each step, I was bleeding internally from my ravaged and brutalized heart.

When we approached the door, I saw her steps falter as Zena stood up with Beaker. Immediately, I knew she'd seen Zena's obviously bulging abdomen. It may have been a trick of my ears or the acoustics in the entryway, but I'd swear she took a shuddering inhale.

Without a word to either of us, she walked out the door. The fact that she gently closed the door with a quiet *snick* resonated with me more than if she'd slammed it. The finality of it ran through me like a sword to the chest. I damn near dropped to my knees.

Why hadn't I asked her to stay? What the fuck was wrong with me?

"Who was that?" Zena asked. Her tone was cold, but when I looked her way and raked a hand through my hair, she had an innocent smile on her face.

"The dog sitter." I replied in a monotone mumble. I was hollow inside. The future I had hoped for had walked out that door, taking every vital piece of me with her.

"Hmm. She's awfully frumpy and disheveled-looking. Did you do a background check on her? Are you sure you could trust her in your home? Maybe you should've had her watching him at her place," she suggested with worry-laced words.

My gaze narrowed as I spun to face her, and I barely controlled my resentment for her.

"I think we have more important things to discuss than the dog sitter, don't you?" I snapped at her in exasperation.

"Can we go sit? I've been flying all day, and I'm so tired. My ankles are starting to swell," she practically simpered as she buried her nose in Beaker's fur.

Knowing she'd follow, I stormed to the family room. The throw blanket Blair loved was bunched up on the couch as if she'd left it to go make her hot chocolate. The open paperback sitting facedown next to it told me I was right. Close to shattering, I folded the blanket and held it to my nose long enough to breathe in her lingering scent before I put it over the back. I dropped onto the cushions with a rough exhale.

Zena also sighed as she sat down, took the blanket I'd just folded, and laid it in her lap for Beaker. Inside, I wanted to scream that it was Blair's blanket and she shouldn't be touching it.

"How far along?" I demanded. The ultrasound had honestly been a little Greek to me, though I'd seen the conception date on the image.

The number she gave me confirmed her conception date right during our dating period as the ultrasound had noted. Weeks before the whole social media thing, if I calculated correctly. Though it was insanity, I again prayed she'd been cheating on me. I also kept hoping to trip her up and catch her in a lie.

"Jordan, I love you. I never wanted us to end. What I did was crazy, but I was so in love and, well, it was supposed to be a joke. I didn't mean for people to believe it was *real*," she pleaded.

I scoffed, rage simmering in my blood at the reminder of why we'd broken up to begin with. "You expect me to believe that?"

"Well. Whether you believe me or not, I'm pregnant, this is your child, and I shouldn't have to do this alone, Jordan," she insisted before pressing her lips flat. "Finding out I was pregnant and coming to terms with it made me realize how awful I'd been. I was crazy, but I was crazy for you."

My jaw hitched as I desperately worked to keep myself from blowing up at her for the situation we were in. Not being pregnant—if it was mine, I was at fault too—but the things she'd done that made this situation a shitty one.

"Fine. We can make an appointment to see a doctor so we can make sure everything is okay. Get care set up for you here, I mean," I offered with a helpless shrug, feeling trapped. I was out of my element and had no clue what to do. Later, I could call Alex and see which doctor Sydney had used.

"I've already arranged that." She rattled off her first appointment, and it was like I was suffocating.

"I'll be out of town for a game," I argued.

"Well, I can't help that," she replied, as exasperated as I'd sounded.

My gaze narrowed because our schedule was public knowledge. She easily could've checked and scheduled around it.

"It was the first appointment they had available. I'll be sure to make the next one after consulting with you," she amended as if she knew where my thoughts had gone and then tossed me another pleading look.

"Thank you."

"I have a favor to ask."

"What?" I heaved out. My brain was exhausted already, and I was pretty sure I was on the verge of losing my fucking mind. Either that or I was stuck in an incredibly bad dream.

"Would it be okay if I stayed here? I sublet my apartment, and since I'm not working at the moment, I don't want to blow my savings on hotels." She must've sensed my hesitation because she immediately added, "If I had family in the area, I would go to them."

Her family was in L.A., and they weren't close. She was only living in Austin because she'd been here for a photo shoot and claimed she fell in love with the area. It hadn't hurt that it was a far cry cheaper than L.A., either. Now I wished I'd found an excuse not to go to that fucking fundraiser, but it had been mandatory since it was held by the Amurs Foundation. Dragging my hands down my face, I sighed as the metaphoric noose around my neck tightened to strangle me. "Sure. But it is only *temporary* until you find a place. We are *not* together. I'm only willing to help you because you're telling me this is my child."

"Thank you, Jordan. And I know this wasn't a pleasant surprise, but I hope that we can find a way to come together in solidarity—for our child," she softly said. Our child. Fuck. Despite not being anywhere near ready to start a family at this point in my life, I couldn't find it in myself to turn my back on my own child. When my dad had left us, I'd been mostly grown, but it hadn't made it hurt any less. I'd never want one of my kids to feel like that.

If it's yours. As soon as it pops out, we're getting a paternity test.

The problem with my inner arguments was not getting attached before then.

"Where is your luggage?"

"In the trunk of my rental. Thankfully, the airport attendants were helpful and lifted them for me." A bright smile lit up her face. Despite everything, I was man enough to admit she was beautiful—on the outside. In her flowy white top and black leggings with knee-high boots, she was all elegance and grace. Soft, wavy blonde hair framed her perfect cheekbones.

Except she wasn't the woman I wanted.

Heart ripping apart at the seams, I hefted myself off the couch.

In the morning, I would end my agreement with Blair. It wasn't fair to expect a casual hookup to deal with all this drama. The limbo I was in sucked. Though all signs pointed to Zena's baby being mine, she didn't exactly have the best track record when it came to honesty. If it was confirmed as my child, that would mean my life would be connected to Zena for at least eighteen years. Though I cringed at the thought, I'd find some way to do the right thing and be there for my child.

No matter how shattered it left me at the thought of never being with Blair again.

THIRTEEN

Blair

"UNWRITTEN"—NATASHA BEDINGFIELD

JORDAN AND I HADN'T SPOKEN IN OVER A WEEK—NOT SINCE he'd texted me the morning after his ex had shown up. Truthfully, I couldn't believe it. He had texted me to end everything between us. *Texted me.* Though I thought about reaching out to him a multitude of times. Like daily.

Maybe several times a day.

I couldn't for the life of me believe everything had been one-sided and he could walk away so easily. No, I hadn't missed the fact that she was pregnant. What sucked was that I remembered him telling me that he'd gotten out of a bad relationship. Yet she comes back knocked up and suddenly their "relationship" is going to be better?

What the fuck?

And how could he not make a single attempt to explain to me what the hell was going on? It didn't make sense that he could walk away so easily while I was unraveling.

Damn, why did it hurt so much? When things ended with Henry, I'd been angry. Betrayed. Shocked. When Jordan ended things, I'd been crushed. My heart decimated beyond recognition. Our fuck-buddy status had gone by the wayside, and my feelings had been involved. Despite our original agreement, we'd both be liars if we tried to say things hadn't spun a one-eighty away from casual.

Trying to keep myself busy since I hadn't been able to take on any extra shifts short notice, I was washing my car. Stupid, because the dirt was probably what held the rusted-out piece of shit together. I realized I was being hateful to a car that hadn't done me wrong. Well, other than not start a couple of times.

God, I missed my Camaro. Not as much as Jordan, though.

Stop! Thinking! About! Jordan!

Forcing myself to keep him out of my head, I focused on my other life problem. My piece-of-shit car. When I ended things with Henry and I found out what he'd done, I knew I wouldn't be able to afford the payments on my beautiful red car. Before my credit went completely to shit, I sold my baby and took out a loan on this little piece of crap. It wasn't worth the papers I signed for the loan, but my payments were a quarter of what they'd been on my Camaro.

The vacuum started making that crazy sound that told me I was trying to suck something up I shouldn't. It made me squeal in surprise. "No!"

Fighting with the plastic bag it was trying to devour, I finally pried the suction off. Then I pulled the bag out, but it ripped apart when I tugged because it was stuck under my seat. Beaker's things I'd completely forgotten were in my car fell to the floor. "Fuck. My. Life."

Ridiculously, I burst into tears and held the squeaky toys and blanket to my chest. I already missed the little guy. The chick using the vacuum next to me looked at me like I had a screw loose.

Maybe I did.

And who was I kidding? I missed Beaker's owner too. I'd gone and done exactly what I said I didn't want to happen. I'd fallen for my sex buddy. Hell, if one wanted to get technical, I'd fallen for my boss. That thought made me snort a little laugh through my tears and confirmed I was indeed losing my mind.

"You know what? I really should bring this stuff to Beaker. He loves this blanket and this squeaky toy. And these are for sure his favorite treats," I insisted, then realized I was talking to myself. Out loud. My vacuum neighbor quickly averted her gaze when I sniffled and caught her staring again.

After convincing myself Beaker needed his stuff, I drove across town to the location that had been beckoning to me like a siren's song. Like a beacon was being sent out into the night sky calling me. "Jesus, Blair, you're losing your fucking marbles. You might be Batnurse, but you aren't Batman, and Jordan's house isn't sending you the Batsignal."

"Excuse me, Ms. Blair?" the gate guard questioned with a crease in his brow as the iron gate rolled open for me. That reminded me, I still had Jordan's extra gate sensor. The security staff all recognized me as Jordan's dog sitter, but I now looked like a lunatic. Great.

"Sorry! Talking to myself again!" By his expression, I wasn't helping myself any. It made me want to flip him off, though I couldn't really blame him.

"Are you okay?" he asked with a concerned frown.

"Sorry, yes, I'm fine. I had some bad news earlier." I tried to shoot him a reassuring smile, but I was certain it came out looking like a horrifying grimace.

"If you're sure." He then waved to me with that look that said he was a little worried for my sanity but glad to pass me off and not have to deal with an emotional train wreck. In response, I gave him another bright, though false, grin and a friendly wave.

My head fell back to the headrest when I came to a stop out front. Breathing deep and slow, I tried to calm my nerves and my racing pulse. Slowly, I rolled my head toward the house. The windows cast warm light out into the growing night. It was a relief because I hadn't reached out to see if Jordan was home before I made the ridiculous trip over to his place.

No, he hadn't said he'd be working out of town, but he hadn't told me anything. Because, hello, again he hadn't called or texted me since that shitty slap-to-the-face day.

After gathering Beaker's things in a reusable shopping bag I found in the truck, I climbed out of the car. For a second, I had to rest back against the door because I got lightheaded. My appetite had been shit, and it was catching up with me.

With a mix of hope and fear, I trudged up the sidewalk lined with fancy solar lights, then up the stairs. Trepidation jolted through me as I rang the doorbell. Not long ago, I would've walked right in. My lower lip trembled at the thought.

The lock turned, and I braced myself to not crumple when I saw him.

Except it was definitely not him that answered the door. It was her.

In all her perfect gloriousness. Bright blonde hair in perfect beach waves that cascaded over her shoulders. Perfectly in shape, other than the perfect little bulge that was all that gave away her current state. Everything… disgustingly *perfect.*

God, please tell me she isn't living with him.

Her chin rose, and she stared down her nose at me. "Can I help you?"

"Is Jordan here?" Boldly, I stared her down. The least he could do was see me one last time. Look me in the eye and tell me it was over without falling apart like I wanted to do.

"No. He's out," she tersely replied.

"Oh, well, I—" I began, but she cut me off before I could finish.

"You think I don't know what you're up to?" she sneered. Her haughty gaze swept over me, leaving me feeling like a big steaming pile of dog shit.

"Look, I just came by to drop off Beaker's things that I forgot were in my car," I explained, trying not to let my gaze fall on her pregnant belly. Because if it did, I might crumble. That ache in my chest might literally crack me open. And I would be assaulted by the questions I had—and there were so fucking many. Like how in the actual fuck could he throw away what we had? How did he know it was even his kid? I took a deep breath to stop my angry runaway thoughts. At his name, Beaker started whining and barking. The sweet dog had me trying to look around her, hoping for one last glimpse of his furry face, but he never came running.

"And don't call him that stupid name. His name is Bubbles," she snidely corrected.

There was no stopping the curl of my lip at the pretentious name. Then I heard the sound of him franticly pawing on his kennel door. "Why is he locked in his kennel?" I asked, knowing it wasn't my place to question but unable to keep my mouth shut. I loved that puppy.

"That's none of your concern," she snootily informed me. "Bubbles and Jordan are my business, not yours. With your cute little dog-sitting act, I'm sure you believed you were fooling everyone. The joke's on you, though. I know you thought you were going to snag yourself an NHL hockey player and sit on your fat ass living in the lap of luxury, but you have another thing coming. Someone like you could never compete with someone like me. Jordan and I are trying to concentrate on our *family*, so I'd appreciate it if you didn't come back."

She yanked the bag of dog items from my hands and slammed the door in my face. For a good minute, I stood there blinking and mouth flapping.

"Hockey player?" I shook my head. The bitch was nuts. What the hell was she talking about? NHL? Jordan was some business suit guy. No way was he a professional athlete and I had no clue. People like that had paparazzi on them and shit. Right?

And I wasn't fat. I was maybe a little thick, but I liked myself. And Jordan certainly hadn't had any complaints.

At least not before.

Accepting the fact that I'd likely never see Jordan again was brutal. Confused and decimated by her hateful attitude, I spun on my heel and practically stumbled to my car. Something kept blurring my vision, making it nearly impossible to see straight. I refused to admit I was crying.

The second I sat in my car, I pulled out my phone. There was no way. With shaking hands, I typed his name in the search. Except I hadn't gotten further than the K in Beck before he popped up. Nothing further needed. There he was.

Between his crystal blue eyes and his gorgeous, dimpled smile, he took my breath away. The fact that he played for the Austin Amurs and was one of the leading goalies in the NHL stunned me. Yet, everything seemed to slowly click into place.

I'd been an idiot.

The day I met him at the stadium to pick up Beaker. He hadn't been going on a business retreat or trip. Not exactly, anyway. He'd been going to a hockey game. The framed jersey on the wall. All the hockey memorabilia. The out-of-town trips all the time.

I had no idea how long I sat in my car in front of Jordan's house, with his pregnant, whatever the fuck she was in there, in a stunned stupor. My thoughts were scattered. My emotions were in complete upheaval. My heart was crushed. The vicious lashes of betrayal beat at me from every direction.

Jesus. Could I have any other jaw-dropping surprises shoved down my throat? Why was my life one big clusterfuck after another?

Not that I knew anything about the game itself, but I'd been fucking an NHL hockey player. One of the area's crowned princes. An Austin Amur.

Except it truly didn't matter to me what he did for a living. I missed him.

"You have to tell him," Tori insisted as I stared at the test in my hand. We miraculously had the same day off, and she had invited me over to hang out. I'd needed to see her something fierce. Phone calls hadn't been enough.

"I can't." The truth of what had been going on with me was staring me in the face, yet I couldn't process it. Because I'd known. Deep down, I'd known, but I'd been worried, so I'd deflected and lived in denial for weeks.

Until I couldn't anymore.

Ten minutes into my visit with Tori, I had become nauseous. The smell of her candle turned my stomach. That was after I'd bitched about my weight gain and how my scrubs were getting too tight. Then I'd looked at her with tears in my eyes and blurted out "I think I'm pregnant."

She'd immediately rushed to her bathroom and returned with the box. I didn't even ask why she had it.

Now as we sat in her kitchen, with the evidence in front of me, I didn't know what to do next, but it wasn't talking to Jordan. Not right now.

"Why not?" she asked, her tone heavy with exasperation. "This is his child too!"

Pepper, their red heeler, lifted his head from his paws and cocked it to the side. He looked at us like he understood every word. Then he barked like he agreed with her.

I shook my head at his crazy behavior.

"Yes, and I'll be damned if I have him come back into my life just because I'm pregnant with his kid. Nor do I want to manipulate him into having something to do with me. I'm not like *her*. If he didn't choose me before, I don't want him to choose me now. Not for any other reason than he wants to be with *me*." I beat my fist on my chest, and a tear escaped, rolling down my cheek. Like clinging to a raft in a turbulent ocean, I tried to hold onto my anger. If I didn't, I might end up losing my fucking mind.

"Then call him. Ask him to meet you. Tell him you miss him and want a relationship. Don't say anything about the baby yet." She wiped my tear away with her thumb.

"Why? So he can think I'm after him because of who he is? He.

Won't. Choose. Me. He already told me he made the decision to do the right thing." My volume grew increasingly louder as I began to spiral into a level of panic I wasn't equipped to deal with. I was barely making it financially. I worked so much I was physically and mentally exhausted. How was I going to afford being a single parent? How was I going to stay sane as I tried to deal with a pregnancy by myself?

"And your baby is less of the right thing than hers?" she squawked, reeling me back in for the moment.

"That's not what I meant. Besides, we both know she's more his type. Not to mention, she's used to the limelight—the fame. I don't know if I could live that life." The truth was, it also hurt that he had once been willing to try a relationship with the statuesque blonde but not me. Then she showed up pregnant and he took her back.

I'd driven myself to the brink of insanity doing internet searches of Jordan after she'd told me he was a hockey player. I hadn't believed her at first. Until there he was. More info than I could've ever wanted all with one Google search. I'd been obsessively looking him up every day since.

The only actual girlfriend I found noted was Zena—that said something in itself. He'd obviously had feelings for her if she was the single, solitary person that he was noted to have been in a committed relationship with. Every other bombshell he'd been photographed with ticked off a specific set of characteristics, even if they were temporary.

Tall. Check.

Beautiful. Check.

Perfect body. Check.

All the things I wasn't.

I'd looked her up because I was a glutton for punishment. She had been a model and a budding actress before getting pregnant. Zena

Bartholomew had been the only person he was documented to have dated long term.

She was also living in his home.

How did I know?

Maybe because I didn't simply conduct a search for her, I stalked her social media and saw the pictures she posted. Granted, she never said anything about Jordan, but she had hundreds of posts of her showing off her growing baby belly in various places in his house. I knew each and every room.

It only drove home the points I had made. He had fooled me into thinking he returned my feelings. More the fool, me. He was out of my league, and I wasn't even swimming in the same lake as the fish he swam with. I was in some little muddy pond. There must've been more feelings for her than he let on if he was willing to take her back so easily.

Still, I'd watched his games. And let me say, not in a million years would I have thought I could become a hockey fan—sports were never my thing. But holy shit. If I thought he was sexy before, seeing him in the net with all that padding was over-the-top badass. Hockey had secretly become another obsession. It was surprisingly an attention-grabbing game. Except the media was saying that he was losing his edge. That this was a really bad week for him.

That little part of me hoped it was because he missed me, but I doubted it.

I'd been such a gullible idiot. He'd fed me lie after blatant or omissive lie, and I'd sat there and accepted it. At any time, he could've told me he was a hockey player, but he didn't. The pictures also gave me one more reality check. He'd never taken me anywhere important. Not once. We really were just about sex to him—no matter what my feelings had evolved into.

"Blair. Stop. It's not like you see hockey players on the gossip rags every day. They don't have paparazzi following them like movie stars do."

"Some of them do," I countered. "Besides, it doesn't matter. I showed you those women. I can't compete with that if I wanted to, and everyone knows that professional athletes have a reputation for having women in every town."

"Enough. You are gorgeous. You always have been. Men have fallen all over you and your perfect curves for as long as I can remember. You're not some little, frumpy troll. You are a sincere, good-hearted, smart, and driven woman. You put yourself through the pre-requisites and then nursing school straight out of high school. You moved across the country to start a new life because you *wanted* to. You pulled yourself up by your bootstraps and dug yourself out of the mountain of debt Henry left you with. You are the most amazing woman I know. But *this*… this, you shouldn't have to do alone." Her soft hands framed my face as she made me look her in the eye.

My bottom lip trembled at the burst of emotion that hit me. I'd never seen myself the way she did. I'd worn a confident mask and lived behind the facade of it to survive. Over the years, I worried I'd give up and slip under because inside I was still that scared little girl, hiding in the closet, waiting for her mom to come back for her.

"The last thing I want is for him to think I'm after his money or that I did this on purpose to trap him or one-up the Barbie living with him," I mumbled as I closed my eyes to avoid her knowing gaze. I rubbed my fist against my aching heart.

"Sweetheart. Let me have Owen talk to Truth—his brother is on the team with Jordan." Once I'd found out Jordan played for the Austin Amurs, Tori had really lost it. I guess one of Owen's club brothers,

Truth, had a brother that was on the team too. The hockey players occasionally went to the clubhouse after home games.

It was such a small fucking world.

"No. Absolutely not." Gaze slightly wild, I opened my eyes wide in denial. And look like I needed other people to fight my battles? Hell to the no.

"I still can't believe I didn't put two and two together. Not that the players hang out there a lot, but the ones close to Alex do on occasion after games. The guy isn't exactly easy to miss. Then again, I wasn't able to hang out a lot because of working nights and every other weekend, and when I do go, I usually hang out with the ol' ladies." She shook her head, and her light brown curls bounced back and forth before they settled to frame her face.

"I mean, you did only see him that one time in the diner. I wouldn't expect you to realize that was who it was," I rationalized. Then, a mortifying thought hit me. I had partied there at one time with Tori. What if he'd been there then? No way. I'd have remembered a bunch of hockey players. People would've been talking about it.

"Maybe."

For a few minutes, we sat in silence. Then she brushed my hair out of my face and tucked it behind my ear. "Right now, you're emotional and overwhelmed. Let me talk to Owen. Jordan is your baby's father too. The other baby doesn't get more priority because he knew about it first. That's bullshit and you know it. Maybe he should've been a little more careful with who he was sticking his dick in," she practically snarled, and I couldn't help the watery laugh that burst from my chest. Tori may have found the love of her life and with that came times where they needed to be together, but I realized that despite the shitshow that was my existence at the moment, at least I still had her as my friend.

"My Mama Bear," I affectionately teased. "I'll tell him. Just not yet."

I'd barely had time to process it myself. To say I was in a disconnect would've been putting it mildly. Shellshocked might be a more accurate term. I'd never given a lot of thought to starting a family. Maybe because I'd grown up with such a shitty example of what family was—other than Tori and her grandma.

I couldn't imagine what kind of mother I'd be. What if I sucked? The responsibility of making sure you didn't totally fuck a kid up was terrifying. Kids didn't come with instruction manuals, nor did you inherit a mom bible when you popped a tiny human out.

"Holy shit. I'm incubating a human," I announced in near-horror after the realization hit me. "I'm not prepared for this. Besides diapers, wet wipes, and all the other baby shit that is expensive as fuck, I'm not cut out to be a mom. I cuss like a sailor and I have terrible luck with men. How am I going to set a good example for this little parasite, I'm carrying?"

"Oh for fuck's sake! Don't call it a parasite!" Her look of disbelief almost made me laugh. Instead, I grabbed my phone and thumbed through it until I found what I was looking for.

"Parasite: an organism that lives in or on another organism (its host) and benefits by deriving nutrients at the host's expense. That's according to the *New Oxford Dictionary*." I pointed at my belly. "Parasite."

"Jesus, Blair," she muttered as she rolled her eyes. "Well, at least it will be a cute as fuck parasite because its parents are both gorgeous."

I gave her an unamused stare as I cocked a brow.

"Hey, Blair. I didn't know you were coming over tonight," Owen piped in from the doorway, nearly sending me out of my skin.

"Babe! I didn't know you were home already. I didn't hear your bike," Tori sputtered, blinking rapidly.

"That's because Slice dropped me off in his cage. Remember, Truth and Lock are starting on my bike first thing in the morning." He sauntered to the fridge and pulled out a beer. After twisting the top off and tossing it to the trash, he leaned back on the counter and took a long pull. Through the entire long drink, he held eye contact with me. By the time he finished, I was starting to sweat. He was totally giving off the vibe that he'd heard everything, and he was trying to break us down like a skilled interrogator.

The good-looking asshole.

"So, which of Truth's brother's teammates needs his ass beat?"

"Shit," I whispered as I dropped my head to my arms on their breakfast bar.

"Babe," Tori softly warned.

"Fuck no. Don't *babe* me. If a guy gets a chick pregnant, he needs to be a man and step up to the fucking plate." Owen was irritated.

"Jordan doesn't know yet," I forlornly whispered.

Then he focused that steely blue gaze on me. "But the chick has to tell him first."

FOURTEEN

Jordan

"CAN'T FORGET YOU"—MY DARKEST DAYS

Against my better judgement, I'd brought Zena to hang out at the little bar we frequented after home games, The Iron Dog. I'd felt bad about her sitting at home alone all the time.

Alex's brother and his club were there, and I kept getting dirty looks from a guy named Black and Alex's brother, Cooper, or Truth as his club called him. But they had nothing on the glares I got anytime I made eye contact with one guy's ol' lady. Though she looked familiar, probably from the club parties, I didn't know the chick. It was incredibly obvious she didn't like me.

"Bro, did I do something to piss off your brother and his club?"

I finally asked Alex when most of the Demented Sons got up to play a game of darts. Mikko had gone with them.

He ran a hand through his shoulder-length hair and sighed before he cast a quick glance their way then at his wife, Sydney. She gave a slight nod, then gave me an apologetic, tight smile.

"So, I guess that girl you were hooking up with?" He paused, and I sat up straighter and leaned in. We both glanced around to make sure Zena wasn't returning from the bar where she'd gone to talk to some guy she recognized from modeling. Head thrown back in laughter, she was still there.

"Yeah?" I asked, not giving two shits that she might be flirting with the dude.

"She's best friends with Black's ol' lady and works with Styx," he mumbled. That had to be the evil eye chick. "They also don't like that Zena's bitch ass is with you."

"I didn't bring her because we're dating or I took her back. I just felt bad for her." I huffed a sigh and ran a hand over my mouth.

"You said 'also.' What else is there? Is she… is she okay?" I asked, hating that I sounded like a sap begging for a scrap of information about the woman. The way my heart immediately leaped at the thought of Blair only confirmed how hung up I was over her. They hadn't even said her name and I was like Beaker when he saw me pull out the treat jar. Fucking hell, I was practically salivating.

"I don't think so."

At his words, my heart stopped, then kicked in again at a frantic pace. "What happened? What's going on?"

"They won't say. Maybe you should call her," he offered with a concerned furrowed brow. Not knowing if she was hurt or sick or in trouble had my insides knotting and bile rose in my throat.

Except I knew I couldn't. I wasn't strong enough. If I heard her voice, I'd need to see her. If I saw her, I'd want to touch her. If I touched her, it was over.

Because I was fucking miserable.

I missed her so much I couldn't focus. My game had gone to absolute shit. I was grouchy and pretty much a dick to everyone around me.

A soft hand curled around the back of my neck, and I winced, knowing it was Zena. I had been trying to be nice, but inviting her had obviously given her the wrong impression. It had been three weeks, and I was ready to crawl out of my skin. Everything about her drove me crazy. Having her in my house was tantamount to torture. At least she wasn't pushing for us to have sex, but her kisses and possessive soft touches tonight were like nails on a chalkboard to me.

"I don't know if I can," I admitted as Zena sat down.

"Can what?" she asked, flipping her blonde hair over her shoulder and practically turning her back to Sydney, Cameron's girl, Bleu, and her sister Crimson. They shot glares her way, and I wanted to cringe. Guilt hit me. I'd brought her, so her behavior was on me.

"Oh uh, make it to his cousin's wedding," I blurted out before realizing that if he could go, I could. We were on the same fucking team.

Thankfully, it had gone over Zena's head since she wasn't interested.

"I gotta piss," I suddenly announced and stood, sliding my phone in my pocket. "Be right back."

The mood at the table immediately became uncomfortable as

Zena gave the women a fake smile, then started messing around on her phone. Alex and Cameron shot me a questioning look.

Kristoffer stood up with me and so did his girl Zoey. "We gotta get going. I don't want to leave the sitter with the twins too late."

I shook his hand and gave him a bro-hug. They said their good-byes as I took off toward the bathrooms. When I hit the sign for the men's room, I bypassed it and went out into the little outside courtyard.

Though I'd adamantly said I couldn't call her, I'd known I would. The thought that something was wrong literally made my stomach cramp.

She was in my favorites, so I unlocked my phone and went immediately to her number. Then I hesitated. What if she was working? What if she ignored me?

Fuck it. If she doesn't answer, she doesn't answer.

Before I could talk myself out of it, I hit the green button. Then I waited. It rang and rang. When it was ready to go to voicemail, I dropped the phone. Except when I heard her hesitantly say hello, I immediately brought it back to my ear.

"Blair?" I questioned and wanted to smack my face. Of course it was her. I'd called her. Fuck, I was a mess.

"Jordan."

Was it my imagination, or did she sound breathy and hopeful?

"Alex said he thought he heard something was wrong with you. Are you okay?" I blurted it out in probably the most uncool display of desperation known to man. The problem was, I couldn't help it. I swear to Christ, since the day I texted her to tell her we would have to call it quits, I'd been half a man. A huge piece of me had been missing.

She sucked in a sharp breath.

"What?" Disbelief colored her tone, and I wanted to kick myself. Shit, Alex was wrong, and now I'd opened the door on my emotions. My chest caved, and my heart ached. "I… I'm fine," she stammered, not sounding overly believable.

"Are you sure? Are you really okay?" I repeated, resting against the outside of the building and shoving my free hand in my pocket. Suddenly, I had nothing to say, but I didn't want to lose the tenuous connection of her voice on the phone. It was the closest to normal that I'd felt since the last day I saw her.

"I'm really all right. Um, does she know you're talking to me? Is this going to cause a problem?" The fact that she had to ask did something so painful to my chest, I couldn't breathe. Not seeing her or being around her these past few weeks had been a real bitch. If I didn't know any better, I'd think I was having actual withdrawals. I mean, could you be addicted to a person?

"Honestly, I don't care. You're my friend, right?" I asked her, knowing she'd been more than a friend to me. So fucking much more.

"At one time, I would've said yes. I don't know how to answer that now." Her honesty burned. "How's Beaker?"

The corner of my mouth lifted in a smile at the thought of my little dog. "He's good, but I'm pretty sure he misses you."

Her laughter rang out and a shiver skated through me at the sound. Fuck I missed that too. "Yeah right, and I'm pretty sure he's forgotten all about me," she shot back.

"There's no way," I returned.

"Oh really? Why's that?"

Because you're unforgettable.

"Because I just know."

"Hmm," she hummed. Silence fell as neither of us said anything. I was worried she would end the call, and I panicked.

"Are you working tomorrow?" I asked her.

"Um, yes, I am," she replied.

"What about Monday night?" I continued, fingers crossed.

"No," she answered so softly I thought I imagined it.

Hands trembling slightly and heart racing, I took a deep breath and slowly let it out. "Can you meet me for lunch?"

"I'll be sleeping," she immediately mumbled.

"Dinner?" I hopefully switched my request. Then I held my breath as I waited for her reply. Several moments went by before she made a sound. With each thud of my heart, I prepared myself for the kick to the nuts I knew was coming.

"Jordan, I don't know if that's a good idea," she whispered.

"Please?" I begged, completely and unashamed if it made me weak. I needed to see her.

"You're with Zena," she argued.

"She lives with me. We're not in a relationship," I clarified, though it might be a bit of a lie. After all, I had brought her with me tonight despite not really wanting her around.

More silence.

"Okay," she finally agreed, and my insides fluttered wildly. "Six o'clock?"

"Yes." My reply was immediate. I'd have found a way to meet her, no matter what time she gave me.

In the background, I heard an overhead page, and I gathered she was at the hospital. The fact that she answered my call while she was at work sent hope shooting through my chest.

"Hey, I need to get going," she whispered.

"Okay."

"Bye."

"Bye."

The call ended, and I stared at my blank screen for a minute before I realized I was standing there smiling like an idiot. Feeling lighter than I had in weeks, I grabbed the handle and swung the door wide. I didn't make it far before the front of my shirt was gripped tight and I was pushed against the wall.

"Hello, puck boy," Truth greeted as he leaned into my space. We were evenly matched in size, but I didn't want to fight the guy, so I bit back my temper and dropped my gaze to where his tattooed hand held my shirt.

"Take your hand off me," I calmly demanded. My ticking jaw probably gave away my inner irritation.

"I'll do that, but first, we have something to talk about," he announced with a curl of his lip.

"Fine. Take your hand off me and speak," I ground out.

"How many other women have you knocked up? And are you ignoring the rest of them too so you can traipse around with your little Barbie Doll?" Truth sneered.

Shooting him a glare of my own, I leaned my face into his. "I have no idea what you're talking about. I'm doing the best I can, and you have no right to judge me."

"Hey, hey, hey, what's going on?" Alex asked as he stepped in to take my side.

"I'll tell you what's going on. Your buddy here likes to stick his dick in women, get them pregnant and then brush them by the wayside." Truth sneered as he pointed a finger in my face. My temper was flaring, and I was about two seconds from burying my fist in his gut, Alex's brother be damned. The rest of his chapter might beat my ass but not before I handed him his.

Before I could get my jaw to relax enough to form words, Alex had stepped up to his brother, poking him in the chest.

"Whoa. What? He has her living in his fucking house. She's here with him tonight. What the fuck is wrong with you?" Alex demanded, getting in his brother's face. Something was off though, because he shot me a sideways glance before focusing on his brother.

"I'm not talking about that rude-ass bitch out there," Truth practically snarled, throwing a thumb over his shoulder.

The reminder that Zena had been embarrassingly inconsiderate had me ready to go get her and drag her out of there. It was a mistake to go hang out when I was in the mood I was in, and it was a bigger mistake to bring Zena.

"What the fuck are you talking about, then?" I snapped. Alex whispered something to his brother, causing him to narrow his gaze, but he didn't let go of my shirt.

"What's this I hear about you and Black's sister?" Truth then asked me. His change of subject had my head spinning.

"Sister?" I questioned, suddenly realizing Black was standing there too. He must've joined us with Alex. Arms crossed, he stared at me. To my knowledge, I hadn't so much as spoken to any chicks outside of my close circle. Unless he was talking about that redhead at the party way back when. I sure as hell hadn't hit on her.

"She's like a sister to my ol' lady, so that makes her a sister to me," Black clarified.

"That still doesn't tell me a damn thing," I said, my words laced with frustration.

"I hear you dumped her for that blonde bitch in there," Truth continued. Though his description was accurate, it chapped my ass that he was talking about the potential mother of my child. Suddenly, I understood who they were referring to, and confusion furrowed my brow. Why the fuck were they bringing up Blair? I had no idea her friend Tori was dating one of the guys from the Demented Sons. And Blair had said there was nothing wrong. What the fuck did they know that I didn't?

"I didn't dump her. We weren't in a relationship like that. We hooked up," I insisted, though the words rang hollow to my own ears. An inner voice screamed that I was a liar. We were more than hooking up, and I damn well knew it.

"Yeah, well, you need to contact her and talk to her," Black practically growled as he glared.

"Not that it's your fucking business, but we're having dinner Monday night," I admitted, though I didn't owe him dick shit for an explanation. This whole situation had my hackles up.

Suddenly, Truth grinned, let go of my shirt, and stepped back. I shrugged my shoulders to straighten my shirt.

"Well, why didn't you just say that in the beginning?" he asked with a friendly grin that had me thinking the guy was nuts. Then he patted the side of my arm like we were best buds. "Good talk."

I snorted in disbelief. He paused and cocked his head. "And if I were you? I'd think long and hard about what you want your relationship to be with that blonde snake in there."

Jaw clenched, I didn't grace him with a reply. Mostly because I didn't want to admit to the guy that he was right, but he had no worries. I didn't have the slightest inclination to be with Zena. If there had been any doubt, having her living in my house had driven that point home. Truth and Black gave me one last glance and walked back across the bar to the group. I glanced around to ensure no one had witnessed that exchange. Thankfully, everyone appeared engrossed in their own conversations. Zena still had her face stuck in her phone where I'd left her.

"What the fuck?" I asked Alex who rubbed a hand over his short beard.

"I don't know why he did that," Alex muttered. "Sorry. Sometimes he's a little quick-tempered and maybe a tad dramatic."

"You don't say," I drawled. "You know what? I'm gonna get Zena and split. He was right—I shouldn't have brought her. I'm just trying to be a nice guy and do the right thing here."

"Dude, I know, but it's making you fucking miserable. You don't love her, and you already know she's crazy. We were all a little surprised when you said you let her move in with you." He gave me a look that told me he questioned my sanity.

"What was I supposed to do? Have her on the street while she might be carrying my kid?" Exasperation bled into my words.

"Now who's being dramatic? She isn't destitute. She could've gotten a hotel until she found an apartment," he argued. He was absolutely correct, and I knew it. I'd let Zena play me and use me out of some unrealistic form of guilt. I hadn't done anything wrong. It was a mistake, and I'd make the best of it, but that didn't mean I needed to be in a romantic relationship with her.

"Well, she caught me in a moment of weakness and completely off guard. I'm going to make sure I clear things up with her tonight. I'll make sure she knows that while she may be staying with me and I will continue to be supportive, she needs to find a place ASAP and leave." I sighed. Relief hit me with my decision, as if a great weight had been taken off my chest. I could still support Zena financially and emotionally without having her in my personal space.

"That's the first sane thing I think I've heard you say for the last few weeks," Alex teased. "Good talk," he joked as he mimicked his brother's earlier actions.

All I could do was laugh.

As we weaved our way back to our friends, I prayed my dinner with Blair would go well and I hadn't fucked things up beyond repair.

FIFTEEN

Blair

"ONE MORE NIGHT"—MAROON 5

NERVES HAD MY GUTS CHURNING. THE ENTIRE DRIVE TO THE diner I wanted to puke. We had decided to meet at the place where everything started. It seemed fitting. I also appreciated that we would be in public where I wouldn't be able to throw myself at him. Because hell if I didn't want to.

I *craved* him.

The last few weeks had made me miserable. I'd been a mess over being worried about what this baby meant to both me and Jordan. If he didn't want anything to do with it, would I be able to do it on my own? Not having a clue as to how he would feel about what I had to tell him left me with an uncertain future that scared the shit out of me.

The other thing I'd come to realize was that I was completely and totally addicted to a man I couldn't have.

I'd seen him sitting in there watching the door as I parked. He stood the second I grabbed the door handle.

"Hey," he murmured as I approached. His dark blond hair was in a sexy disarray, as if he'd been nervously running his fingers through it. His T-shirt clung to his defined muscles, damn near causing me to drool. His crystal-blue eyes searched my face and I wanted to dive into them and lose myself in them. He was beautiful.

Then I noticed the shadows under his eyes and the subtle indicators that he'd possibly been as miserable as I had been.

Pain clawed at my chest, seizing my heart in its vicious grip. It hurt so much I couldn't breathe but for stuttered gasps. In that moment, I knew I was in trouble.

He had become more than the father of my baby—he'd become *important* to me. My body and mind craved him.

I fucking loved him. Mind, heart, body, and soul.

"Hi," I replied and winced when my voice cracked. We both laughed nervously, and I knew we were thinking the same thing.

We sat at the booth where he'd been waiting. Cat was working tonight, and she stopped at the table to get our drink order. Neither of us said anything until she dropped off my water and his lemonade, and took our orders.

"You look good. I've been worried about you," he started with, and I froze. Feeling like a deer in the headlights, I stared. Had someone told him? If it was Owen, I would kick his ass.

"Oh?" I questioned before taking a drink to delay.

"Alex said he thought there was something going on with you, so I was concerned you were sick or something."

"I'm not sick." It wasn't a lie. After all, a pregnancy wasn't an illness.

Relief softened his features, and I melted a little. Even looking exhausted, he was so good-looking it should be illegal.

"So I, uh, told Zena under no circumstances would we have a romantic relationship ever again. And if it turns out that the child is mine like she insists, I'll be there for her financially and I'll be there for my kid, but that's it. She'll be moving out. I offered to help her find an apartment," he explained, and my heart thumped wildly. Hope fluttered in my belly.

"What does this have to do with me?" I asked, hating that my question ended in a squeak.

"I miss you, and I can't stand that we haven't seen each other for almost a month." The pain in his gaze matched what burned inside me.

"I've missed you too," I admitted. The little black-and-white image in my purse seemed to cry out, but I was afraid to tell him. Not on the heels of all of this. I rationalized that despite being further along than I'd thought, so much could go wrong, and I was afraid to jinx things. I also needed to see exactly what he wanted. If it was to go back to just sex, I didn't think I had it in me. My heart wouldn't survive that. Not now that I had accepted the truth of my feelings—I loved him.

He nervously spun his straw like a tiny baton.

"Beaker misses you too," he added.

A soft smile lifted the corners of my mouth. "So you've said."

"We want you in our lives," he whispered.

"What?" I held my breath, afraid I'd heard him wrong. Blood was whooshing in my ears. To keep him from seeing how his admission affected me, I tucked my trembling hands into my lap.

"I know we said we were both happy to be casual, but somewhere along the line that changed for me," he admitted, gaze locked on mine.

Though I wanted to climb over the table and into his arms, the thought of all the shit I saw online had me hesitating. Zena's happy pregnancy posts in his home, their history that it seemed he'd minimized, and the fact that he'd hidden that he was a professional hockey player all had done profound damage to my heart and in turn, my trust. Swallowing the lump in my throat, I struggled to bring forth words that made sense. Because I didn't want to say no, but I wasn't sure I could truthfully tell him yes.

"It changed for me too, but that's before I knew you were a celebrity. Why would you keep that from me? When Zena threw that in my face, I was in shock. I thought surely she was full of shit. Only she wasn't. Do you know how that made me feel?" I pleaded as my heart ached.

"Blair, it wasn't my intent to make you feel lied to, but you have to see where I was coming from. As soon as people find out who I am, things change. Then I never know if they like me for me or for my money and fame." A crease formed between his brows, and I empathized, but I needed to look out for myself and my child too. This wasn't only about him.

"I would've thought by now you would understand and believe I'm not like that. I never cared about the fact that you obviously made more money than me. Not once did I take advantage of your affluence. If I'd never seen your beautiful home, your multiple vehicles, and your lifestyle, I still would've wanted you—for *you*. But honestly, I don't know if I can deal with people invading our personal life because of who you are. Not to mention, we both know I'm not part of your usual diet."

When it was just me, I thought I could handle the lack of privacy a relationship with someone of his celebrity status would entail. After finding out I was pregnant, it made me analyze the situation from a completely different angle. There was another tiny, helpless human's privacy at stake. The thought of my child's picture being all over social media or in gossip rags because of who its father was made me nervous. People were crazy.

"My usual diet?" He cocked his head and frowned in confusion.

"Your type."

"How would you know that?"

"I've looked you up," I admitted, embarrassed.

"You Googled me?" The wolfish grin that he shot my way did something to my insides that left them feeling jumbled. It also affected me a little lower, making me squeeze my legs together.

"Stop it," I whispered, dropping my gaze to break the spell he so easily wove with his gorgeous eyes and that completely treacherous-to-my-heart dimple.

Our food came, and we ate in companionable silence, though it was evident we both had a lot on our minds. As the minutes ticked by, I found it harder and harder to keep myself from reaching over the table to touch him.

He was magnetic.

Sitting across from him close enough I could smell the tantalizing spicy scent of his cologne but with a gaping chasm still between us made my chest seize. I'd missed him so much it hurt. A part of my soul settled simply having him near, but I was afraid of him breaking my heart again. Could I find a way to shove the worry away?

Then I thought about what my life would look like if I never saw him again. The bleakness of that picture brought tears to my eyes that I quickly blinked away. I'd done a lot of thinking and I knew I could raise this baby on my own. It wouldn't be easy, but I was capable and prepared, if need be. I lifted my gaze to his pleading crystal blue eyes and found myself slipping. Because the moment I made that connection, I got another picture. One that included us with a family together. It was beautiful and showed what we could have if we took a chance and made the leap together.

If we didn't try, we'd never know either way—and that might be the biggest tragedy of all. To waste something precious because we let fear dictate our choices.

I wanted him. Not only his body in mine, but his love, his trust, his secrets, his pain, his dreams—I wanted it all.

Like he'd read my mind, he froze and dropped his fork to his plate. His chest rose and fell rapidly, and his eyes were blue fire. It became increasingly difficult for me to breathe, let alone swallow my food. I too set my silverware down. Then I wiped my mouth with my napkin.

"Do you want to leave?" he asked in a strained tone.

"Yes. But I want you to come with me," I whispered as a ripple of need hit my chest, then fluttered in my stomach before moving to my core.

He didn't waste a second. While he scooted out of the booth, he was digging out his wallet. Then he grabbed my hand, approached the counter with me in tow, and set some cash down in front of Cat. "That should be enough—keep the change."

Cat gave him a knowing smirk, then shot me a wink. I waved over my shoulder as Jordan practically dragged me out of the restaurant.

"I can't believe you referred to it as my diet." He chuckled as he escorted me to my car.

"Are you going to deny that you chew women up and spit them out?"

He full on laughed, then he raked his heated gaze from my head to toe. His expression could only be described as… hungry. Completely validating my statement.

"Well, I don't think I chew women up and spit them out, but I am going to devour you."

Oh God.

My heart raced, and my breath caught as he stalked closer. When he got into my bubble, I backed up with each of his steps until I hit the driver's door of my car.

One large hand slapped the roof of my car, effectively bringing us closer, causing me to jump a little and my heart rate to gallop dangerously. He slowly trailed the other up my arm in a delicately soft sweep before he brushed my hair away from my shoulder, then speared his fingers into my hair. They curled into the dark brown strands until he could use them to pull my head to the side, further exposing my throat.

"Oh, Blair. Not an inch of you is safe," he whispered against the sensitive flesh, his lips brushing up the slope of my shoulder to feather against the shell of my ear. A shudder ran through me with his actions, and it wasn't from revulsion. His cocky chuckle told me he knew it too.

"I've missed you so much," I practically sobbed out.

He inhaled deeply at the crook of my neck. "Not as much as I've missed you," he breathed. "I've been lost and miserable without you."

"I know. God, do I know."

"I would say your place or mine, but I think your place would be better right now," he murmured before he sunk his teeth into the tendons on my neck. A cross between a sigh and a moan escaped me, and I clutched his shirt. Before, I couldn't get enough of him. Now, whether it was pregnancy hormones or simply because he was sexy as fuck, I needed him. Desperately.

"Okay," I gasped out as he sucked where he'd bitten.

"Want me to follow you, or drive?"

"Follow me." I didn't want to have to go back for my car. When I fumbled with the keys, he gently took them from my shaking fingers and unlocked my door. Before I knew it, he had me seated and buckled up. He cupped my cheek with his big hand and dragged his thumb along my lower lip. The black of his pupils practically swallowed the blue as he stared at me. My lungs seized as I touched his thumb with my tongue, and he sucked in a hissed breath.

Ensuring I was safely inside, he closed the door and turned. His stride was purposeful as he closed in on his truck. One last glance to lock eyes with me, and he climbed in and then he was waiting on me.

The trip to my apartment took no time at all. We both got out of our vehicles, and for a brief moment, we stared at each other. Without waiting, I moved to the stairs and to my door, assuming he would follow.

His rapid footsteps on my heels told me he did.

"This is a bad idea. You know that, right?" I tried to reason with my wayward emotions and him. He walked forward, forcing me to move back or his body would be flush with mine. If that happened, my fight was over because I couldn't refuse the man when he touched me.

"I disagree. I think this is a brilliant idea."

"You're going to be a father," I tried again.

"Maybe," he stressed as he closed and locked my door without looking at it once. "I'm still not convinced it's mine."

Well, this one is. God, how do I tell him I'm pregnant given the situation?

"She's living in your house," I added.

"Not for long," he countered, closing in on me. "And not because we're together."

"You didn't choose me," I whispered, finally admitting what the real issue was. Saying it out loud ripped off the Band-Aid. No, it was like taking a wrecking ball to a dam. What started as a small crack soon exploded, and all the hurt and devastation at being set aside flooded me, nearly drowning me in the violent surge. I trembled head to toe as I frantically fought to stay afloat.

One hand curled around the front of my throat, holding my jaw with his thumb and forefinger. He threaded the fingers of his other hand through my hair, and he gripped it tight as he tugged my head back.

The tenseness of his jaw paired with the slight flare of his nostrils told me he was struggling with what to say. Finally, he ground out, "And I was a fucking idiot."

Relief followed his admission, and a tear broke free and slipped down my cheek, followed by another.

His mouth slammed to mine, and he ravaged me with his wicked tongue. Teeth nipped my lip before he soothed it with his tongue and sucked it gently. I whimpered as the hand on my throat slowly skimmed down and over my nipple before he gave my breast a squeeze. He caressed and gripped me in needy exploration. With each second that ticked by, my heart galloped at light speed. Any minute it was going to explode.

"Fuck," he muttered when he slipped his hand into the waistband of my leggings and cupped the soaked center of my panties. "So fucking wet for me," he whispered against my cheek. Involuntarily, my hips jerked toward him, seeking the friction he could give.

I was almost there that quickly, but before I reached that perfect explosion, the reality of our situation washed over me like ice water. We still hadn't defined where we were headed with this. The last thing

I wanted was to slip back into a pattern of sex with no clear relationship boundaries. Nor did I want to fall into bed with him without him knowing I was pregnant. That was more important than a few orgasms, no matter how phenomenal they might be.

"Stop," I gasped. He immediately released me, his eyes wild as he searched mine.

"What did I do?" he demanded as he frowned, and worry filled his gaze. "Did I hurt you?"

Seeing the immediate concern in his eyes hit a tender spot in my heart, and I cradled his face with my hands. Words eluded me, and I could only shake my head. I was afraid to tell him because it could change everything. Yet I knew what I had to do.

Shaking head to toe, I stepped back. I needed space. I needed to breathe without inhaling his goddamn intoxicating cologne.

"You didn't do anything. But I c-c-can't do this," I stammered.

"What?" he snapped as he blinked rapidly and gave himself a shake. His chest heaved, and one hand brushed over the short stubble on his chin.

"I wasn't going to tell you like this. I had it planned out just right, I mean. Oh God, why am I in this situation?" I began to pace and gripped my hair in my hands. I couldn't keep my mouth from blabbering. "I was diligent. Never missed switching my patches. Never had one fall off. You didn't come in me. It doesn't make sense. Yet here we are."

"Blair!" he practically shouted my name, and I paused. From the look on his face, he'd likely called out to me more than once.

"I'm pregnant!" I blurted out on a choked sob. Beginning to cry, I struggled to hold my shit together by wrapping my arms around myself. My chest ached as I watched his expression morph from emotion to emotion, none of which was anything resembling acceptance. Not that I expected him to jump for joy, but I hoped for more than knocking him senseless.

He stumbled back until he hit the wall. It seemed to be the only thing that held him upright. "How?" he whispered in disbelief.

"How? How do you think?" I shouted. Jesus, how the fuck did he think I got pregnant? "Sperm, egg, fertilization, baby. It's a minor miracle when it happens, but it's a pretty simple concept."

He shook his head. Denial was all over him as his mouth opened and closed but nothing came out. His horrified expression was the last straw, and my anger flared.

"Don't you dare tell me this isn't yours because I will throat punch you right now," I growled through clenched teeth. Now that I'd blurted it out, a weight had lifted from my shoulders, and I wasn't going to let him deny this child. Whether he wanted to be with me or not, I was having his baby.

"I… fuck," he muttered as he stared blankly at the wall behind me. No, I hadn't thought he'd want to throw a goddamn party, but I sure as hell didn't expect the devastation I watched charge through him. His reaction told me all I needed to know. He found out Zena was pregnant and moved her into his motherfucking house and shitcanned me. I told him I was pregnant, and he emotionally disintegrated before my eyes.

Well, fuck him. I'd survived this long on my own, and I'd fucking deal with being pregnant and being a mom to this baby by myself too.

"You can feel free to let yourself out," I gritted out, trying to rein in my temper. Then I spun on my heel and stormed to my room, slamming the door. Fighting to bring oxygen into my nonresponsive lungs, I fell back much like Jordan had. My hand clutched my chest as if I could hold my aching heart together.

Part of me had thought he'd follow me and demand we talk about this. When all I heard was silence, then the click of my front door closing, my heart I'd tried to protect, shattered. I slid down, my ass hitting the floor. Then the dam broke, and my tears burst free.

I'd never felt so alone in my life, and I'd practically raised myself.

I cried myself to sleep on the floor, and that was where Tori found me the next morning.

SIXTEEN

Jordan

"TAIL LIGHTS"—BLACK TOP MOJO

NEVER IN A MILLION YEARS HAD I EXPECTED THAT NEWS. Now
the shifty way everyone had acted at the bar made sense. They
had all known. Even Alex. Without putting too much thought
into it, I drove straight to his address.

As I approached his front door, I clenched my hands and tried to
get them to stop shaking. Unsuccessful, I banged on the door.

Movement appeared behind the textured glass of the door before
it swung open. Alex stood there barefoot and only wearing jeans. No
shirt, he frowned at me like I was crazy. Hell, maybe I was.

"Can I come in?" I asked, breathing deeply.

"Sure," he agreed, though warily. He stepped back to let me pass.

Sydney looked over the back of the couch as I entered the living room Alex led me into.

"Hey, Jordan," she said with a smile. When I didn't return it, her expression went guarded like her husband's.

"You knew," I accused. Alex sighed, and Sydney gave me a sympathetic wince.

"I only found out that night after the game. My brother confronted me about it. I didn't have any idea he was going to do that shit. I wanted to give her a chance to discuss it with you on her own," he explained.

I dropped into one of the chairs, and my head fell back to rest on the leather.

"So, I'm guessing she must've told you?"

"Yeah. After she gave me a case of blue balls," I muttered, then cast an apologetic glance to Sydney. "Sorry."

"No problem," she assured as she unfolded her legs and slowly stood. She braced a hand to her very pregnant belly, and I couldn't breathe. An image flashed through my mind of Blair like that, and it took my breath away. On its heels was one of Zena which soured everything.

"You don't need to leave," I declared, feeling bad that my surly mood was chasing her away.

Her smile was kind, and I found myself more than a little jealous of Alex. "It's okay. I think this might be boy talk, and I'm ready to go soak in the tub."

She slightly waddled over to Alex, with him grinning at her affectionately the entire way. He stood so she didn't have to bend over, and she kissed him before she murmured something quietly. A pang of envy ripped through my chest as a vision of that being me and Blair hit me. Then she ruffled my hair as she went by and headed to their bedroom.

"Her pregnancy was a surprise too, right?" I questioned, knowing the answer but needing the affirmation.

"Uh yeah, definitely."

"I don't know what to do," I sighed helplessly. I'd gone from being on top of the world with my career as my only focus to having two women pregnant and making a fucking mess of it all.

"Well, first thing you need to decide is where you see yourself. Do you see yourself with either of the moms? Do you see yourself as a dad? Or do you want to sign off on both and pay out the ass?"

Anger surged at the thought of not being a part of my children's lives. It was strange because starting a family hadn't even been on my radar six months ago. "Fuck no, I'm not stepping down. And I thought I saw myself with Blair. I planned to tell her that tonight. I mentioned it, but we didn't get a chance to discuss things before she blurted out that she was pregnant, and it fucking knocked me over. Literally. If I hadn't hit the wall, my ass would've been on the floor." I leaned forward, placing my elbows on my knees and burying my face in my hands.

"Then my first suggestion is to discuss things with Blair, sooner rather than later. Why didn't you talk to her tonight after she told you?" His head cocked in question.

"I freaked out. She got pissed and went to her room. I was reeling. Nothing seemed to make sense, so I left to clear my head."

He groaned.

I dropped my hands, and they dangled between my knees. Dread burned in my throat. "I fucked up, didn't I?"

"Dude, if you have to ask, then the answer is a definitive and resounding yes."

He didn't need to tell me that, since I already knew. Blair had put up with so much from me, and the first sign of the unexpected with her and I bailed. What the fuck was wrong with me? But I needed to bounce my thoughts off someone who'd been somewhat in my shoes.

"Should I go back to her house? Or should I call?" My stomach was in knots, and I was a little nauseous. This was completely uncharted territory for me, and I was adrift without a motherfucking paddle. Fear settled in my chest that I'd really done it this time. It was bad enough that my stupid ass didn't take five minutes to talk to Blair before I had dumped her the second Zena showed up pregnant. But this? Holy shit, I'd really messed up, and I didn't know if I could fix it.

"Well, at this time of night, I would recommend calling her or sending her a text."

"You're right. It's late." I whipped out my phone and then tried to figure out what I should say. Though I'd rather talk in person, I first owed her an apology. A big one.

Me: I'm sorry. I reacted poorly. I'm an asshat. Can we talk?

I waited for the dots to pop up, but nothing happened. The message just sat there as delivered. But she didn't read it. Not that night and not the next day.

By the third day, two flower deliveries, and maybe a million text messages that she didn't read, I was about to lose my mind. Zena was being a pain in my ass, and I was preparing for a three-game road trip.

"Pick up, pick up, pick up," I chanted.

"Bro, I don't think she can hear you like that," Mikko said as he climbed on the bus in front of me. I rolled my eyes at him.

All the way to the airport, I tried to call her. I must've left a dozen messages. My stomach was sick, and my chest hurt. It was obvious by then that she was ignoring me, and it was driving me crazy. She was pregnant with my kid, and she was ignoring me. She might as well have carved my beating heart out of my chest because I was dying without her.

Over the last few days, I'd done a shitload of self-reflection. On the ice, I could make split-second decisions without pause. In my life, I had been a bumbling dumbfuck. Zena had shown up saying she was pregnant with my kid, and I was ready to be the gallant knight, riding up to be the dad I wished mine had been. Then the same thing happens with Blair and I lose my fucking shit.

The only excuse I could come up with was that with Zena, my emotions weren't tied up in it. There had been panic and disbelief, but I put on my responsible hat and was ready to deal with whatever came at me. When Blair told me she was having my baby, I panicked in a different way. Sure, part of it was the "oh fuck, I somehow knocked up two chicks despite using protection." But I think the bigger piece of the puzzle was that Blair had my heart and that scared me.

I was terrified I wouldn't be good enough for her and I'd be a disappointment to her as a father. Until I really thought about it. No new parents were really prepared. Parenthood was a houseful of Ikea furniture with no manuals. It was a lot of trial and error and working together. Except so far, I'd fucked it up. I'd lost half the screws, and I didn't know what to do next.

No, that was a lie. I needed to find a way to get Blair to talk to me. If I had to beg on my knees, I would. The thought of her giving me the cold shoulder for the rest of my life made me want to scream and break shit.

"Blair, it's me, but you probably figured that out. I have no idea if you're even listening to my messages, but I want you to know that I plan to be there for you and the baby. I'm not a douche or a deadbeat.

I swear. And I." I paused as I glanced around to make sure no one was listening to me be a sappy fucking wuss. "I miss you."

There was more I needed to say to her, but it had to be in person. So I could look her in the eye when I told her what she meant to me.

"Beck... did I just hear you say you missed Zena?" Dmitry stood up and leaned over my seat.

"Quit listening in on my conversations, asshole," I grumbled. Surly as fuck, I wasn't in the mood to discuss how bad I'd fucked up.

"Please tell me you aren't falling for her bullshit again," he begged.

I swatted at him. "Get out of my airspace and sit your ass down."

"I'm tryin' to look out for you. That's all."

"Well, I got this. But thanks."

"It's not Zena he's talking to," I heard Jericho tell his cousin. I sighed and rolled my eyes.

"Huh?" Dmitry grunted.

"Rumor has it he knocked up that nurse he's been banging," Jericho whispered, but the dude wasn't quiet. I palmed my face and dragged it down before I raised myself off my ass and glared at them over the seat back.

"You guys gossip worse than a group of teenage girls," I muttered. "Mind your own damn business and don't talk about me banging Blair again."

In a huff, I dropped my ass back to my seat.

"Told you, man, you got it bad," Mikko gloated with a smirk.

"Shut it." I closed my eyes and ignored everyone the rest of the way to the airport. It was obvious I was the talk of the team at the moment. Just great.

To top off my shitshow of a life right now, for our first game, we were playing our archrivals—the Nashville Falcons. I'd been off my game since my life imploded, and with them, I couldn't afford to be. The problem was, since I'd been a fucking idiot and ended shit with Blair, my skills and instinct had sucked. After the clusterfuck I'd made of things when she told me she was pregnant, it had only gotten worse. The last few days at practice were so terrible that Coach talked about pulling my starting position from me. I'd been sucking balls that bad.

There was talk that "The Wall" was crumbling, and it pissed me off. My contract was up at the end of the season, and if I didn't get my shit together, I was in danger of being traded.

As we suited up in the locker room before we hit the ice, I tried Blair one more time.

Me: The game will be starting soon. I wanted you to know I was thinking about you. Please answer me. I need to see you when I get back. Please?

Not that I expected her to answer, but when there was no response, not so much as a "fuck you," it was depressing. As I went through my usual routine, I tried to clear my mind.

"Are you guys fucking kidding me? Who the fuck smashed my goddamn Ding Dong?" Alex barked out, sending laughter through the locker room. "It's not funny! And if I play like shit tonight, I'm blaming all of you." Dude had the weirdest superstition about having one of those nasty little chocolate cakes with the cream filling before each game. I had no idea what he'd do if they quit making them.

"It's not gonna matter if it's intact or smashed, Kosinski. As long as you eat it, it's gonna come out the same either way," Kristoffer told him. He grinned though and patted Alex on the back. It was nice to see them getting along now. When Alex had first been traded to us, there was a shitload of tension between them because Kristoffer thought Alex was chosen over a good friend of his simply because of who Alex's dad was. The Kosinski name was as legendary as the Beck name despite his career being cut short due to injury. Alex's dad had been a beast on the ice, but it hadn't had dick shit to do with why the Amurs picked him up. Alex was damn good. Eventually, they figured their shit out.

For a moment, I closed my eyes and tried to meditate. Anything to get my head in the game.

"That's right, Beck, find your zen place. You got this," Mikko told me.

"But do I?"

"Fuck, yes. Stop with the negative bullshit," he insisted as he scowled at me.

I sighed.

He shook his head. "You're letting this chick get in your head. Let it go. When we fly home, you can pour everything you have into winning her back. Between home games and off days, you'll have over three weeks to wear her down."

Scrubbing my face with my hands, I agreed. It was doable. *If* I could keep my focus.

Grabbing my gear, I stood up.

"Let's do this," I announced as we all made our way to the ice. The second we hit the sheet, the crowd started their chirping. That was fine with me. The win would be all the more glorious afterward.

As the music played to hype up the spectators, I roughed up the ice in the crease. Adrenaline began to course through my veins, and I stretched some more and warmed my muscles back up. Through it all, I breathed deeply and did my best to shove my personal life into a little box in my head until after the game.

The puck dropped, and it was on.

Washburn, the Falcons' star forward, wasted no time and within the first three minutes scored with a backhand into the net that went right past my glove. It pissed me off and cranked my focus up a notch. Better to allow that frustration to clear my head than cloud it. They may have scored early in the game, but it wasn't happening again if I could help it.

"It's okay, Beck. Shit happens. We got this," Alex encouraged. My jaw hitched, but I nodded.

My problem was Blair. At the worst times, she was taking over my thoughts. Worry gnawed at me. Fear that I'd fucked up too bad to fix it sizzled in my spine.

The Falcons scored again.

"Goddamn it!" I shouted when the crowd cheered.

Kristoffer skated up to me, and I groaned.

"I know," I sighed.

"No, you obviously don't. I'm not sure what's going on in that head. Maybe not the exact details, but I get it. You can't do a fucking thing about the situation right now. I'm not saying forget about it, but I'm simply saying put it on the back burner for this game. Then I want you to ask yourself something. Do you want to tell your kid that the first game you played after hearing they were on the way was an absolute shitshow, or do you want to tell them it was the best game of your fucking life?" He stared at me, waiting for what he'd said to sink in.

For a second, I dropped my attention to the ice at my feet. Breathing heavily, sweat dripping off my brow, I blinked slowly and then I realized he was 100% correct.

I was going to make my kid proud. I would find the most effective way to grovel and fix my fuckup once and for all. Because come hell or high water, Blair would be mine.

Lifting my head, I gave him a single determined nod. Then I got back in the zone.

The satisfying whack of the puck as it hit my pads or glove drove me forward. Never still, I darted to the sides, dropped to my knees, and hell, I dove after the puck three times. With each attempt, I was successful.

It was a tight game.

With twenty-eight shots on goal by the end of it, I was pretty happy with the fact that only two got by me. I would've been happier with a shutout, but we won, and in the end, that was what matters.

"Fuck yes!" Dmitry shouted as he slammed into me after the final buzzer. The rest of my teammates weren't far behind. There were smiles on each of their faces. It was a sweet, sweet victory.

"Looks like you have one helluva story to tell your kid one day, Beck," Kristoffer declared with a blazing grin that I answered in kind.

"Fuck, yeah, I do," I agreed. That got me thinking about Blair and our baby. I'd been so wrapped up in the shit with Zena and wanting to be a good dad and now I had to ensure that happened two-fold. I worried that Zena might try to turn that child against me because, let's face it, she was nuts.

The contrast between the two women was like night and day. There was no question in my mind that Blair would be an awesome mom. She might be a firecracker at times, but she was caring and kind. I imagined the three of us as a family, and it made my stomach flutter like fucking crazy.

The only thing that would make this night sweeter was if there was a return text from Blair when I checked my messages.

We skated off the ice, coach gave us a congratulatory speech, and we cleaned up. By the time we were dressed and I was climbing on the bus, my phone was in my hand.

Problem was, I still hadn't heard from her.

The ache in my chest told me I was all in, whether I wanted to admit it or not. We may have started out as a casual fling that progressed to friendship via a little, fluffy black puppy, but it was definitely more now. I'd like to say my love for her hit me like a freight train, but it didn't, because I think I'd always known. There had been a crazy connection from the start. Probably why I'd given her my number that first day. She was really the one. Not only relationship material, but she was the whole shebang.

She was my person, and I'd fucked it up.

Good thing was, I was dead set on turning that around.

When my mom Facetimed me that night, I braced myself for the fall out when I told her what a shitstorm my life had become. During my explanation she was quiet. I didn't miss the way she gasped and covered her mouth, nor did she hide her tears well. I finished and waited for her to lose her shit.

Except she surprised me.

"Oh Jordan. I'm sorry this is all hitting you at once, but you have some serious and life-altering choices to make. I'm not going to presume to know how you feel, but from what you explained, I'm afraid you jumped into Zena's bullshit with good intentions, but for reasons that aren't practical." She sighed.

"Son, your father and I were so young when we met. We rushed into marriage because we were foolishly in love with the *idea* of being in love. He was newly drafted and I was just starting at the university. We struggled with schedules and distance, deciding that it would be a poor time to start a family.

It wasn't until your father was a seasoned player that we had you kids. While I wouldn't trade you and your sister for the world, we did it for the wrong reasons. We thought it was what we needed to bring us back together. Unfortunately, young children don't make it easy to work on unresolved issues. The tension increased and your father… well, he made bad choices. I wouldn't say he was completely to blame, because I was wrapped up in raising you two.

When you showed an interest and aptitude in hockey, he found some common ground with you and things got better for a while. He was so proud of you. He still is, you know," she softly added.

"I know. It's just rough sometimes," I tried to explain as I leaned against the headboard of my bed in the hotel room, resting my phone on my knees. I'd stayed behind when the guys decided to go down to the hotel bar for a while.

"Why? Because you feel like he replaced you and your sister?" God, she hit the nail right on the head.

"I…" I started, but I couldn't get it out due to the burning in my throat. I cleared it and asked her to continue with her story.

"Okay. By then you and Everly were in school and he was traded. I made the choice to go home to the Yukon. He came home to us as often as he could at first, but then they became fewer and farther between. His schedule, travel, practices, training camps, there was always a reason he wouldn't make it. When he did, we fought. I'm so sorry you kids had to see that.

When he retired after too many unsuccessful knee surgeries he came back to us. But he wasn't happy. Everything he was, his entire identity, had been stripped from him. All he knew was hockey. He tried to switch that identity to being a dad but he didn't know how. We held out until you two were almost adults, but we couldn't do it anymore.

I hold a lot of guilt for how you and your sister grew up. The poor example your father and I set for a marriage and a relationship. We both tried to show you two as much love as we could, but I sometimes worry it wasn't enough.

Anyway, what I'm trying to say and not doing a great job of it is, don't try to be a better person and father than yours was by taking on the responsibility for that woman." Her lip curled when she said 'that woman' and I couldn't help the snort that escaped. My mom didn't like Zena and I swore she went out of her way to not say Zena's name.

"Mom, I swear, I'm not in a relationship with her. I'm only trying to help her get on her feet. She had a lot invested in the overseas job she took and when she found out she was pregnant, she lost it all. I feel a little responsible," I admitted.

"Why? It took two of you to make a baby. That doesn't mean to take on all of her troubles to either make yourself feel better or out of some misplaced sense of responsibility. You are responsible for making sure you contribute to her medical care to ensure the baby is healthy. Then you owe her to help with the child's needs—food, clothes, a safe place to live, and your time as a father. You don't need to support her 100% because she's a grown woman and she's half responsible for the situation and herself. Your duty is to your child. Both of them. Now I'm not saying you should jump into a relationship with either of these women, but what I can tell you is that when you spoke to me about Blair, what I heard in your voice was something many people spend their entire life looking for. It wasn't only what you said, it was how you said it. The unspoken things. Like the way you smiled when you said her name, how you looked off when you told me something about her, the corners of your mouth tipped up as if you couldn't help but be happy when you thought about her. You're absolutely adorable."

My mom was embarrassing the shit out of me. I dropped my head and massaged my forehead. "Mom," I cut in as my face heated.

"Jordan, I only want you to be happy. You can't be with someone strictly out of responsibility, thinking you're going to be better at it than your father was, but neither can you shy away from someone who might just be the best thing to ever happen to you because you're afraid it will only end up like your father and I. Life is full of risks, we just have to find a way to choose the right ones to take."

For a moment, I felt like the little boy who was sad because his dad didn't make it to his hockey game and my mom was doing her best to cheer me up. The memories of those days hit me hard, but what my mom said finally sunk in. I wasn't my father, nor was Blair my mom. We were our own people and our path wasn't predetermined based on my history or my parents' history.

She gave me knowing little smirks as I told her more about Blair.

"Son, I hate to tell you this, but if you have any hopes of getting that girl to forgive you, you're going to need to do some serious groveling."

"Oh trust me, I'm well aware of that," I snorted. I'd been a fucking dumbass and I was well aware of the fact.

We talked a little longer before I heard the guys coming down the hall.

"Oh and Jordan?" my mom called out before I ended the call.

"Yeah?"

"Regardless of what you decide is best for you, I'm excited to meet my grandchildren."

We both smiled.

SEVENTEEN

Blair

"DYING ON THE INSIDE"—NESSA BARRETT

"How long are you going to shut him out?" Tori asked me with her arms crossed.

"Why do you care? You're the one who said he wasn't worth the heartache," I grumbled, glaring belligerently.

"Yeah, well that was before I knew you were in love with him."

"I am not."

"Lies."

I growled—because she was right.

"Like I said… you have been absolutely miserable since you told him you were pregnant and the guy left your apartment. Maybe he feels like a grade A dickasaurus. Didn't you say he texted and called to tell you he was sorry? I know he's sent you a small fortune in flowers, edible bouquets, and healthy snacks. He must've found the best website in the world for what to get a woman when she's pregnant because he's totally spoiled the shit out of you with those massages and lunches he had delivered to you at work. He obviously realizes the error of his ways and wants to talk. I don't know why you're being so damn stubborn." With her last words, she dramatically threw her hands above her head and stood from the couch. I rolled my eyes at her sudden shift to team Jordan.

"Yeah, well, I'm still a little pissed at Maddox for telling him my schedule for this week," I grunted with a scowl. Though inside, I secretly loved the sweet little notes Jordan had included with each delivery or gift he sent.

"Christ, Blair, he meant well. Where's your wine?" she shouted from the kitchen.

"In the fridge in the deli drawer—where it always is," I explained with a sigh because she knew this. "You might as well drink it all because I sure as hell won't be for a while."

"Good. I need it."

"Okay, so on another subject, what's gotten up your ass? You're extra specially grouchy today," I called out as she loudly rummaged through my drawers, I assumed looking for my corkscrew.

At her "aha," I smiled. I could hear her opening the bottle and the pop of the cork. She then came back to the living room where she plopped onto the sofa and poured her first glass. The bottle went to the coffee table, and she lifted the glass to her lips where she proceeded to empty half of it in one gulp.

"Well?" I prompted.

Slouched down, she eyed me over the rim. After one more drink that emptied the glass, she sighed. "I think Owen is getting tired of me."

"What?" I spat out in shock. He was head over heels for her. There was no way—she had to be imagining things.

"You heard me. He's been…different. When I try to get him to have sex, he brushes me off and he never initiates it on his own. It's been *two weeks*, Blair," she moaned in comic despair.

Slapping my palm to my chest, I gasped in mock horror. "No! Not two whole weeks? As in fourteen whole days? Say it ain't so."

"This is no joking matter," she huffed. Despite her comment, I laughed.

"You know, not everyone has sex every day, Tori. Maybe the guy has a lot on his mind," I tossed out.

She rolled her eyes my way. Then she blinked slow.

"Hey, it's possible," I argued.

"We're not talking about me. We're talking about you, your baby daddy, and Junior Jones there in your belly." She motioned to my still flat abdomen. My hand reflexively rested there at her words.

"Well, like you said to me, maybe you should talk to him," I threw her advice back at her with an arched brow. She lifted a middle finger at me. "And I don't know. Maybe I'd like him to fight for me. Maybe I need to feel like I truly matter and it's not just because I'm *another* baby momma he needs to support. Maybe it would be nice to know that he actually wants this baby—because I do. At first it was a shock and I was terrified. Then I realized what a miracle this little bean is, and I was humbled by the fact that its tiny soul chose me to be its mom."

Her bottom lip shot out. "Aww, honey. He or she is a miracle, and I'm so glad you're happy. Also, never forget that Aunt Tori is always here to help as much as she can."

"That means a lot. It's been one helluva roller-coaster ride since the day I met Jordan. The ups and downs and loops have left me wondering which end is up. I've been happy, sad, angry, but most of all, without him, you're right… I'm miserable. But he has to show me that he's in this for the long haul. Not just willing to buy me shit. Whether we work out or not, this is our baby. I'll be fine on my own, but I'd prefer to be a team. You know?" I explained.

"Well, he gave you his schedule in detail in case you wanted him to be there for your appointments. I'd say that's an attempt to be there for you, at least as much as he can be right now. And as much as you're letting him." She pursed her lips and cocked a brow at me.

"I'm just torn. On one hand I stubbornly want to be able to do this myself. On the other, I want there to be an us through all of it," I admitted.

"I understand. I'm glad you see how strong you are, and I'm also glad to see you being honest with yourself when it comes to Jordan."

"Yes, I am. I can and will be the best mom possible. And I am trying my best to open my heart to him again, but it's hard after being twice bitten." I rested a hand on my lower abdomen, and I mulled over everything. Then I sighed. "You know, what really shocks me is how much I love my itty-bitty human already. How does that happen?" I murmured, more than a little in awe of human nature.

"It doesn't always work out like that. Some people are simply incubators but don't have a single scrap of motherly love or instinct," Tori sagely spelled out.

We were both quiet for a bit. From what I remember of my mom, she loved me. She wasn't a bad person, but she just had shit taste in men. Hmph. Like mother, like daughter, I guess. Tori's mom, on the other hand… she'd split when Tori was a baby. Dropped her off with her grandmother and was gone.

I wrapped an arm around my friend. Then I leaned over and kissed her cheek.

"I love you," I whispered.

She smiled, then turned her head to face me. "I love you too."

"Thanks, chica. Now let's plan a seduce Owen mission." I evilly rubbed my hands together.

The paper taped to my door fluttered in the breeze that blew through the landing of my apartment building. My heart matched its arrhythmic movement. A shiver shot through me, and I juggled my grocery bags so I could reach for it.

Was I getting evicted? I'd been late on my rent a few times, but I knew I'd paid it every month. God, what if it was from Henry. He'd texted me after the day Jordan bailed on me, but I never answered.

After darting a glance around to see if someone was watching, I plucked the fluttering page from the metal, unlocked the handle, and rushed inside. Like I had stolen something, I slammed the door and locked it. My grocery bags hit the floor. Then, with trembling fingers, I unfolded it. It wasn't what I expected.

Blair,

I don't know where to start. There are things I want to say to you in person, but I can't if you won't speak to me. What I need you to know is that you mean something to me. I reacted like a jackass. We might not have planned any of this, but after having time to process, I want this baby with you. I can't wait to be there for you as you

181

go through your pregnancy. My hope is for my kid to grow up and tell people I was a good dad. No, a great dad. I'll figure out the stuff with Zena, but it's you I want by my side. It's you I need. Please call me.

Jordan

By the time I read the scrawl of his signature, there were tears in my eyes. When I blinked, they spilled out over my cheeks. More than anything, I wanted to rush to his house and ask him if he meant it.

Except I was scared.

He'd essentially rejected me twice. What if he changed his mind again? My heart couldn't handle that. Because Tori was right and so was Jordan. We were supposed to be casual, with a little friendship thrown in because of Beaker. Yet somewhere along the way, I'd messed up—I'd fallen in love with Jordan Beck.

The other question was did I want to have to share him with another woman? Because even if he wasn't in a relationship with her, he would always be tied to Zena through their child. And she was a bitch. Then again, I was pregnant with his child too, so there would be a connection between us whether I was with him or not.

Could I handle seeing him each time we exchanged the baby for visitation, knowing he wasn't mine? Could I survive having to watch him with someone else when he eventually moved on? The churning in my guts at the thought told me the answer to that. I'd hate it with a burning passion.

After thinking about everything with a clear head, I realized I could never keep his baby from him. It wasn't about the money or what he should or shouldn't be responsible for. It was the fact that he had a right to see his child and that child had a right to have his or her father in their life.

So many what ifs, though. Turmoil reigned in my heart as much as my head.

I dug in my bag for my phone and pulled up his number. Praying I was doing the right thing, I tapped out my message.

Me: Okay. We can talk. If you're not busy, I'm off tonight and at home.

It took a few minutes before the notification chimed telling me I had a message. To prepare myself for what it might say, I inhaled deeply and exhaled slowly. Then I flipped my phone over.

Sexy Giant: I'll be over shortly. Please don't leave?

Me: I'll be here.

Sexy Giant: OMW

My heart fluttered erratically at the knowledge that he would be here soon. Then I hurried to put away my groceries and slid around the corner to rush to the bathroom. A long look in the mirror showed me that I was a hot mess. A quick sniff of my armpits made my nose wrinkle in distaste.

Having no idea how far away he was, I didn't know if I had time to shower. Yet, I didn't want to smell like I'd forgotten how to wash my ass. Quickly, I cranked the water on, stripped out of my clothes, and hopped in the tub. In record time, I soaped and conditioned my hair, scrubbed my body, and dried off. I pulled on a pair of pajama shorts and matching tank but then thought better of it. Maybe I'd be giving the wrong impression. I whipped them off and switched them for a pair of running shorts and a T-shirt.

The doorbell rang, and I squeaked.

"Shit!"

No time for makeup. I ran a quick brush through my hair and wrapped it up in a wet messy bun. Then I rushed to the door where I gave myself a quick pep talk and took a few cleansing breaths.

Once I had myself as calm as I was gonna get, I flipped the lock and whipped the door open. My mouth fell open, and I was speechless.

"Hey, Blair. Can I come in?"

"No!" I snapped, but Henry pushed past me as if I hadn't said a word. Dumbfounded, I stood with my hand on the knob and watched him pace my apartment.

"We need to talk. You won't answer my calls or my text messages," he finally said as he stopped and gave me puppy dog eyes that at one time would've had me melting.

"Absolutely not. And there's a reason I don't answer you. It's because I have nothing to say to you. Get. Out!" I snarled through clenched teeth as I jabbed my finger toward the landing.

"Blair, please," he begged.

"I think she was pretty explicit with her answer," Jordan growled from the doorway.

Well, shit.

"Who the fuck are you?" Henry sneered and crossed his arms. Pretty brave considering Jordan's massive form filled the only exit unless Henry wanted to jump off my balcony.

"Me?" Jordan asked innocently as he splayed a hand on his broad chest. "Oh, I'm the guy who's going to beat the living dog snot out of you if you don't remove your ass from the lady's apartment like she told you to do once already."

Henry seemed to weigh the situation and opted for the safest choice. He stormed toward the door. Jordan kept his exit blocked until the last second. With an intense stare, he slowly stepped to the side, but Henry had to brush against him to pass through the doorway. It might've been my imagination, but it sounded like Jordan grumbled at him.

Watching to ensure Henry indeed left, Jordan stood with his arms akimbo. Then he slowly spun and kicked the door shut behind him. The angry expression had fallen off, and there was nothing but naked hunger in its place.

"Before we let our hormones speak for us, we have some things to discuss," I blurted out before I could race to climb him like a tree.

"I agree."

Neither of us spoke though. We simply stared at each other until my pulse was soaring sky high and my heart tried to bust through my ribs.

"I love you," he finally admitted with a daring lift of his chin. My mouth fell open.

And my heart exploded. As did the dam that held back my tears. In a few long strides he was in my space, his arms wrapped around me with my cheek pressed to his hard chest. "Please don't cry," he murmured while pressing kisses to the top of my head.

"I can't help it," I cried. "I'm so stinking emotional. And you just told me you l-l-love me."

One large hand cupped the back of my head and the other tightened around my waist. Warm air hit me with each of his breaths as he seemed to bury his nose in my hair.

"Shhh, I don't expect you to say it back, but I needed you to know how I feel. I've fucked up too many times, and I don't want to do it again. You snuck your way into my heart, and I can't get you out—not that I've tried. Beaker misses you too. He runs to the door every time someone comes over, and it's like he visibly wilts when it's not you."

Gripping the front of his shirt, I pushed back to look him in the eye. Sniffling, I tried to blink away the tears that kept sneaking out. When I finally got them under control, I bit my lip as I tried to decide the best way to word what I needed him to tell me.

"What about Zena?" I simply blurted out.

"I think he kinda hates her," he whispered with a smirk that told me he was well aware that wasn't what I was asking. Though it kind of made me feel better to think Beaker liked me better.

"That's not what I meant."

"I know." He sighed. "I'm still helping her find a place to live. I'm also not a hundred percent convinced the baby is mine, but if it is, then I'll do my duty and be the best dad I can be, but I'm not doing it with her. I can't. The more I thought about how unhappy my parents were while I was growing up, the more I realized I couldn't do that to myself or a child."

"I was afraid of you thinking I was like her. Or that I was only after your money and fame. I wanted you to be with me for me and not because I was having your baby," I whispered.

"That rationale is the most ridiculous bunch of drivel I've ever heard. You are *nothing* like her. And I'd want you whether you were having my kid or not. I was a fucking idiot to think I could be without you." The rough calluses on his hands scraped my sensitive skin in the best way as he cradled my head and stroked my cheeks with his thumbs.

My heart leaped into my throat. It was now or never because I'd known how I felt about him for a while.

"I'm not just saying this because you did," I started before my gaze searched his. "But I love you too."

His inhale caught before it stuttered. "Then what the hell are we doing denying it and avoiding each other?"

"I don't know," I honestly replied. I was still afraid, but if I was truthful, I was more frightened of not trying. The thought of missing out on what I knew could be incredible, simply because I was gun-shy was a worse thought. I wet my lips and my gaze dropped to his mouth, then back to his beautiful blue eyes.

His groan told me he'd noticed. "You are killing me," he announced before he dipped his head and swooped in for a demanding kiss. It took my breath away in its intensity. And in that moment, my heart took the leap—risked a chance on us.

Happiness burst through me like a mini fireworks show through my veins and in my chest. Things might not always be perfect and there would likely be days where we had frustrations with the learning process, but we were taking the first steps. Together.

When his tongue slid along my lip and darted in my mouth, I moaned. He tasted me with abandon, sucking on my lower lip before sinking his teeth into it and tugging. My worries dissipated like smoke on the wind for the time being. I simply wanted to feel him and be together.

I smoothed my hands over each hard plane I could reach, reacquainting myself with all of his physical details.

Unable to stop myself, I worked his shirt free of his jeans and spanned his trim waist and skimmed over his rippled abs with my hands before slipping around to his back. My nails dug into his skin as I held on for dear life.

"I need you," I gasped when we broke for air.

It was all he needed to hear. Like a man on a mission, he lifted me into his arms, and I wrapped my legs around his waist. Hungrily, I kissed him as he blindly made his way to my bedroom.

Gently, he set me on my feet. As if I was a priceless gift, he reverently removed my clothing, one item at a time. Wildly, he pressed his lips to my neck, then nipped and sucked as if he couldn't get enough. My head lolled to the side as I moaned. It felt so fucking good. My nerve endings were firing like mad, and arousal rushed through my veins.

He dropped to his knees at my feet where he kissed the side of each breast before pressing a soft kiss to my abdomen. A shiver shot through me as his teeth scraped along my hips. Then I sucked in a startled gasp when he grabbed me and tossed me on the bed.

"You are so beautiful you take my breath away," he whispered with his hands caressing every sensitive spot I had. His hot kisses trailed my skin, and I threaded my fingers through his tawny hair. When his wicked mouth found my dripping wet core, he lapped and sucked on my clit until I was writhing on the comforter, desperate for more.

He never let up, and when he added his fingers to the mix, it only took a few beckoning curls to send me flying. Violently, I tugged at his hair as I ground myself against his talented mouth. With one last suck, he sent me over the edge. I froze, and bright flashes of light burst behind my closed lids. Each pulse had me panting before I arched in a silent scream and the finale rocked my world.

When I was once again coherent, I was breathless and still so damn needy.

"Jordan, please come here so I can feel you," I begged, pulling at his T-shirt. He did that sexy move where he grabbed the back of his shirt and tugged it over his head. My heart fluttered, and a needy tingle made my pussy clench. As he settled between my legs, I let them fall open further to grant him better access.

Focused on watching his finger swirl through my wet heat, he stroked his thick cock. I was mesmerized by the clear bead that appeared at the tip, and my tongue yearned to lick it off. But I wanted him inside me too much.

"This time when I fuck you bare, I'm coming inside you—filling you with every drop I have. Because you're mine, and this pussy belongs to me." The crass words damn near set off an orgasm as I clenched around his teasing fingers.

All I could do was nod.

As he lined the head of his cock up and began to work it inside, he glanced up at me in question—as if he was making sure I hadn't changed my mind.

"Yes," I gasped as my legs tightened around his, desperate to pull him in.

Gripping my ass, he drove his thick length into my pussy, and I screamed at the slightly painful but utterly amazing intrusion. He hissed as I wiggled my hips to get him to move.

"You need to give me a sec or this will be over before it starts," he ground out through clenched teeth. The tendons in his neck stood out as testament to his barely leashed restraint.

"God, Jordan, just fuck me. If you come too soon, I'll suck your cock until you're hard again," I wildly pleaded, causing him to groan.

But it worked, because he slowly dragged his throbbing shaft out, then plunged back in. It was so good that my eyes rolled and I tore at the bedspread. He repeated the motion, and a satisfied groan escaped me.

"Are you okay?" he questioned with a worry-laced gaze.

"God yes, but I won't be if you don't move," I practically shouted.

A wicked grin hooked his mouth, and he let loose. True to his word, that round didn't last long. Not that I was complaining, because the second his cock pulsed inside my core and his hot spurts of cum filled me, I lost it. My orgasm hit me like a runaway train.

"Jesus Christ," he moaned as he gave a last shuddering thrust.

For a few moments, we both sat there fighting to regain our breath. During that time, I watched him and thought about everything that had transpired. The depth of my love for him almost scared the shit out of me, but I couldn't find it in me to regret taking the chance. Needing the reassurance that I wasn't dreaming, I smoothed my palms over his sweat-slicked surfaces.

"Give me a minute and I'll be ready again," he muttered before he dropped to his elbows and buried his face in my neck. Soft kisses along my damp skin sent shivers down my spine. Unfortunately, it dislodged him, and we both cried out in disappointment.

He rolled his weight off me and flung an arm over his eyes. "Holy shit. That was...."

"Yeah," I replied. When I could move again, I climbed out of bed and practically hobbled to the bathroom to get a warm washcloth. I cleaned myself, then padded back and wiped him off. He sucked in a startled gasp, and his arm fell to the side.

When I was done, I tossed the cloth to the floor. Slowly, I

crawled up the bed and straddled his legs. Heat filled his gaze as I wrapped my hand around his soft but still impressive shaft. Immediately, he twitched in my hand and began to harden. I cast a smirk at him before I scooted down and lowered my head to circle my tongue around the soft crown before sucking.

"Sweet baby Jesus," he whispered as his fingers combed through my hair, then he slowly wrapped my hair around his hand. With gentle force, he guided my rhythm as I drew him into my mouth, going deeper each time. By the time my nose touched his groin, he was hard, and he pulled my hair to make me stop. Another tug told me he was getting impatient. Happily, I crawled up his glorious body until I was centered over his now throbbing, stiff cock.

He lined up, and I dropped onto him as he drove upward.

"Holy shit," he groaned as I whimpered.

His hands wrapped around my hips, and he rolled them in a sensual rhythm perfectly synced with his own. Our eyes locked as my fingers splayed over my sensitive breasts, catching the nipples between them. Insanely, I was willing to swear my boobs had gotten bigger over the last week.

"Fuck yes. Play with those amazing tits. They were beautiful before, but I swear they are goddamn mesmerizing now." He punctuated the statement with a hard upward thrust that took my breath away.

Well, that answered that.

As I continued the slow grind on his rock-hard cock, he smoothed his rough hands up my sides. I moaned when he slid them under mine to take over massaging and pinching the taut peaks until I could barely stand the stimulation.

Never ceasing the smooth, steady movements of his hips, he

curled himself upward and captured a taut nipple in his hot, demanding mouth. With a gasp, I clutched his hair, and my back arched. After laving his tongue in circles around the now peaked tip, he nipped it and moved on to the other.

"Jordan," I pleaded as I rode him faster and clung to him.

"Are you going to come?" he whispered, his breath blowing warm over my damp flesh. Between his hands and his mouth, he seemed to wrap around me—consume me. Paired with the steady friction of his thick shaft relentlessly stroking my core, I was indeed on the verge of a full-body meltdown.

"Yes," I admitted, my voice raspy with pleasure. It was all too much, and I was ready to explode.

"Good," he replied with a powerful surge deep inside my needy pussy. Faster, I rode him as he held me tightly in his protective arms and alternated between kissing and sucking on my skin. Shivers of desire coupled with all the ways he moved, and he owned my body.

Hell, he owned my heart and soul.

The pressure grew until I knew I was either going to come or shatter. A well-placed thumb on my clit and he played me like a well-tuned symphony. I came in an explosion of sensation. My vision was filled with bright flashes of light, and my entire body convulsed as my sheath pulsed around his still-driving shaft.

"Jordan! Oh God, Jordan!" I shouted, uncaring that my neighbors could probably hear me.

"Fuuuuuuck!" he groaned as he held me close, and his fingers dug into my side and my shoulder.

By the time he filled me with every drop of his release as he promised, I was a satiated, boneless heap. He carefully rolled me to lie on the bed and drew me into the shelter of his large body.

Wordlessly, he pressed kisses to the curve of my neck, eliciting mewls of satisfied bliss from me.

"We're going to be parents together, babe," he murmured behind me, his tone one of awe. It made my lips curve happily.

"Yeah, we are," I softly agreed.

"I'm glad it's with you," he rumbled quietly as he squeezed me in his thick arms. Then he brushed my hair back over my shoulder to rain kisses along my sensitive skin.

"Me too." I pressed his arm to my chest.

"I love you," he whispered into my neck as he wrapped one thick arm around me and tucked his hand under my breast.

"Love you too." I drifted off with a smile on my face.

EIGHTEEN

Jordan

"BLEED INTO ME"—TRIVIUM

T WAS THE THIRD HOME GAME THAT BLAIR HAD ATTENDED, AND
she was there to watch me each time. If that made my chest puff a
little, so be it. For tonight's game, I'd arranged for extra tickets so she
could invite several of her friends. Alex had gotten his brother tickets,
so most of the section behind the bench was our friends and family.

As we entered the rink for our warm-up, I glanced up and spot-
ted Blair with her friend Tori. I'd officially met her about three weeks
ago—the day after Blair and I had figured shit out. Well, maybe not
figured it out, but we were on the right track and were working on it.

We'd met her for breakfast, and she'd seemed vaguely familiar. I
wasn't sure whether it was from one of the club parties I'd attended or
from that first night at the diner. At the parties, I never messed with

a chick that was with someone, and I'd honestly only had eyes for a chestnut-haired beauty that had so explicitly been describing her sexual desires in the diner. It had been impossible not to be amused that night. Tori teased us about that experience—about how I must've shown Blair how it was done.

I'd snorted orange juice out of my nose. I liked her.

"It's cool that your brother's club could make it," I told Alex as he and Cameron skated into the rink after me.

"Yeah. That's one of the best parts of being picked up by the Amurs—being close to him," Alex admitted. His brother's club surrounded all the wives and girlfriends that were attending. It made me feel better to know no one would fuck with them during the game with the guys there.

Another glance at where Blair was sitting sent a rush of longing through me. In my head I imagined her there with our kid. She'd point out to the ice and say, "Look! There's Daddy!" Then maybe she'd bring him or her down to the boards, and I could see their little smile as they waved and I fist-bumped them through the glass.

Unable to shake my grin, I brought my attention back to the task at hand.

Ensuring I was limber, I stretched while everyone else skirted the boards as they circled the ice. Then, as they passed the puck in pairs, I blocked my teammates' shots as everyone warmed up.

"Let's get this show on the road," Cameron said as he backhanded a puck and it went past me.

"Dick," I grumbled, but my smirk belied my words. Then I stole one last peek at the girl who had me in knots. Having her there was one of the best feelings in the world. Over the years, I'd had friends and family attend my games, and it was cool, but Blair being there was different. It was nerve-racking, because no one wanted to look like a loser in front of their girl, but it was also more. Like my desire to do well skyrocketed to another level, amping up my motivation. Her smile took my breath away, and I knew I'd need to limit the attention I gave her after the game started.

Black, the dude Tori was dating, sat next to her, but they both looked like they were irritated. I wondered if they'd fought before taking their seats because I thought they seemed okay earlier.

"You're so fucked," Mikko teased in a sing-song voice with a wide grin.

"Maybe I like it that way," I shot back as my mouth hooked in a half smile.

"Are we going to braid each other's hair next, or are we going to warm up?" Kristoffer questioned as he stopped quick, spraying snow all over us. I removed my glove to flip him off.

As everyone chuckled, including me, we got to work. Shaking the distraction, I returned my attention to my job. Or I tried to anyway.

"That your nurse?" Jericho asked as he skated backwards and motioned with his chin toward the stands.

It was impossible to keep the grin off my face. "Yeah."

"She's cute," he said with a shit-eating grin as he watched me and handled a puck. "If you ever want to unload her, say the word."

"Yeah right. You're such an asshole. You realize that, right?" I said as I caught his shot in my glove.

"Of course. Did you expect anything less?" he teased, then skated off with a laugh. If I didn't know him so well, I might've wanted to beat his ass, but he was harmless.

Mostly.

Mikko and Mikhail passed the puck from the line toward me.

Mikko hit me with a slapshot that went through the five hole, and I cussed that I'd been a hair too slow to stop it.

"Better luck next time," Mikko called out as he skated away. There wasn't a second to reply because Kristoffer and Alex approached next.

Dodging left, then right, dropping to my knees, and snagging a few pucks in my glove, I went through all the basics. When we were done, we slowly left the ice to make our way through the tunnel to the locker room.

"All right, listen up!" Coach boomed. The chattering in the room dwindled, and he had our full attention. There was an occasional rustle, but all eyes locked on him, and all ears took in every word he spoke. Nick Soderburg hadn't become the youngest coach in the NHL by being unable to command a room.

His pregame speech was designed to motivate us, but it was also meant to remind us why we were there. He'd also been one of the greatest players to ever take the ice. He'd been a rookie when my father played. If he hadn't taken a bad hit that messed up his knee and left him with one helluva concussion, he might still be on the ice.

"So yeah, it might be a game and yeah, we want to have fun, but we're going to play hard, and we're going to make beating their asses the most fun we've ever had," he concluded to the shouted agreement of every player there.

Each player finished gathering their crap and doing whatever last-minute superstitious bullshit we believed in. Alex shoved a fucking Ding Dong in his face as Mikhail shook his head at him. Then Mikhail kissed his necklace and tucked it under his sweater.

Kristoffer stood in front of me and leaned over until our noses damn near touched. He stared in my eyes and asked me, "Who are you?"

"The Wall."

"Who?" he repeated.

"The Motherfuckin' Wall!" I thundered, adrenaline surging through my veins. My teammates cheered, and I got to my skates. Then, with me leading the way, we headed out.

The second we took the ice, I had a bad feeling. Something seemed off, but I couldn't put my finger on it.

Blair waved, and I watched her mouth "I love you" and "Good luck" before I pulled my focus to the ice. That would never get old. I stretched, then went through my usual routine of roughing up my crease.

The puck dropped, and we got down to business.

By the second period, everything was going smoothly, and I was beginning to think I had been wrong about my initial misgivings. We were up by two, and I'd stopped sixteen shots already. Too early to celebrate, but we were playing damn well.

Alex scored his 25th goal of the year and Kristoffer, his 31st.

Greg Washington, the center for San Jose, had played with me my first season. We had both been sent down to San Antonio, our AHL developmental team. Though he'd been traded at the end of that season, we'd kept in touch off and on, and I generally considered him a friend. With a pretty badass breakaway, he was barreling down the ice toward me.

Keeping my eyes on not only the puck but his actions, I waited. My heart raced, but I maintained my usual calm as I zeroed in on his body language—analyzing each of his movements. Those would be what would give away his last second actions in an attempt to get the puck past me.

"Go, go, go!" I heard the crowd chant as Dmitry, Jericho, Kristoffer, Cameron, and Alex tried their damnedest to catch up.

As he faked left, a couple of his teammates charged up, along with ours. He shot, and I dove for the puck, right as Washington and Jericho hit each other. The collision didn't look that bad until Washington lost his balance and did a nosedive. Everything seemed to happen in slow motion.

In reflex, I jerked my head back to avoid getting kicked. That turned out to be my downfall. The sting told me his skate had caught me under the neck guard as I'd thrown my head back. Despite the more protective design of modern goalie helmets, it was the perfect storm.

"Beck!" I heard Alex shout right as I looked down and saw the blood spray out in front of me. The red on the ice registered. My next reflexive action likely was my saving grace, as my hand went to the slight burn on my neck. Shock hit me.

Holy shit. This is bad.

Blood leaked from between my fingers as I got to my knees. Eyes wide, I cast a glance around.

Fuck, my family is watching. Please God, don't let them see me die.

Our trainer, Joe Larson, jumped over the boards and ran toward the net. He reached me as I struggled to get to my feet. With the help of people I wasn't even aware of, he ushered me off the ice. Numbness settled in, and I barely noticed any pain. Did that mean I was dying?

Panic was setting in, though I tried to fight it as they were laying me down. Pressure hit my neck, and my gaze darted up into a pair of eyes I didn't recognize.

"Hey, I'm Josh. I'm a medic up at Fort Hood. Buddies and I came for the game. We were getting a beer. I'm sorry, I reacted and tossed my beer before I jumped the rail. Thought security was gonna tackle me until I told them what I did for a living. We're pretty up close and personal right now, so stay with me, okay? You can buy me a new beer after this." He gave me a friendly smile that didn't quite reach his eyes. That scared me.

He maintained pressure as they cut my gear off me. He was pushing so hard that I couldn't breathe. Suffocating, I grabbed his hand.

"If you need to breathe, we have to be quick," he solemnly started, then continued. "I have to keep pressure as much as possible. You are *not* dying on my watch."

All I could do was rapidly blink my eyes and squeeze his hand. When he let up, blood sprayed, I sucked in a breath, and he immediately reapplied pressure.

Jesus, I'm going to die. I have babies on the way. I'm not ready yet.

The doc practically skidded up to us. He took over holding pressure for the guy while I sucked in another breath. I could barely keep up with everything around me.

I had no idea where the young medic went as I tried to gain control. Hell, at that point I wasn't sure if I had imagined him. I signaled for air again, and the process repeated. Then they rushed me into the waiting ambulance, and with people shouting, they raced me to surgery. In the background, I was vaguely aware of quiet commands and rushed actions. The sterile smell practically choked me with each desperate breath I was allowed.

The helplessness that washed over me was suffocating me as bad as the person smashing on my throat. The panic that threatened earlier bubbled to the surface. My mind was in a whirl, vacillating between losing my fucking mind and giving up.

I'd never given much thought to dying, but I did then. I still had so much to do that I couldn't believe I had reached the end already. But I was terrified I'd never wake up again. I wanted to scream. With the pressure they had on my neck, I couldn't say anything.

Couldn't tell anyone to tell my family I loved them.

Couldn't say I needed Blair or that I loved her with all my fucking heart.

Couldn't say I hoped people made sure my kids knew I'd wanted to be there for them.

"You're in good hands," a nurse said to me as they prepped me for surgery—still holding pressure while I lost blood with every breath. A weird little part of my brain wondered if she knew Blair.

I didn't want to close my eyes. If I did, they might never open. I'm not embarrassed to say I was terrified.

Despite my fears and fighting to stay conscious, blackness crept in, and I could no longer keep my eyes open.

NINETEEN

Blair

"IF IT MAKES YOU HAPPY"—SHERYL CROW

TONIGHT WAS THE START OF MY THIRD PROFESSIONAL HOCKEY game I'd attended, and I counted myself a lucky girl that my boyfriend was on the team. Watching him play live was so much more exhilarating than following the game on TV, from videos, or replays online.

The last couple of weeks had been both amazing and terrifying. Jordan had several days without games. He would go in for practice and the gym, but after that, we had time to ourselves. His home games, I attended. I was totally addicted to watching him play.

During Jordan's free time, we took Beaker to the park when he could get the little dog out of the house without his bitch of an ex catching him.

The frightening part of all of it was having our reality settle in. I was pregnant, and his ex was pregnant. We were really doing this. Not that we had discussed marriage, but we were definitely together. Zena was a two-faced bitch. She was sappy and sweet any time Jordan was around, but if he left the room, she was cutting her eyes at me and sneering. I avoided going over there as often as I could.

And through it all, I fought the fear that things would end. Nothing in my life except for Tori and nursing had lasted. For years, I'd wondered if I was destined to have everything and everyone I loved ripped away. Daily, I reminded myself that Jordan loved me and between the two of us we had enough determination to hold onto anything.

"This is gonna be so good," Truth said as he dropped into his seat next to me, pulling me from my musing. He held his bag of popcorn my direction in an unspoken offer, and I grabbed a handful. As I chewed, I cast a sidelong glance at my best friend on my other side.

Owen and Tori were on edge. I tried to pretend I didn't notice as I watched each play, but I was worried about them. Especially after the discussion Tori and I had a while back.

Slice was there, but things were awkward for only a moment until I acted like nothing had happened, and he seemed to breathe a sigh of relief. That was all in the past, before Jordan.

The game was intense. Both teams were playing with high energy and aggression.

"Yes! Did you see that?" Truth excitedly whooped. The announcers told us it was Alex Kosinski's 25th goal of the season—that was his brother. Truth and I high-fived with huge grins. Everyone around us got in on the action as we all celebrated with Alex and his team.

As we were cheering, they dropped the puck, and the game was on again. Halvorson shot, but it was redirected off their goalie's stick.

We watched with trepidation as one of the opposing players seemed to dart toward Jordan before anyone realized what happened. Though our players were on the guy's ass, he had a significant head start.

"Go! Oh my God, go!" a lady a couple of rows back screamed at our players to catch up. We were on the edge of our seats.

What happened next seemed to unfold in slow motion, yet it was likely only seconds.

There was a collision, and the guy from the other team took a fall as Jordan dove for the puck. Jordan's body jolted when the guy appeared to catch him with his foot. Before I could see exactly what was going on, Jordan was prone on the ice.

Slowly, he pushed up to his elbows.

Then his glove flew off and his hand hit his neck and held. He rose to his knees, and I tried to make sense of what I was seeing.

The second I saw blood on the ice in front of Jordan, I was on my feet and running down the steps to the glass. No way to get to him, I started beating on the thick acrylic in front of me and screaming his name as the puddle appeared to spread at an alarming rate. In my mind, I was estimating blood loss, and it was terrifying me. Truth and his brothers tried to guide me away from the horrors in front of us as they led Jordan off the ice, but in my panic, I initially fought them.

"Easy, we're going to find out where he's going and take you there, okay?" Their president, Smoke, murmured in my ear as he wrapped me in a bear hug from behind and his wife clutched my hand. Heaving breaths shook me as I trembled. Maddox was there with his wife Gwen, and my frantic gaze sought his. He was not only one of Truth's club brothers, but he worked in the ER with me.

"Why am I panicking?" I babbled through my tears as we hurried to exit the arena. "I work traumas for a living. Maddox?" I pleaded, though I didn't know what for.

"Because this hits close to home," he calmly explained despite our rapid pace out of the stadium.

They bustled me into an SUV and then we were racing down the road. No one spoke, and not once did I ask how they knew where to go. All I could concentrate on was Jordan.

We pulled into the ER parking lot, and though I recognized it as my hospital, it all seemed so foreign. It was like I was watching everything play out from a distance.

Maddox spoke quietly to our receptionist, Frances. She motioned down the hall as they finished up.

"Let's go," he murmured to everyone standing around us.

By the time we headed toward the surgery waiting room, I'd begun to go numb. We paused long enough for Smoke to get something from one of the vending machines.

"Here. Drink this," Smoke quietly instructed as he handed me a water bottle. Without a second thought, I took it and tipped it back. The memory of all the blood on the ice made me swallow wrong and I choked. Realizing I was falling apart, I shot him a wide-eyed stare.

"I don't want you going into shock on us. Everything is going to be okay. Keep it together," Smoke warned as he led me into the waiting area.

Tears leaked from my eyes and trailed down my cheeks. "I'm pregnant," I whispered.

"Shit," he murmured. Tori arrived out of breath.

"Sorry, we couldn't find a freaking parking spot," she explained in a rush before wrapping an arm around my shoulders.

Whether it was the warning from Smoke, the arrival of my best friend, or the support I was getting from people who barely knew me, I sobbed but began to focus. I took a deep shuddering inhale and slowly let it out. Shaking worse than I had in my life, I placed a hand over my stomach where my little bean nestled, completely unaware of the events that could significantly change its life, and settled into a chair.

"I'm so scared," I cried as Tori tried to soothe me. "What if he doesn't make it?"

"Shhh, we're going to think positive. You hear me?" She pressed her forehead to mine. "He's a big, tough dude—a fighter. He has you and your baby to live for."

The wait for news seemed to take years. People started to filter into the waiting room, but all I could do was absently stare at the pattern on the carpet. Vaguely, I noted most of them seemed to be his teammates. The restlessness in my chest was reflected in their nervous movements, despite the solemn silence.

Jordan's friend Mikko sat on my other side and gave me a sad but encouraging smile. Catching both lips in my teeth, I again fought breaking down.

The wait continued. My mind reeled as I thought about what I would do if Jordan didn't survive. I couldn't fathom it. Initially, I'd wondered what it might be like for my little bean to grow up without its parents together. Now my child might be without a father at all. The devastation that slammed into me was soul shattering.

The ache in my heart grew with each minute that ticked by.

Several times, someone from our group approached, asking if I needed a drink or a snack. To each one, I shook my head and whispered "no thank you." The thought of consuming anything at all made me nauseous.

"Family of Jordan Beck?" an exhausted looking nurse called out from the edge of the waiting area. Heads swiveled my direction, and I fought the sobs that threatened. It should've been his parents or sister, but they were still trying to get last-minute flights out of Canada, but everything had been booked.

"Y-y-yes?" I stammered.

"Are you Mrs. Beck?" she asked.

"She is," Kristoffer, their team captain, announced, surprising me. Everyone's attention zeroed in on him, but he remained stoic. I didn't know he had any idea who I was, let alone was willing to lie for me.

"The surgeon will be out to give you more details, but Jordan made it through surgery."

Cheers erupted, and my heart damn near exploded as I hugged Tori tightly. We both knew things could still nosedive, but for now, he was alive—and I'd take every bit of good news I could get.

The sound of heels on the hard hallway floors echoed, and heads swiveled in that direction. Perfectly coifed blonde hair topped an artfully made-up face of Jordan's pregnant ex. As usual, she looked disgustingly amazing, and I wondered if she'd spent the entire time we were there waiting, getting ready.

A few grumbles went through our little crowd.

"How is he?" she cried out to their coach, completely ignoring me and Jordan's teammates.

"Don't tell me that's her," Owen grumbled next to Tori. Despite the discord I sensed in them earlier, he'd still driven her here and had stayed with us the entire time.

"Fucking bitch," I heard one of the hockey players mutter.

I couldn't agree more.

As she sobbed without tears to the coach, I glared, and my lip curled in distaste.

"Are you sure she isn't an actress?" Tori asked with a disgusted sneer.

"She's actually been trying to get parts for after the baby's born," I informed Tori as I kept myself from jumping up and ripping out her extensions—the ones I knew Jordan paid for. He couldn't see it, but she was milking him on all four tits. I'd be willing to bet she hadn't actually looked at a single place to move.

"Seriously?" Tori deadpanned.

"Right?" Despite wanting to kick her out, she was likely pregnant with Jordan's kid, too. It wasn't the baby's fault that its mother was a scheming bitch. If she hadn't had an ultrasound showing all the information, I would've sworn the baby was someone else's. Jordan thought she might've cheated on him, and I wouldn't put it past her.

"Mrs. Beck?" Though it seemed strange, I looked up. An outraged gasp followed my movement as I stood. When I approached the man in scrubs and a surgical cap, those fucking clicking heels rushed after me. The guy looked as tired as the nurse had. While I'd never worked in surgery, I'd had some traumas that had been exhausting, so I felt for them.

"Yes?" I questioned, desperate for another scrap of good news.

"You aren't his wife," Zena sneered. "I'm his fiancée," she smoothly purred to the surgeon.

"What?" I exclaimed in outrage at her audacity.

"Didn't he tell you yet?" she asked with saccharine-filled sweetness. "We've decided to work things out."

She held up her hand as she wiggled her fingers, the sparkle of a massive diamond glittering in the bright hospital lighting. My chest seized as I told myself that was impossible.

"There's no way," I insisted, but my doubt came through in the waver of my voice.

"Aww, are you the last to know?" Mock sympathy rolled off her and I wanted to gag, then choke her.

The poor doctor watched the shitshow playing out in front of him, unsure of how to proceed.

Finally, Jordan's friend and teammate, Kristoffer, stepped between us. He turned his back on Zena as he locked his gaze with mine. "Don't listen to that. Jordan didn't say any of that. You know him. You know how he feels about you. She's a conniving leech."

Then he switched his attention to the waiting surgeon. "I'd like that woman to leave before you speak." He jabbed a thumb over his shoulder at the outraged blonde. "If she doesn't, then you'll need to call security."

A gasp preceded Zena's hissed reply. "How dare you!"

Kristoffer spun on her. "Oh, I dare. Now you have until the count of three. One." He tapped his foot as he crossed his arms. "Two." Zena clenched her teeth, and her hands curled into fists. "Three. Coach, call security if the doc can't."

The coach attempted to pacify Zena by getting her to step down the hall to talk to him. She flashed a hateful glare at Mikko, then me before she spun on her heel and followed the coach. Unable to watch her pathetic acting job as she pretended to sob again, I tried to ignore her.

"Jesus, she's nuts," Mikko mumbled.

The doctor waited until the coach put Zena on the elevator as he quietly spoke to her. Once the doors closed, he cleared his throat and nodded to me and Mikko. I figured he knew who Jordan was and that the majority of the massively large men standing and sitting around the area were his teammates.

"I'm Dr. Tenski. I was the main surgeon who operated on Jordan. Did I hear you're a nurse here? ER, right?" he asked.

"Yes, Dr. Tenski. I'm down in the ER—night shift."

"Good, you'll understand a lot of this. I have to say, he's an extremely lucky young man. If I had to estimate, he lost over a liter of blood. We repaired his internal jugular—it was severed which accounted for the amount of blood loss. The blade just missed his internal carotid artery which was what saved him. Had it cut that, he wouldn't have made it off the ice alive. Then we repaired the tendons and muscles that were cut. All in all, he has a total of over two-hundred stitches inside and out. And I'll reiterate, he was an incredibly fortunate man." He sighed and shook his head. "Pretty amazing. Anyway, he'll go to ICU for the night, and if everything goes well, which I anticipate it will, he'll move down to the Med/Surg floor—sorry, medical/surgical." The last he directed at their coach and the players who surrounded us, eager for news. He explained what to expect when we saw him.

I wasn't sure if the severity of what had happened had really sunk in with them. As a medical professional, I understood why the doctor was saying Jordan had been lucky. Because he certainly was. Thinking that I could've lost him to a freak accident had my heart bottoming out into my stomach.

Time passed in a blur of disbelief until I was able to go see him.

When I stepped into the room, my knees buckled. I grabbed the doorframe, and Mikko caught my other side. Despite the surgeon's assurance that he was alive and would be okay, the fear still lingered. Seeing him in that bed, chest slowly rising and falling, was both surreal and a relief. The man was usually so full of life and energy that it was hard to believe it was him.

Mikko wouldn't let me move the chair. He scowled when I tried, then carried it closer to the bed for me. Trembling, I sat and gripped his hand.

"He might be in and out for a while but won't really be cognizant," the nurse explained as she documented on the computer. "He woke up in PACU, but he'll be in a chemically-induced coma for a few days. Then, he'll be on some pretty heavy-duty painkillers after they bring him out."

I nodded, but my attention had already returned to Jordan.

Besides being sedated, he had a hard neck brace to keep him from making any sudden movements and ripping his stitches. His face seemed a little swollen, but he was still the most handsome man I'd ever seen.

Mikko had given me Jordan's phone, so I'd been communicating with his mom and sister as they fought with international travel plans.

One by one, his teammates and coach had cycled in and out to check on him. Despite the fact that he was still alive, I think seeing him in that hospital bed worried them. His coach had talked to me briefly.

"A long time ago, something like this happened and that guy was back on the ice in ten days. While that may be possible, the general manager spoke to me, and we don't want him rushing his recovery. We'd rather have him at 100% for the long term than coming back too soon and losing him to complications." He stared at Jordan the entire time he spoke until he was finished and then his bold hazel eyes bored into mine.

"Okay?" I frowned in confusion.

"While Jordan has been a typical guy in many ways, he has a good head on his shoulders. I've watched his talent and skills grow over the years, from when I still played and he was an up-and-coming rookie until I became his coach. He is a pretty private person for the most part, and he's a helluva good goaltender—maybe one of the best. Not only because his family has played in the NHL for unprecedented generations, but because he has talent and drive." He ran a broad hand through his hair.

"What does this have to do with me?" I cautiously questioned.

"He already had one woman burn him, and unfortunately, now she's back in his life. If you have anything less than the best intentions toward him, don't let me find out," he warned.

Initially, shock hit me, then a simmering anger. My nostrils flared as I held my temper in check. "I'd like to tell you to fuck off, but I realize you have his best interests at heart, so I'm reining in my temper. Instead, I'll tell you this—if you think threatening me will chase me off, you can kiss my ass. I love Jordan, and while our relationship may have unconventional beginnings and timelines, that doesn't diminish the fact that he is my world."

Unsure if he'd told his coach I was pregnant, I kept that to myself for the moment.

For a moment, he studied me with a narrowed gaze. Then a smile spread across his face. "I'm glad to see you're a fighter and you're willing to protect him. He needs someone who looks out for him as much as he does for them. Take care of our boy. He's going to be okay."

With that, he gave me a nod with a half grin and left the room.

I heaved a sigh as I turned my attention to the man who had stolen my heart with his easy smile, his good heart, and the cutest little dog in the world. He dwarfed the hospital bed, and despite what he'd been through, he looked so peaceful. Normally, family wasn't supposed to stay in the ICU rooms, but because I worked at the hospital as a nurse, they had made an exception. As long as I kept the curtain drawn so no one else saw, that was.

They had him in a C-spine collar brace that was open at the front to allow for airflow and assessment. The bandage over his injury was stark white against his skin. The wound had been on the left side of his neck, just below his jawline. My fingertips feathered over his forehead and down his cheek. Carefully leaning forward, I placed a soft kiss to his slightly parted lips. Then I took his hand in mine and rested my head on the edge of the bed and closed my eyes.

Being by Jordan's side was where I belonged. Every time we were apart, the world was livable but seemed skewed and almost uncomfortable. When we were together, that internal restlessness I'd experienced for most of my life faded away. Like two pieces in a puzzle, we simply fit.

I sent up a word of thanks to whatever higher power had spared him for me and our child. With it, I added the promise that I would do everything in my power to make him as happy as he made me.

"You shouldn't be laying like that," I heard whispered and jerked upright. Heart slamming against my rib cage, I stared into the bright blue eyes of the man that owned me heart and soul.

"Oh my God, I was so worried," I blurted out. They ended up keeping him in the chemically-induced coma for a couple of days to minimize strain on the vessel that might occur with increased blood flow and to ensure he remained calm until the laceration could begin to mesh. Each night, I slept with my head resting on the bed next to him.

"Do you still love me now that I have another person's DNA floating through my body?" he continued in a hoarse whisper. The corner of his mouth kicked up in a lazy grin.

A shudder ran through me. "Don't remind me of how much blood you lost," I replied in a sleep-raspy voice. "I could live a lifetime without ever seeing something like that happen to you again."

"Has anyone told my family I'm okay?" For a second, he looked like he might cry, but I blinked and it was gone.

"Your general manager called them as soon as they took you to the hospital, and Mikko gave me your phone so I've been talking with them since you came out of surgery. Your mom and sister flew in on the earliest flight they could get seats on. They're staying at your house, and they'll be here"—I glanced at my watch—"shortly. She texted me early this morning to find out when they would be waking you up. Your dad flies in this afternoon."

Relief flickered through his gaze. "Okay. Thanks."

He squeezed my hand tightly, and we sat in a thankful silence. His voice cracked as he softly admitted, "I was so worried they would be watching and that I was going to die in front of them—and you."

"Same," I murmured before I kissed the back of his hand, my heart lodged somewhere in my throat.

"How are you? Is the baby okay? Like the stress of seeing that didn't...." He trailed off helplessly. The worry and pain in his gaze was nearly debilitating. At a time when he nearly lost his life, he was concerned about me and our baby. There was no way this man was real. Any moment, I expected to wake up from the crazy dream I found myself in.

"We're both fine. But you probably shouldn't be speaking too much," I insisted.

"The nurse was in here before you woke up. She said I was fine to talk but not to do anything to put unnecessary stress on my sutures for the next twenty-four to forty-eight hours. So, no gym, no hockey, and no sex. I'm not happy about any of that," he hoarsely grumbled.

A knock on the door had me glancing over to see who it was. Jordan's mom peeked in, and when she locked eyes on her son staring back at her, she covered her mouth, and tears welled.

"Mom," Jordan whispered, his tone full of regret and sorrow.

His sister burst past her and came into the room, breath heaving. "Sorry, I dropped mom off at the doors and parked the rental. I didn't want to miss you being awake."

"I'm going to let you three visit while I go down to the locker room and take a shower. Is there anything you need me to bring back?" I asked the two women I wished I'd met under different circumstances as I stood and stretched my aching muscles.

"No thank you, Blair," his mom kindly replied. His sister was already talking softly to Jordan, and I wasn't sure she had heard me at all. Feeling awkward about showing affection in front of Jordan's mom and sister, I cast a small smile at him, grabbed the backpack Tori had dropped off, and excused myself. He had glanced at me as I turned for the door and returned my smile, but that was it.

They hadn't said anything about my pregnancy, and I began to wonder if Jordan had told anyone. His coach hadn't said anything. His family hadn't. Maybe I was the one losing my mind. What if this was all bullshit and Zena had been telling the truth? What if they were engaged again and I was the side piece?

No.

No way.

If that was the case, that nutso wench would've thrown a shit fit to be here in my place. I was getting wrapped up in my own head, likely from the shitty sleep I'd gotten since the accident.

Thankful I had access to the ER locker room and the on-call room, I quickly showered. As the hot water ran down my aching back,

I worried about my finances and the hit my paycheck was going to take from the lost hours. I had some sick time, but that wouldn't include my differential pay. With a sigh, I figured I'd cross that bridge when I came to it. By the time I was done, I could barely keep my eyes open. I was exhausted—mentally and physically. While his family was with him, I decided to catch a quick nap before I went back to Jordan's room.

Except I didn't get to so much as lay my head on the pillow before Tori was barging in.

"Blair!" she whisper-yelled.

"I'm not sleeping yet. What's wrong? Is it Jordan?" Panic that something had happened had my heart thundering, and I was wide awake.

"Owen didn't want me to say anything yet, but I told him that was bullshit. You needed to be prepared." Eyes wild, she stared at me with her phone clutched to her chest.

"Prepared for what?" I asked, dread settling in my stomach.

"The only reason I'm showing you is because I don't want you to be blindsided by this. There were some, um, people at the front desk already trying to get information." She chewed on her bottom lip, and her brow furrowed. Then she glanced down at her phone before she held it out.

Initially, I shied away from it as if it would bite me. I was afraid of what it would show. Finally, I couldn't stand it, and with a tremble in my hand, I took it. My heart plummeted when I saw what she had pulled up.

Austin Amurs' Star Goaltender Caught in Love Triangle With Baby Mamas the title of the article read.

"Oh my God." I read what was obviously an online gossip article with growing horror. It had painted me as a money-hungry harlot who had tricked Jordan into getting me pregnant. It went on to say I was trying to break Jordan and Zena up and that I was extorting them both for money. They mentioned my relationship with a "doctor" and implied that he broke up with me because he found out I was using him to pay off *my* credit cards. They knew how much fucking debt I had for fuck's sake! Debt that I only had because of that piece of shit "doctor."

"Why would they write all of this? And how did they get my personal information?" I cried out, nausea roiling in my guts.

"Do you think it was Zena?" Tori asked.

"I don't know. Maybe?" I absently replied as I continued to scroll.

The pictures were almost worse. There were several of me looking horrible, obviously taken after a long shift and on my way to the doctor's office after being sick all morning. Then a shot of me getting out of my shitty car in front of my doctor's office, but the worst was the one of Jordan appearing to be consoling a sobbing Zena.

I tried to tell myself it had to have been an old photo, but upon closer examination, I could see her pregnant belly in the image. My heart shattered.

Unable to stand it anymore, I shoved Tori's phone at her and ran to the bathroom where I vomited until I thought my stomach was turning inside out. Good friend that she was, Tori rubbed soothing circles on my shoulder and held my hair back.

Wiping my mouth with toilet paper, I then flushed the toilet and sat on the floor to lean against the wall.

"Owen said Radar is looking into it all, and they are going to find a way to fix this." Tori looked like she was a cross between sick and furious.

With my stomach still dry heaving and tears leaking from my eyes, I wondered how anything could fix this.

TWENTY

Jordan

"CHAOS"—I PREVAIL

THOUGH MY RECOVERY WAS SURPRISINGLY WITHOUT complication in the two weeks since my discharge from the hospital, I was struggling. Not so much physically, but it was the emotional toll of everything that snuck up on me. The shitstorm that blew up after my accident had my agent and the team publicist doing damage control as best as they could. I'd lost one sponsor already because they said whether it was true or not, it didn't look good for their brand.

Add to that the reality of my own mortality, and I was sleeping like shit. My dreams nothing but nightmares, I woke up in a cold sweat most mornings.

"I really like Blair. Didn't you tell her we wanted to visit with her?"

my mom casually dropped as she set her fork to her empty plate and leaned on her elbows. "Why hasn't she been by?"

That was the million-dollar question. I understood that she had been hounded by the press for a few days after the bullshit gossip was posted, but I'd offered to let her stay with me. She had adamantly refused. Not that I could blame her, with Zena still at my fucking house.

That was another bone of contention with me. I was sick and tired of her being in my home. I'd recently hired a real estate agent to help her look for a place to rent or buy, but still no luck. It had been two months—she needed to go.

"She has been working a lot, and Zena being here… it complicates things," I muttered, not meeting my mom's gaze. Guilt hit me that I hadn't told my family about Blair's pregnancy before they heard about it through social media. It had been a nightmare. My dad had been shocked and my sister had been so pissed at me.

"Speaking of which—that's so not fair to Blair. You need to kick that evil woman out of your house," my sister complained with a groan. "I'm sorry that she's having your kid, but God, she's a bitch. She's also a damn snake in the grass. How can someone not find an apartment in the amount of time she's been staying with you?"

None of this was something I hadn't already told myself a million times.

We were sitting at my kitchen table having breakfast that my mom had made. My dad had come and gone with very little issue between my parents. They were thankfully amicable, so that was one less thing to stress. He'd given me the "you're tough" and "I remember when so-and-so had something similar happen when I was playing. He was back on the ice in three weeks" speech. I'm sure he didn't mean anything derogatory, because he'd truly been trying to give me a motivational pep talk, but it put a lot of pressure on me.

Then the shit had hit the fan with that bullshit article, and social media ran with it. Of course, Zena swore she had nothing to do with it. My sister wasn't convinced, and honestly, neither was I, but I had no proof.

Now, the constant tension between the three women in my home was reaching a boiling point. I had only seen Blair once in the past two weeks. That was when she told me she thought it would be a good idea if we cooled things until this blew over. Except I hadn't liked how she had looked and sounded so emotionless and detached.

She cited work. Which may be true—I knew she had to make up for the time she'd taken off while she was staying with me in the hospital, but I couldn't help but think there was more to it. Something told me she was pulling away, and that terrified me.

I missed her desperately, and I was worried about her. I'd offered to pay her for her time because it made me feel awful that she lost wages to be with me. The fact that she stayed by my side through that entire hospital admission was a testament to her dedication. It was touching, and I appreciated that she hadn't left me alone in what was a terrifying time for me.

"I honestly don't know," I muttered. The last thing I wanted to talk about was Zena. Because the truth was, every place we'd looked at, Zena had found fault with. This one was too close to ABC, or that one was too far away from XYZ. It was obvious she was stalling, but I didn't know why. She knew I was with Blair and that she and I would never be a couple.

"She doesn't think she's actually going to get you to change your mind, does she?" my sister asked as my mom watered Herman. I was worried that he might not have survived while I was in the hospital and the days after I got home where I was limited on what I could do and had forgotten about him. Mom assured me he could handle a while without water and told me she took care of him as soon as they got to my house.

"I was very clear. I don't see how she could."

My sister snorted. "Uh, maybe because she's batshit crazy? And if you let her take Beaker again, I will disown you."

Thankfully, the woman in question wasn't here as she had a breakfast date with a couple of her girlfriends down in south Austin. I ran a frustrated hand through my hair before I buried my face in my hands.

Obviously, hearing his name woke Beaker from his comfy sleep because a bark from the tiny canine in question had me scooting my chair back to pick up my furry little man. I nuzzled my nose into his soft wavy fur. As if he knew I was losing my mind, he licked my cheek and jawline. I was sure he missed Blair too.

"You shouldn't be bending over like that," my mother scolded, though she paused by my chair to love on Beaker. She took a seat at the table again to finish her coffee.

Despite all the bullshit swirling, I softly laughed. "Mom, the doctor and my physical therapist said I could move freely now, I only have to listen to my body and not overdo anything. If my next checkup goes well, I can start light workouts and have some time on the ice during practices." Missing out on game days had nearly made me almost as sick to my stomach as the thought of losing Blair after I'd just gotten her back.

Then there was the concern over being replaced since Landon was kicking ass and missing being there for my team was real.

Crazy truth though?

I'd give it all up if I could make the gossip mess go away forever and have Blair here in my arms. She had burned herself on my soul, and I didn't know what to do without her.

"Are you sure you don't need us to stay longer?" Mom asked. Her worried gaze searched mine for possible untruths.

"No, you have both been away from your jobs too long."

"It's only been a couple of weeks. And we've been able to do some things remotely," my sister argued. "My boss said I could stay if you needed me. He totally understood."

My eyes narrowed as I studied her guileless expression that seemed phony as shit. Her willingness to stay better not have had anything to do with Jericho. She'd "gone shopping" on several occasions since they'd arrived. She had indeed returned with a few shopping bags, but one time she looked just-been-fucked, and I almost vomited. Not how I wanted to see my little sister. Didn't matter how old she was. Nor did I want her with a player like Jericho. I might have been a bit of a playboy, but I was at least more discreet than he and Dmitry were.

And so help me, if I found out they'd been with her together, I'd kill them both. They'd been known to do shit like that occasionally. To each their own, but not with my fucking sister.

"Look, I know you're a grown man and I probably should keep my mouth shut, but I'm not going to. I'm your mother, and I'm always going to be blunt and honest with you. I never liked Zena. While I'm excited to have not only one but two grandbabies, I'm sorry that she will be one of their mothers—tying you to her for the rest of your life."

Lordy, that made two of us. Knowing I would have to interact with her for the next eighteen years minimum grated on my fucking nerves.

"Blair seems like a sweet and down-to-earth girl. Maybe you didn't plan on the pregnancy with either of them, but if you love Blair like I think you do, you need to get off your ass and go after her. Don't just sit around waiting for things to work themselves out. You've never been that person, and I can't believe you're allowing yourself to be like that this time. Where's the son I raised that fought tooth and nail to be known for his own accomplishments and not the legacy of your father's family? I think you need to find him," my mom insisted. She leaned back in her chair, crossing her arms. Her cocked brow dared me to argue.

As I let what she'd said sink in, I absently tapped on the tabletop, staring at it like it would reveal all the answers of life to me. Finally, I looked up to catch both my mom and sister watching me.

"You're right."

My mother's smile was megawatt, and my sister clapped her hands in excitement. I shook my head at them, but the corner of my mouth lifted in a crooked grin.

"You sure you're okay to drive us to the airport?"

"Of course," I assured her.

"All right, then I need to finish packing the things I used this morning," Mom announced as she pushed back from the table.

"Me too," my sister added, though she seemed less than enthused about the prospect of going home. I'd like to think it was because she didn't want to leave me, but I kind of doubted it.

After they both left the kitchen, I made a decision.

"Come on. We have things to do," I said to Beaker.

He barked enthusiastically.

With Beaker as my audience, I changed out of my sleeping pants and T-shirt. I pulled on a black Amurs hoodie, some track pants, and slipped on a pair of running shoes. Then I got to work.

It didn't take me long to accomplish what I had planned. Before either my mom or my sister was out of their rooms, I'd made a phone call and had my stuff stashed in the back of my truck. As I was scooping up my dog, they came out rolling their suitcases behind them.

"Ready?" I asked.

"Not really, but yes." My mom sighed.

"Beaker wants to come with us," I told them as we went out to the garage and loaded up their things in the backseat. My sister insisted on holding Beaker on the way.

"He wants to spend a little more time with auntie Everly," she cooed as she snuggled him. I rolled my eyes.

As we backed out of the garage, my mom asked, "Um, why is Herman in your cup holder?"

"I figured he would like a little sun. He also likes to go for rides sometimes," I replied with a shrug.

When I cast a sidelong glance at my mom, I saw her blinking at me like she was afraid I was losing it.

"What?" I challenged.

She shook her head.

The drive to the airport was bittersweet. Though I hated the reason they'd come down, I'd loved having them. I did miss my family. I hated to see them leave, but I knew I'd be okay without them, and they had lives to get back to.

My mom was already crying by the time I parked in the unloading zone.

"Mom, don't," I begged after we had their stuff on the curb. I wrapped her in a big hug.

"I can't help it. I nearly lost you, and leaving you after that is hard. Please take care of yourself. And call Blair. Talk to her." Her voice was slightly muffled as she smashed her face into my shoulder.

"Are you trying to smell my armpit?" I teased, trying to lighten the mood.

Mission accomplished, she laughed and pushed back to look up at me. She reached up to frame my face with her hands. "I will be down when the babies are born. I love you, Jordan."

"I love you too, Mom."

"I love you too," my sister added as she threw herself against us, making it a group hug with Beaker in the mix.

When she stepped back, she smiled and grabbed her suitcase. "See you around, big brother."

She started for the terminal, and my mom reluctantly let me go and wheeled her suitcase after Everly.

"Hey, Sis!"

"Yeah?" she asked, peeking over her shoulder.

"Aren't you forgetting something?" I crossed my arms and looked down my nose at her.

"Hmm, nope. Got everything," she told me as she took another few steps.

Loudly, I cleared my throat. "My dog?"

"Oh! I totally forgot about that!" She blinked innocently and wide-eyed surprise lit her face.

"Right," I drawled. She snickered and rushed back to hand Beaker over.

"Nice try," I deadpanned.

"It was worth a shot," she admitted as she unapologetically grinned.

Laughing, I watched them disappear into the airport. Then I held Beaker up to my face. "You ready?"

He barked in reply. We got back in the truck, and I drove away from the congestion of the drop-off area. Determined, I made a call I should've done a long time ago. It went better than I thought. When I hung up, I hoped I was doing the right thing. As the miles passed, I second-guessed myself a hundred times.

With determined resolve, I parked at my destination. Then I got out, opened the tailgate, and set Beaker down. "Sit."

He did as he was told, but his little butt wiggled in suppressed excitement. Keeping an eye on him, I slung my duffle over my shoulder, grabbed his kennel, and tucked him inside. He seemed to glare at me. "It's only for a few minutes."

The little shit actually huffed and pouted. I jogged to the open truck door, grabbed Herman, then juggled everything while I shut the tailgate and locked the doors.

"Here goes everything," I whispered. The steps seemed to go on and on, though I knew there were the same number as always. Using Herman's pot, I knocked on the door. When there was no answer, my shoulders slouched. "Well, shit. This backfired."

"What backfired?" I heard a voice from behind me and spun. The woman who took my breath away stood there with her keys in hand and a bunch of mail in the other.

Her hair was up in that messy bun that I loved on her. Little wisps had escaped and blew across her beautiful face. Staring at her, I devoured every detail, cataloguing the tiny differences the past two weeks had brought. It might've been my imagination, but her belly seemed to be a little rounded now, and I wanted to drop to my knees and kiss it.

"I thought you weren't home," I admitted in a rush. "I didn't think this through very well."

"Didn't think what through?"

"Can we go inside?" I practically begged. For a moment, we had a silent stand off, and my heart plummeted to my toes. "Please?"

Her gaze dropped, and I braced myself for the rejection I felt coming.

Then she sighed and squeezed past me to unlock the door. Sure she was going to slam it in my face, I was surprised when she motioned me in.

"What's with all the stuff?" She motioned to the kennel and duffle I set down. Beaker was already pawing madly at the kennel door. The second I opened it, he darted out and practically jumped into her arms when she crouched down.

Her laughter at his exuberance made my chest oddly flutter.

"This is Herman," I awkwardly announced as I held up the little succulent. Her soft gaze lifted, and she cocked her head in curiosity.

"Um… thanks?"

"No, I brought him with, um, never mind." I took a huge fortifying breath and huffed it out in a rapid gust before placing Herman on her counter. "Can I stay here?"

Slowly, she stood to her full height. There was a cute little wrinkle between her eyes when she drew her brows together. "Stay here?"

"I can't stand this. I miss you. I'm so, so sorry that someone put that shit out about us—you, me, and Zena," I clarified. "If you can forgive the fact that it's my fault because of who I am, I… well, I need you."

I tucked my hands in my pockets, and my lungs seized as I waited for her reply. When she didn't say anything, I tried again. "I meant what I said before. I love you. There is nothing in this world I want more than to be a family with you, Beaker, Herman, and Junior. We may not have planned any of this. We may have said we were happy with the opposite, but we were wrong. There are times in our lives when fate gives us what we need, not what we expect or think we want. If you choose us, I can't guarantee that the media or fans won't say stupid shit again, but what I can promise is that I will love you, and I'll tell all of them to fuck off."

Her lips pursed, then the corners of her mouth twitched and a smile broke free. "That was probably the weirdest but most romantic thing anyone has ever said to me. But why do you want to stay at my place? I can't have dogs."

"Not true. You can, but they have to be under twenty pounds— which I'm pretty sure that little bit of fluff is—and they required a deposit. I called. I'll pay the deposit and cover anything he might damage. But we both know he's a saint so he won't." I tipped my head hopefully.

"You are crazy. You have a big, beautiful house and you want to stay here?" She swept one arm out to indicate her nice but small apartment.

I pulled my hands from my pockets and held my arms out in surrender. "It's where you are," I simply offered. "Unless you want to move into my place. We kind of have a roommate who's a bit of an entitled bitch."

"About that… why don't you kick her out? It's your house."

My arms dropped. "That's what my family said. Honestly, it was because of the baby. The thought of her being on the street or bouncing from friend to friend seemed like a shitty thing to do to the mother of my child no matter what kind of person she is. But I actually called her and told her she had until the end of the month to find something. If she didn't have anything figured out, I would pay for a hotel for up to two months. After that, she's on her own. She's a big girl."

"And she agreed?" she cautiously questioned.

"Yeah, she did," I breathed, still surprised and relieved that Zena had been so amicable.

"Wow."

"That's what I thought."

"So, you wanna be roomies, huh?" Chin lifted, she placed her free hand on a hip, cocked a brow, and waited. Her mouth twitched, and I could see she was trying not to smile.

"No. I want to be your boyfriend who lives with you. And hopefully, one day, something more than that." My heart slammed against my ribs as I put myself out there.

"More?" Her voice broke as her lower lip quivered.

Slowly, I closed in on her. When we stood toe to toe, I cradled her face in my hands and tipped her head back to look her dead in the eyes. "You are mine. There is no one else for me, and there never will be." I dropped one hand to rest over her lower abdomen. I might have imagined it, but I was pretty sure it seemed firmer than it used to be. As my hand circled lightly, I glanced down. I was right, in the past couple of weeks, she had developed a barely there bump. My stomach flipped, and my chest tightened.

It had me dropping to my knees to hold her hips and rest my forehead against the hard curve. Just like I imagined earlier. Then I kissed it before I glanced up at her hopeful gaze. "Yes. More. What do you say? Do you want to be a family with me, Beaker, Herman, and Jordan Junior?"

A slow smile kicked up the corners of her mouth. Then she caught her lip in her teeth and nodded.

"Speaking of, I have something to show you," she whispered excitedly. She reached over to the counter for her purse that sat next to Herman. Then she rummaged through it for a moment. Whatever she took out, she whipped behind her back. "Close your eyes."

A chuckle escaped, and I did as she said. "Okay."

"Open them," she instructed.

The slightly shiny black-and-white image was reminiscent of the copy of one that Zena had handed me. But this one… this one brought a huge smile to my face as I reached for it. Ignoring the slight tremble of my hand, I took it from her. My heart was so full, I was sure it would burst. I traced the little white blob that already had definitive features, up and down a little arm, over the tiny belly, and around the curled-up legs. I settled my fingertip over the little black spot I knew was its heart.

Swallowing the lump in my throat, I glanced up at her. "This is our little bean?"

"Yeah," she whispered, her voice one of love.

"I love him," I insisted with a grin. "Or her," I amended.

"Me too. And Jordan? I wasn't leaving you. I just needed some time to process what it meant to be with someone of your status. That mess shocked me. Shook me to the core. The invasion of my privacy." She sucked in a breath.

"I'm so sorry about that," I interrupted, but she placed a finger over my lips.

"It was a lot. It did hurt, though I believed it wasn't true, but I came to the conclusion that it doesn't matter. As long as we know the truth, that's what matters. So yes, you can stay here until the wicked witch of the north is gone." She raked her fingers through my hair, and I practically purred as her nails scraped my scalp as she did.

Nothing had felt more like home in my life.

TWENTY-ONE

Blair

"HEARTBEAT"—THE FRAY

HAVING A SIX-AND-A-HALF-FOOT GIANT IN MY RATHER SMALL apartment was an adjustment. I loved it, but he made the space seem much more crowded than it used to. He had been cleared by his doctor and physical therapist to resume light workouts and ice time. There were restrictions, but he seemed to be bouncing back well.

A couple of nights I'd had to wake him from what were obvious nightmares that had him soaked in sweat and tangled in the sheets. I was a little worried and encouraged him to see a counselor like his coach and doctor suggested.

"There's no shame in talking to someone. You had a significant life event." My chin rested on my hands where his heartbeat pulsed under them. His chest rose and fell before he turned his head to look at me.

"It's embarrassing. It's not like I was at war or something. I got injured playing hockey."

I sat up next to him, ignoring how his gaze dropped to where my nipples peeked through my hair that fanned over my chest. "You didn't simply get injured, Jordan. You had your throat sliced open and damn near bled to death on the ice. You were less than inches from death. That would mess with the strongest of men or women. Though I am here for you, I think it would help if you got some input from someone more qualified than I am."

He lifted his arm, and his large hand cupped one of my breasts as his thumb skimmed over the now hard peak. "I like you being here for me," he softly murmured.

"And I love being here for you."

"Good," he said with a wicked grin before he gripped my hips and lifted me to straddle him. "How wet are you?" he whispered. His length was hardening, and I moaned as he moved my body so I slid along his smooth shaft. His echoed groan accompanied his fingers digging into my flesh when he found out the answer to his question.

"Jordan!" I gasped as he reached between us to circle my clit with his thumb. Our conversation was a distant and fuzzy memory by then.

"What do you want?" he taunted while his thumb worked its magic.

"Oh God," I rasped as he increased the pressure and lifted to press up into me. I could feel his hot, thick length throb as it slid along my slit. Needy, I attempted to raise up to get him inside, but he stopped me.

"Uh-uh," he chastised. "Not until you tell me what you want."

"You," I pleaded as I stared down into his intense ice-blue eyes.

"Use your dirty words. Now, tell me what you want," he repeated.

"I want your cock in me. I want you to fill my pussy with that thick cock. I want you to fuck me. Hard." I boldly held his sultry gaze.

"Fuck yes." He sighed as he stroked the cock in question and then we fumbled a bit to get lined up before I slowly sank down little by little. We both panted as I felt him pulse once, and I squeezed him with my inner muscles. "Easy," he warned.

As I held myself still, I closed my eyes, bit my lip, and splayed my hands on his inked chest. God, I wanted to move. I needed to feel the perfect friction of his silky skin against mine as he stroked in and out. A thought occurring to me, I opened my lids and licked my lips. "Will you talk to someone?"

"What?" he frowned in confusion.

"A counselor," I clarified and tightened around him again.

He hissed through his clenched teeth.

"Yes or no?"

"Blair," he ground out.

Though I didn't want to, I started to get off him. His eyes went wide, and he desperately grabbed my waist.

"Yes or no?" I repeated.

"Are you really blackmailing me with your goddamn pussy?" he incredulously asked.

I cocked a brow.

"Ugh! Fine," he conceded before he held me and in one swift motion had me flipped to my back. Then he rested over me and drove his cock in exactly the way I liked it—hard. "I'll go." He thrusted again, his groin grinding over me, eliciting a gasp. "Because you want me to."

"You can't go just for me," I argued, out of breath from my desperation for him to keep moving.

"I'm not," he admitted as he locked his solemn gaze with mine and paused. For a split second, I searched his blue eyes for his sincerity. When all I saw was raw honesty, I gave an encouraging shift of my hips. It caused him to slide further inside me, and I gasped. I loved the perfect way he filled me. There had never been anyone that reached all the magic places like he did. I let my legs fall open to allow him more room and hooked my ankles around his thighs.

"Oh fuck," he hissed when I tilted my pelvis and he went deeper.

Mouth slightly parted, he held my gaze as he worked my body over like a goddamn pro. He did this thing with his hips that made me see stars with each stroke.

Sweat broke out over his forehead and upper lip as he drove relentlessly. Our skin slapping, soft grunts, moans, and the creak of my bed were the only sounds that broke the silence of the early morning.

I reached up to brace myself on the headboard because he was pushing me up with each piston of his cock. No matter how good he felt, I didn't fancy my head being bashed into the wood.

Shifting his weight to one arm, he used the other to lift my leg, then wrapped it around his waist.

The increased pressure and depth had my back arching and my eyes rolling back. I groaned and met each thrust with one of my own. The moment was animalistic, and our rhythm grew slightly uncoordinated as we were consumed by primal need. There was no need for words—our bodies followed instinct bred into us since the beginning of time.

When he let go of my leg, it slipped a bit, but I didn't care because he played with my nipples one after the other. They were so sensitive that when he leaned down and fought the shaking from our movement to suck on one, I screamed, and my pussy clenched tight before the explosion hit me.

"Fuuuuck!" he cried out as he picked up the pace and madly fucked me through each erotic contraction that squeezed his shaft. My nails scored his slick skin as I rode the waves of ecstasy. One last thrust and he froze above me. His face twisted in the bliss that sucked him in as he roared. Each pulse of his cock told me he was filling me—marking me as his. My lids slammed shut as I savored the sensation.

He dropped his head next to mine as he fought to catch his breath.

Equally as breathless, I relaxed against the linens with my eyes still closed. I drowned in the heady rush of euphoria consuming me. With a huff, he rolled over and dropped to the bed. He tucked me into his body with his big arm. Sometimes I wondered if he realized he did it.

I lost track of time as we found our way back to earth. Slowly, he stirred, but when he lifted his head to look over at me, his hair was in disarray, soaked and stuck to his forehead with parts of it sticking up from where I'd tugged on it. He was handsome in a way most men wished they were.

"Holy shit," he muttered in awe.

"Ditto," I replied, snuggling into him again. "By the way, if it's a boy, we are not naming him Jordan. He's not going to be a junior."

He huffed. "Jordan is a nice name. I like my name."

"For you, maybe. But our son would need his own name to forge his own identity."

"Our son… I like the sound of that. Our daughter doesn't sound half bad either but then I'll need more guns."

I lifted my head from his chest where I'd been listening to the comforting thud of his heart. His scar was right in front of me as I looked up, and I gently traced a finger along its raised surface. He was lucky in many ways. The surgeon was good, and the scar was pretty thin, all things considered.

"Don't," he whispered as he gripped my hand, stopping my movements.

"I love it. Do you know why?"

He grunted.

"Because it's proof that you lived. Through what could've killed you, you lived. And it's a part of you. I love everything about you, and I always will," I promised.

He raised my hand to his lips and pressed a kiss to it.

"I love you too. And I love the little bean even though I haven't met him or her yet. I even love Zena's baby, though I can't stand its mother." He chuckled.

Part of me was sad that she would have her baby first. Jordan would share first time fatherhood with that conniving witch. She was a hateful person, yet I hoped for the baby's sake that she turned herself around after it was born. Because God help the poor child, if she didn't.

"I'm so glad you were able to come to days finally!" Tori squealed as we all sat at the nurse's station. Things were fairly slow so far that morning. Maddox winced.

"Not so much with the screeching," he grumbled with a wince.

"Did someone party too much?" Tori asked with a wicked grin as she rested her chin on the heel of her hand.

Since Jordan had pretty much moved in, he insisted on paying my rent for the month. We'd argued over it for days, but I finally relented when he said it was for selfish reasons because he wanted me to work day shift so we could see each other more. I agreed on half. He wasn't overly happy, but it was my final offer.

"No, I didn't. The baby kept me up all night." He sighed and flopped back in his chair, absently staring at the ceiling.

"But he's so cute," I cooed. He and Gwen's little boy was only two weeks old, but he was a darling.

"Yeah, well he's not so cute when he's colicky and screaming all night. The only thing that quiets him is the vacuum. I can't sleep with the vacuum going the whole time," he muttered.

"But think about how clean your house is now," Tori teased with a giggle.

Without lifting his head, he flipped her off.

My phone vibrated in my pocket. My heart immediately raced, hoping it was Jordan. Since the ER was dead, I pulled it out to see. A smile nearly split my face.

"Must be lover boy," Tori piped in. I rolled my eyes and swiped to answer.

"Hello, handsome," I purred.

A chuckle carried over the line. "Hello, sexy. Work must not be too bad if you were able to answer."

"Nope, but whatever you do, don't say the Q word!" I warned. Tori and Maddox agreed.

"I wouldn't dare," Jordan promised with a laugh.

"You getting ready to leave?" I asked, a little sad because I'd miss him. It was the first away game he would be attending since his accident. He was going as the EBUG or emergency backup goaltender, which he hated, but he was happy to be there at least.

"Yeah, but I spilled coffee on my suit, so I need to run by the house to grab a clean one," he explained. I immediately frowned and grunted.

"Is she going to be there?" I tried not to sneer when I asked. I couldn't stand the idea of her possibly cornering him at the house and weaseling more time out of him or something. Maddox and Tori were behind me trying to figure out what they were going to order for lunch today. I glanced over my shoulder, but they didn't seem to be paying attention to me.

"I have no idea. Probably, but I doubt she'll be awake. She rarely rolls her ass out of bed before eleven. I'll likely be in and out without her having a clue." He snorted in disgust.

"Well, watch yourself, just in case. I don't trust that rabid jackal." I wouldn't put it past her to sneak in while he was changing then post on her social media that they had a quickie before he left. She was an honest-to-God psycho.

"I'll be extra stealth," he joked.

"You do that," I concurred. A call light went off, and Tori got up to check on her patient. At the moment they were the only one we had, and they were waiting to be transferred to the Med/Surg floor.

"I'm gonna miss you. I've been spoiled being around so much," he said, his tone going serious.

"I know. I'm gonna miss you too. But at least I'll have Beaker," I added with a smile. That was another thing that had pissed Zena off. She hadn't been home when Jordan had left and snuck him to my house. When she found out, she demanded he return him. Which was stupid because she always had him in his kennel when she had him. The only time she did anything with him was when she went out and could show him off because he was cute. She loved the attention.

"Give him kisses from me. He's going to miss me," he insisted, and I rolled my eyes.

"You just left him, and you'll only be gone two days. He'll survive." My coworkers snickered, and I knew they were done discussing lunch and were listening to my conversation.

He gasped, and I couldn't help but giggle at his sound of mock outrage.

"Okay, well, I'm pulling into the neighborhood. I'll try to give you another call before I get on the plane. If not, I'll text. And tell whoever was listening that they shouldn't laugh—Beaker always misses his daddy."

I snorted.

"It's Maddox and Tori, and I'll let them know. Talk to you soon. Love you," I told him with my face heating because I knew my friends were going to give me shit.

"I love you too, baby."

Maddox and Tori were making smoochy noises. I shook my head at their antics.

The call ended, and I sighed.

"You know Radar has been looking into Zena," Maddox reminded me. I tucked my phone back in my pocket and lifted my gaze to his.

"Yeah, but I figured he hadn't found anything significant since we haven't heard a word," I muttered. Simply talking about the woman ruined my mood.

"I'm sorry, my brain is fried due to sleep deprivation, or I would've told you right away. Radar wanted me to have you or Jordan call him tonight. He said he was checking into a couple of things further and he should have something by then," Maddox informed me as he sat up.

"Really?" I immediately perked up. Except it was going to drive me crazy waiting.

"Yeah," he confirmed. "Hopefully it's something worthwhile, but who knows?"

"I just want her gone," I complained.

"I know people that can make that happen," he quietly offered.

My eyes bugged. "Maddox!"

"What? I do." He shrugged.

"Well, regardless of what a piece of work she is, she is still carrying Jordan's child. Much as I hate it, I don't wish her harm. At least not too much," I teased.

He laughed, and we got back to work.

TWENTY-TWO

Jordan

"SURVIVOR"—POP EVIL

O F ALL THE SHITTY LUCK. IT WOULD HAVE TO BE TODAY. THE first away game I was slotted to play since my injury and Beaker had gotten excited and jumped in my lap while we sat on the couch. He'd immediately put his paws on my chest right as I was taking a drink of my morning coffee. Now I had to drive over to my place and back to the stadium. Thankfully, I'd gotten up when Blair did, so I was ready early.

"I'm at my house, but I was just calling to tell you I needed to swing by to change. I'll be there ASAP," I said to Mikko through my speaker.

"See you soon," he replied and ended the call. He'd rung right as I hung up with Blair to see if I needed a ride.

I whipped into my driveway and parked there. It was quicker to run up to the door than to wait on the garage. In no time at all, I had punched in the code to open the lock and paused the security system.

Trying not to wake the beast, I was as quiet as I could be. But when I heard glass break from her side of the house, I hurried that direction.

Her door was open, and the en suite door was cracked. On the bed was a weird pillow, and a string of curses came from the bathroom. Afraid of catching her naked, I tapped lightly on the door. Then another loud noise echoed through the room, and I figured fuck it. If she was injured, that could mean the baby was hurt too.

"Zena?" I questioned, confused at what was in front of me. She had a towel around her, and she was swaying a bit as she leaned over the counter. It was what was on the counter that had me seeing red. There was a baggie of pills, a pill crusher, and two lines on the granite—one of which was half gone and scattered a bit. If there was any question as to what she was doing, the white residue under her nose cleared that up.

"It's not what you think!" she immediately cried out as she held an imploring hand out to me.

"Really? Well, please tell me what it is, because it sure as hell looks like you're snorting some kind of fucking pills!" I shouted, on the verge of losing my ever-loving mind.

"It's just Adderall. I take it to stay awake during demanding photoshoots and to keep my weight down. It's prescribed to me for my ADHD," she rationalized.

"You don't have fucking ADHD, remember? When we were together, you tried to get several doctors to give you that diagnosis when one of your friends said the meds helped them stay alert. All of them told you that didn't have it," I sneered. "And you're fucking pregnant! You shouldn't be taking that at all, let alone snorting the shit! Is this why you keep conveniently scheduling your doctor's appointments for days I can't go?"

"The last one was on your off day," she argued.

"I was in the hospital after I had my fucking throat cut!" I roared, and I felt bad for a second when she flinched. Then I remembered why I was pissed in the first place. Gritting my teeth as I clenched my jaw, I tried to rein in my temper. "Get dressed. We're going to the doctor. Now."

"W-what?" she stuttered, eyes wide.

"Get. Dressed."

Trembling with anger, I spun on my heel and exited the bathroom. As I passed the bed, that weird pillow caught my eye again. I paused. It wasn't a pillow. Not even close. Things began to click in my head, and I shook it slowly in denial.

A sickening feeling settled in my guts. Chills skated over my skin, and I had to force my lungs to breathe. Roughly, I ran a hand over my face and fought to remain calm.

"Jordan," she whispered behind me. I picked up the piece of silicone and spun to face her. It was fairly heavy and jiggled oddly in my hand like a giant fake boob. The horror on her face was quickly replaced by tears that were as fake as the pregnancy belly in my hand.

The mix of horror and rage within me had me trembling so violently I thought I might explode. I knew she was nuts, but I didn't believe she could be that vile. To fuck with a man's emotions and fake a *baby*? I actually had no words to describe her—vile wasn't accurate enough.

"Save it," I gritted out. "Pack your shit. All of it. Get the fuck out. You have thirty minutes or I'm calling the cops. Beaker stays with me. I paid for him, and you don't really want him anyway."

She amped up the sobs as she rushed at me and gripped my arm. "Jordan, please. It was the only way I thought I could get you to give us another chance. Then that damn dog-sitting nurse came along and wove her web around you so you couldn't see what was right in front of you!"

Coldly, I dropped my gaze to where her manicured fingers clutched my suit jacket. Another thing I'd paid for.

"Get your hand off me," I snarled in a low and vicious tone. Anger surged through me so violently I wanted to break shit.

She released me as if she'd been burned.

"Clock's ticking," I told her and walked out.

Practically trembling with rage, I paced my living room. Yanking at my hair, I tried to make sense of what she had done. Photoshopping pictures was low. Faking a pregnancy was disgusting. There were women all over who would give their right eye to be pregnant, and she'd made a mockery of it. She turned my stomach.

Timidly, she came out of her room wheeling two suitcases after her. I stopped and glared at her.

"Is that everything?" I motioned to her bags.

"I have another one in my room," she softly replied. My sympathy for her was nonexistent. I turned my back on her and retrieved the last one. Then I opened the side door to the garage. I whipped open her Mercedes and tossed the suitcase in the trunk. I'd been paying the payment on it too. Then I marched to the door, grabbed the other two from her, and puzzled them into the vehicle. Before I closed the passenger side, I snatched the remote from her visor. The entire time, she stared at me forlornly with tears running down her cheeks.

"Jordan, you have to know, I was only desperate," she tried again.

I held my hand up in front of her. She snapped her mouth shut.

"You are truly a despicable human being. You need help. Serious help," I told her.

"You bastard! I just needed you to love me! You're a selfish asshole!" she screamed in my face as she began to hit and claw at me. Not once did I raise a hand to her other than to protect my face.

"Zena!" I barked, but she was like a wild woman. She began to hit me with her purse.

"Goddamnit Zena, don't make me call the police!"

That got her attention, and she stepped back, heaving and staring at me with crazed eyes. Wary, I watched her in case she came at me again.

Like something from a movie, she squared her shoulders, smoothed back her hair, and primly put her purse over her arm. Then she sauntered to the driver's side with her nose in the air as if she hadn't done a thing wrong.

I was literally speechless. It was like watching a real-life Dr. Jekyll and Mr. Hyde. I was left questioning what I had just seen. It also showed me that I needed to contact my attorney for a restraining order sooner rather than later.

Any minute, I expected to wake up from whatever bizarre nightmare I was stuck in, because I was looking at pure insanity standing in my driveway.

One hand fisted, I hit the opener, and the garage slowly filled with sunlight.

As she started to get in, I called out "wait."

The insane hope on her face made me want to laugh.

"How did you plan to explain it when you never gave birth?" If she told me she was going to substitute a baby and hope for the best, I might take my old hockey sticks to her car.

Obviously realizing she was finished, she curled her lip at me.

"I was going to take a trip to see my family and tell you I lost it," she heartlessly tossed out.

When I thought her evil treachery couldn't get any worse, she spewed that out. I was sick to my stomach.

"Go. Oh, and if you post a motherfucking thing about me any- where, I'm pressing slander and assault charges against you. My at- torney will be emailing you a statement you can post. Otherwise, you keep my name out of your mouth and off your fucking social media." Her nostrils flared, and she pursed her lips before she got in and slammed the door.

It was the last thing I said to her. The second she backed out, I closed the garage door. First, I called my attorney and asked him to file that restraining order and told him what she'd done. He ad- vised me to call the police. I declined. The last thing I wanted was for this to get out. I simply wanted to quietly erase her from my life. Then I notified the gate and told them she was forbidden to enter the neighborhood.

Another smart move I made was to take pictures of the scratches and red marks from her attack and emailed them to my attorney.

Then I changed out of my ruined suit and rested my hands on the bathroom counter. My head hung as I breathed slow and deep to calm myself. Once I let go of the anger at her audacity, I actually laughed. Maybe a little maniacally, but I wasn't splitting hairs.

"I'm not having a kid with her," I cheered to the me in the mirror. "Thank fucking Christ."

My next thought was to call Blair, but I needed to get my ass in gear. I dialed as I strode outside and to my truck. It was ringing as I started it, and the Bluetooth took over.

"Getting on the plane already?" She answered her phone in a tone laden with confusion.

"No, I'm on my way to the stadium now. But you aren't going to believe what just happened," I announced. A rapid inhale carried over the speakers.

"What did she do?" she asked, trepidation heavy in her voice.

Funny that she immediately knew it had something to do with Zena. I quickly explained everything. When I finished, I had to check to see if she was still on the line because there was only silence.

"Blair?"

"I'm here. Oh my god. I am quite literally speechless. That's psycho-level stuff there. You realize that, right?"

"Oh, I do. As far as I'm concerned, I dodged a bullet the size of a tank round."

"I'm just… wow."

"Same."

Relief left me feeling lighter than I had in months. Ironic that the thought of an unplanned pregnancy with Blair made me want to shout it to the rooftops. Such a drastic difference from the lead weight I'd carried at the prospect of having my life forever connected with Zena.

I did have to admit that I was a little sad as I'd been actually looking forward to being a dad to the child. It was for the best though, and I would be able to be the best fucking dad in the world to my baby with Blair. I loved it already, and I was head over heels for its mother.

I grinned the rest of the way to the stadium.

Though I hadn't been able to play, simply being in my uniform and pads on the bench was akin to heaven. I had to admit Landon was good. For a young kid just out of college, he had a lot of raw talent. He reminded me of myself at that age. Not that I was ancient, but I was twenty-six. Almost twenty-seven—still young for an NHL goalie. And I was excited to see what the future held for our team.

"I cannot believe that crazy nut job was milking six different guys," Alex grumbled in disbelief. When I'd called Blair the minute my ass hit the bus seat after we deplaned, she told me the news. I guess Alex's brother's club had done some digging on Zena.

Turned out she had six of us on the hook for false pregnancies. She was mooching off me while she let them believe she was here doing makeup commercials, and they sent her money. Despite me trying to be nice, she was arrested this morning on fraud charges. I guess one of the guys she'd been stringing along was either disgustingly rich or well-connected, and he was a pissed-off motherfucker. Blair didn't know which. I didn't care.

"That's insane. See, that's why I don't mess with chicks like that," Mikko noted with a firm nod. "Single and ready to mingle."

The guys around us groaned and laughed at his corny saying. It was funnier because of his accent.

"Regardless, I'm glad she's out of your hair," Kristoffer added from the seat in front of me.

"Amen," I concurred. Truth's club had also found out that Blair's ex, the weasel I chased out of her apartment, was the guy who had contacted the gossip sites. He had broken into her apartment looking for shit in her home and on her computer. He got paid a pretty penny for his bullshit information. I wanted to call my attorney, but Alex told me not to worry—the club handled it. I was afraid to know what that meant but decided maybe I was better off leaving it alone.

For the rest of the ride, some of us chatted, and others listened to music or played on their phones. Cameron was FaceTiming with Bleu in the window seat across from me where he sat with Alex.

I stared out the window for the forty-minute drive back to the arena. All the dirty things I wanted to do to Blair ran rampant through my brain.

"Sure you don't want to join us?" Mikko asked.

The single guys were all gathering at Mikko's place to watch Nashville play. They were running neck in neck with us for the playoffs this year, but I was anxious to get home. I'd told Blair to stay at my house since Zena was gone. She said Beaker was happy to be back in his own home where he had a yard to run.

I hopped in my truck and pulled out of my spot with a wave. The drive seemed to take forever. Each mile closer had my heart racing faster. By the time I pulled into my garage, I was damn near feeling my heart up in my throat.

The door flew open, and she stood there, chestnut hair framed by the light of the house. Long strides brought me to the bottom step, putting us nearly at eye-level.

KRISTINE ALLEN

"I missed you," she coyly murmured. Beaker danced at her feet, whining in his excitement.

"Not as much as I missed you," I replied before I grabbed the back of her hair and pulled her in for a kiss. Her hands rested on my shoulders, and she leaned in, tongue diving in to toy with mine. It was like fuel to a tiny flame because my need flared to a fire of epic proportions as I wrapped my other arm around her and brought her chest to mine.

By the time we broke apart, we were breathless, and her lips were rosy and swollen. Hazel eyes shone with passion, and I scooped her up. A squeal left her as I moved with a purpose toward my bed.

Despite my voracious appetite for her, I slowly peeled away her layers, unwrapping her like the gift she was.

"Jordan," she breathed as I swiped my tongue through her wet slit. Head thrown back, breasts heaving, she whimpered. With her shining chestnut locks in disarray over the sheets, and fingers tangled in my hair, she was a goddess. Reverently, I worshipped at her altar and gave thanks over each inch of soft skin I revealed. I wanted her to know I valued her and everything she gave me by loving me back.

Once I'd covered every bit of her front, I flipped her to her stomach, careful of her slightly rounded belly. "Is that okay?" I asked, mindful of her comfort.

"Mmhmm," she replied, then hummed in satisfaction as I kissed her spine between her shoulder blades. Goose bumps broke out, and I smiled, knowing the effect I had on her.

"You are beautiful," I whispered against her silken flesh. Using my hands, I sensually touched the satin soft planes of her back, shoulders, arms, legs, then moved up the insides of her legs, teasing over her swollen, wet pussy. She raised her ass, seeking more, but I denied her.

She huffed and whined, wanting me to touch her there. Instead,

I kissed each ass cheek, then bit each one eliciting a needy groan. Writhing, she again attempted to get me to go where she wanted. I slid my body up her back and whispered in her ear as the surface of my front melded with her backside.

"You need me to taste that pussy?"

"Yes!" she enthusiastically returned. A wicked grin hooked the corners of my mouth.

Seductively, I slid down until I could kiss the light-red mark I'd left when I'd bit her. Then I raised her ass until her glistening pink slit was revealed and on display. Despite my need to keep the upper hand as I teased her, I groaned. Then I dropped my head and licked up from her clit to the tight pucker of her ass.

"Oh, sweet Jesus," she hissed, and I smirked in satisfaction.

Gently, I slipped my middle finger in to her tight, wet sheath. The heat of her surrounding me nearly made my eyes cross, but I persevered. Another finger joined the first, and she clenched around me, breathing faster and pressing back into me.

Torturously slow, I pushed them in and drew them out. The sound it made drove me crazy and told me how ready she was. "Fuck, you're so damn wet."

"You're killing me," she panted, and I darkly chuckled in response.

"Lies," I taunted before I removed my fingers and licked them clean. "Delicious," I whispered.

"Jordan," she pleaded, but I showed no mercy. I dove in and shoved my tongue into her heaven. She was a buffet, and I was a man who hadn't eaten well in a lifetime. It was messy and loud, but I didn't care. Her nails scratched at the covers, bunching them up as she buried her face in the pillow and screamed into it. The pulsing of her core around my tongue was accompanied by a flood of her release.

Not wasting a drop, I licked and sucked her clean, then wiped my face on my shoulder before rising to my knees to straddle her legs. I dropped to one arm, trailing feather-soft kisses along her sides and back as I swirled my thumb in her still-contracting sheath.

"I want to try something, but you tell me if you don't like it, okay?" I instructed, heart pounding fast and bold.

She spun her head to the side to look at me, and her hair covered her face. She shoved it out of the way and stared at me with a deep groove between her eyes. "Something like what?" she warily questioned.

"You'll see," I evasively replied. Then I got back to my knees. With her chest still on the bed, curves for days, long legs together and between my own, her pussy in the air like an offering, she was stunning. "God, I fucking love this body."

First, I leisurely fucked her with my thumb. She was whimpering and making sexy little noises by the time I teased her with the head of my cock. Joke was on me though, because that tiny bit of sensation damn near had me blowing my load.

"Deeper," she demanded, and I grinned.

"I want you begging for it," I taunted.

"Please!" she shouted without pause.

Done with the games, I gave her a few shallow strokes before I buried my cock in her tight pussy. I hissed through my teeth at how good it was.

"God yes, like that," she mumbled into the pillow.

To her disappointment, I kept a lazy pace. She was desperate by the time I rewet my thumb and trailed it up to circle the puckered hole. She froze, stiffening at the sensation.

"Yes or no?" I questioned. Testing her, I pressed in slightly—not deep.

For a few heartbeats, she was quiet. I was prepared for her to say no, so I was a bit surprised when she pushed back on my thumb. My dick throbbed, and I sucked in a sharp breath.

"Do it," she prompted, and I pushed harder. I wasn't in far, but it was the thought. My fingers spanned one ass cheek as I watched my thumb move in and out in time with my strokes.

"Holy shit," she whispered with awe in her tone.

About to lose it, I needed to give her a push. I leaned forward and pinched her clit, causing her to shout. Then I alternated between circling it and pinching it as I thrust harder and faster. It was uncoordinated at best, wild at worst, but goddamn did she feel good.

By that time, she was panting, and her little satisfied mewls were muffled in the bed. Sweat trickled down my spine, my heart raced overtime, and my fingers worked her swollen nub furiously. "Come," I demanded.

"I'm close," she gasped. "Oh God, I'm so close."

The first telltale flutters began, and I knew I needed to see her face when she shattered. Jerking out, I breathlessly chuckled when she whined and whimpered.

"Turn over," I told her. She quickly did as I said.

The slight curve of her stomach caught my attention, and she covered it with her hands. My eyes snapped to hers as I frowned.

"Don't," I growled.

"It's not exactly sexy," she whispered as she avoided meeting my gaze.

"The hell it's not. I can't wait to see you heavily pregnant with my child. Call me a caveman, but there's nothing sexier than the mother of my child rounded with a baby I put there." I meant every word.

She chewed on her lip indecisively. Finally, she gave me a tentative smile and let her legs fall open in invitation.

Fuck.

It was so fucking hot.

I grabbed a pillow and shoved it under her ass to help lift her, then lined back up and fed my cock into her slick, hot pussy. Thankful for the brief reprieve, I held off my orgasm for a bit, but damned if her walls tightening around me didn't make my eyes roll.

"What are you waiting for?" she asked in a sultry whisper.

"Just savoring," I explained as I slowly stroked in and dragged out before doing it all over again. My thumb went back to rubbing her clit as I picked up the pace.

"Yes," she encouraged as she cupped her full tits and pinched her nipples.

"Ohmyfuckinggod," I muttered as I watched her mesmerized but never relenting in my pursuit of her orgasm. When she licked her finger and reached down to push my hand out of the way, I almost lost my fucking mind.

Taking advantage of the use of my hands, I unceremoniously threw her legs over my shoulders and fucked her with a desperation I'd never experienced in my life. I planned to make her come, then get mine, but I was beginning to realize that wasn't going to happen.

"I'm going to come. Fuck, baby, I'm gonna come. Fuck, fuck, fuck," I chanted as the familiar sensation zipped down my spine and settled in my balls. It wasn't going to be long.

"Yes, yes, yes," she moaned in time with my rapid thrusts.

When she stiffened, her mouth falling open in a silent scream, and held her breath, I went insane. It was sweaty, primal—man and woman at their most carnal.

She squeezed me so tight I grunted, then the pulses of her release began, and I couldn't stop myself. "Fuuuuck. Oh fuck. Yes. Milk my cock with that perfect, tight little cunt. Jesus fucking Christ. Oh God," I rambled as I shot what had to be the mother lode into her magical pussy. It seemed to go on forever.

When she clenched me one last time, I gave a shudder of bliss and dropped to my hands so I didn't smash her. Sweat dripped from my brow, and I knew it landed on her chest, but I didn't give two shits as she pulled a final spurt from my poor depleted dick.

"Holy shit. What the hell did you do to me?" I asked between ragged breaths.

"Made you feel as good as you did me, I hope," she languidly murmured.

"Christ, did you. Hang on."

I cautiously rolled us over, trying to keep myself seated in her. We both huffed when it didn't happen. Then she collapsed against my side and nuzzled into my neck. After a massive sigh, she kissed the side of my throat.

"I love you," she sleepily whispered as she hooked one leg over mine and snuggled in closer.

My arms reflexively tightened around her. "I love you too," I sighed, utterly drained and satisfied.

As I floated in and out of sleep, I absently rubbed her back. This. This right here was what life was all about. Not hockey, though it was a close second. This feeling of completeness. The melding of two souls. This was what some people spent a lifetime in search of, and I'd been lucky enough to stumble upon it in a random little diner in central Texas.

Life was good—no—life was fantastic.

EPILOGUE

"**D**ADDY, LOOK! RIGHT BETWEEN THE PIPES!" MY OLDEST GIRL shouted after her sloppy but adorable slapshot sent the puck into the net at the practice arena.

"Great job, Tessa!" I shouted as Cora slapped her hands on my head. I held her legs as she sat on my shoulders, watching her five-year-old sister on the ice. "Sissy did good, huh?"

"Goot!" Cora cheered.

Tessa skated over, a little unsteady but determined. She stopped in front of us, sending a tiny spray of snow off her blades. That was one of her favorite things.

"I'm gonna be in the NHL like you, Daddy," she insisted, full of a child's exuberance.

I chuckled. There was plenty of time to tell her girls didn't play in the NHL. But who knew? Maybe by the time she was grown, they might. It was a crazy world. No promises on how well I'd hold myself back if some guy slammed her into the boards. I could feel my temper flaring at the thought.

"Mommy! Did you see? Huh, huh? Did you?" she hollered out, clutching the top of the short wall. I glanced over my shoulder to see my beautiful wife waddling down the stairs on her way back from the bathroom. Her sleek chestnut hair was braided and rested over her shoulder, and one hand rested on her large, rounded belly.

I had to tell my dick to behave, since this wasn't the time or place, but damn I hadn't been kidding all those years ago. The sight of my wife heavy with my child was the sexiest fucking thing I'd ever seen.

"You only got it in because I had something in my eye," Alex's oldest son, Gavin grumbled as he lumbered over in his goalie pads. He was older than Tessa, but they had become best friends. Blair and Sydney liked to tease us that they were going to be sweethearts one day. The first time they said that, Alex and I had frozen and blinked at them like they'd spurted out pure blasphemy. Now they liked to whisper it just to get under our skin.

It worked.

The rest of the kids headed our way, a couple wiping out. Off-season, we taught our kids and their friends to play. We shouldn't have been surprised that we raised hockey fanatics. After all, it was in their blood.

"Daddy! Watch me!" Tessa shouted as she prepared to race Kristoffer's twins. They were about Gavin's age, but they were dainty things despite their lack of fear. Adriana and Adeline were identical, just like Alex's girls. The only way I could tell them apart was that Adriana was a tomboy from the get-go. You wouldn't think so if you saw her off the ice, but she gave Gavin a run for his money as a backup goalie. Their son Aaron was Tessa's age but bigger than all three girls.

"Say when!" Adriana shouted to her dad.

"One… Two… Three… Go!" Kristoffer called out, and the three musketeers took off.

Blair stood on her tiptoes and kissed me, then I held Cora's hands and crouched a bit so she could lean over to kiss her mommy.

"Wuv you Mommy! Sissy goot!"

Blair laughed. "Yes, Sissy is good."

Cora giggled and bounced on my shoulders as the kids skated off and started goofing around. Their laughter echoed over the ice. Practice was done so now they were just having fun.

Blair wrapped an arm around my waist and smiled up at Cora.

"How are you feeling?" I asked her as I took in her huge belly and noted the pinched look on her face.

"Tired. Your son is a beast, and he's doing a number on his poor mommy."

I huffed a laugh. "*My* son, huh? You had absolutely nothing to do with it, right?"

"None. You got me drunk and took advantage of me," she grumbled. The little twitch at the corner of her mouth ruined the stern image she was going for.

I snorted.

"You laugh… I think he's going to come out wearing skates, pads, and carrying a hockey stick."

Alex burst out laughing as he held one of his twin girls. I honestly had no idea which one it was. He and Kristoffer both had twin girls, but Kristoffer's girls were closer in age to Gavin and Tessa. Now that practice was over, Cameron and Bleu were helping their son get his skates on. He must be about three now. It was hard to keep track of them all. I knew he was a little older than Cora.

"Ellie! Wait for me!" Sydney demanded as a giggling girl zipped past us. Guess that answered that question—Alex was holding Emma. Sydney was pregnant with their fourth child, but we didn't know what it was yet. That would be next week after practice.

"I feel you, Syd. That's why this one is up here." I motioned with my chin toward Cora up on my shoulders.

"Unfortunately, Alex can only handle one at a time," she replied in a harried tone before she scowled. "The next time Jericho gives them candy, I'm beating his ass. Better yet, his day is coming soon. Revenge will be so sweet. Pun intended."

Her scowl morphed to an evil grin, and I almost felt bad for Jericho.

We all watched Cam help his son onto the ice and slowly skate backward as he held Rowan's hand. He'd been so excited when Bleu got pregnant two years into their relationship. They hadn't been trying either. You never would've known it. He'd insisted on a gender reveal thing. Sydney and Bleu had seen something online so they thought it would be a great idea to make a puck that had the color stuff in it. They had Cameron out on the ice where he whacked it with his stick, and blue powdery shit blew out in a big puff.

Not gonna lie. It was pretty cool and started a tradition with each of us since. That was how Alex and Sydney would find out what this one was—same as how we knew Blair was having a boy this time.

Watching these kids learn to skate and play hockey brought back so many memories. Maybe none of them would make it to the NHL, but maybe they would. Who knew? I figured as long as they had fun, that was all that mattered. Because to this day, I still enjoyed playing. I hoped I had many more years left in me—it would be a sad day when I finally had to throw in the towel.

"Who would've thought you guys would all still be together and chasing kids around?" Zoey asked as she patted their youngest daughter's back. Ember was sound asleep on her mom's shoulder. Kristoffer skated up and came to a stop at the boards.

"Hey, sexy. You should give me your number," Kristoffer teased Zoey.

She cocked a brow and feigned disdain. "Puh-lease… I'm a married woman, and my husband is a professional hockey player."

Kristoffer leaned his forearms on the boards and grinned. "Oh yeah? I bet I could take him."

"Hmph!" she scoffed. "I doubt it. He's the team captain, and he's a badass."

"I'd fight him for you," he continued, suppressing his laughter.

"Would you now? Well, sir, I'm sorry to say, I'm happy with him. Even if he got a bit of a dad belly in the off-season." She smirked, and we laughed at Kristoffer's open-mouthed disbelief.

"I most certainly did not." He clearly enunciated as he stood upright and crossed his arms.

Zoey giggled and stepped closer to our side of the boards. "Teasing," she whispered before she held Ember's back so she could lean forward to give him a kiss.

"I was gonna say!" Kristoffer huffed. Zoey planned to give him a peck, but he shot his hand out, cupped the back of her head, and pulled her back in for a kiss that had everyone whistling catcalls and cheering.

"Get a room!" Dmitry shouted from the other side of the ice.

Kristoffer broke the kiss with a chuckle as he licked his bottom lip. Zoey stood there openmouthed and starstruck with a pink tinge to her cheeks.

"We can drop Tessa off if you want to go home to rest," Bleu said to Blair. "You look exhausted. Not much longer, Momma."

"That sounds like a good idea. Maybe we can put the little one down for a nap, and I can give her mommy a massage," I murmured quietly to Blair. It had the desired effect because she blushed and smiled.

"Don't wanna nap!" Cora yelled, obviously figuring out we were talking about her.

Alex snickered behind me, and I let go of one of Cora's legs to flip him off.

We said our goodbyes, buckled Cora into the backseat of Blair's SUV, and went home to the neighborhood damn near all my teammates lived in. Despite Cora's adamant insistence that she wasn't tired, she was sleeping by the time we got home.

I spent the next hour massaging my wife. With my hands, lips, tongue, and cock. Of course, I did all the work. When we were both well satisfied, I pulled her back up against my front. She used my bicep as a pillow, and I wrapped my left arm around her with my hand splayed possessively over her rather large belly. It was my favorite thing.

"I love you," I softly breathed into her hair as she lightly snored in my arms. Holding might've been a hockey penalty, but I'd pay every fine in existence because I was holding onto her for the rest of our lives.

ACKNOWLEDGEMENTS

If you're actually reading this, damn, you really do like my writing. I thank YOU first and foremost! KISSES! Okay, now hang on, this is gonna be a little long.

Holding was dedicated to four people this time. And here's why. I am proud to say I have watched all four of these guys get their start in professional hockey. I actually have a picture with Jake Oettinger—ask me about it and I'll share it with you. Adam is such a cool guy and a great goaltender. He didn't even call security when we waited forever to see him after a game to have him sign our posters. Hahahaha! And the two Matt's (that actually cracks me up because it's pretty cool) were dropped into a season that put a lot of pressure on them and instead of caving to that, they came out swinging.

Thank you to all the hockey players in the Stars franchise, both NHL and AHL, for feeding my hockey obsession. I'm proud to say I'm with you guys through thick and thin. No fair-weather fans slowed around here. Go Stars!

Thank you to my readers who keep giving me a reason to write and hit "publish." Your constant support and encouragement is awesome and there are no words to express my gratitude.

Most of this will be the same as always because all of you are always in my corner and I love you to pieces. So bear with me… or bare with me, but don't get arrested. Public indecency is a thing I hear.

Again, I want to thank **Brenda Keller** and **Michele Brooks** for inviting me to the first Texas Stars games and getting me absolutely addicted. Originally coming from up north, I've always enjoyed hockey, but I never really took the time to understand it. Now I'm a fan for life. You've created a monster! Bwahahahaha!

Thank you to **Pam, Kristin, Brenda, Lisa** for being my betas and letting me bounce ideas off you at all hours of the night. You're my squad. I couldn't do this without you.

Kristine's Street Team! Here's your shout out! Y'all mother-freaking rock! Especially my top promoters **Pam and Chasity**. You ladies continually go above and beyond for me and my books. Never in a million years could I thank you enough. Hugs and kisses! Also send out the best of vibes to Chasity as she's going through a rough spot and she can use all the good juju.

Kat, thank you for stepping in last minute when my life imploded and I fell behind. I have a confession… for a few days I really hated all that yellow (you know what I mean). I moaned and grumbled, and cursed. But then, I appreciated you. So dang much. Because you showed me something I could do better and I love you for that! Thanks again!

Penny. Where do I start? My beautiful forever friend. Thank you for always believing in me, even when I didn't believe in myself. <3 Every time I tell you how good things are going and you tell me you're not surprised, I want to cry. Your faith in me is eternally humbling. The light is there at the end of the tunnel. You WILL be tacking that RN onto the back of your name before you know it!

Lisa and **Brenda**, y'all are the best and I cannot thank you enough for your support, advice, and friendship. And wine. To think it all started with a lunch born from the love of books. Life has gotten crazy and our girls' nights have been fewer, but we're still rocking this friendship shit! Always with wine.

Avery Kingston, you are a design goddess! Thank you for

taking on this project and bringing my visions to life. I'm so glad we met that day in Dallas. Everything happens for a reason and I pray we remain friends forever! Chef's kiss to you, babe!

Eric McKinney, thank you so much for this fantastic image! But I'm gonna need you to stop tempting me with all those images you post. You're a terrible influence and enabler. LMAO. **Philip,** I love the image and I have received so many compliments on your cover. **Avery's** artwork brought everything together and we made magic! Thank you for blessing me with your beautiful image for my cover! The minute I saw Eric post this one, I knew you'd be perfect for my goalie. ☺

Stacey of **Champagne Book Designs**, never, ever, ever forget—you are a goddess. Every single time, you make my pages sparkle. Okay, maybe not literally, but you get me like so many others don't. LOL. Thank you for making the guts of yet another book baby shine! Hard to believe we've been doing this for 5 years this month! 27 books, if we include the DSMC Boxset and I counted correctly! We rock!

Ladies of **Kristine's Krazy Fangirls**, every one of you are the bomb-diggity. Every single one of you are my personal little cheerleading team and I love you all! I thank you for your comments, your support, and your love of books. Come join us if you're not part of the group www.facebook.com/groups/kristineskrazyfangirls

The military has had such a huge impact on my life, and even in a hockey book, I found a little way to weave them in. From having multiple family members who served, to being a military brat, to a military spouse, and then working as a nurse in the military system, it's in my blood. With that being said, my last-but-never-least is a massive thank you to America's servicemen and women who protect our freedom on a daily basis. They do their duty, leaving their families for weeks, months, and years at a time, without asking for praise or thanks. I would also like to remind the readers that not all combat injuries are visible, nor do they heal easily. These silent, wicked injuries wreak havoc on their minds and hearts while we go about our days completely oblivious. Thank you all for your service.

OTHER BOOKS

Demented Sons MC Series - Iowa

Colton's Salvation

Mason's Resolution

Erik's Absolution

Kayde's Temptation

Snow's Addiction (An expanded version of a short story in the Twisted Steel Anthology II)

Straight Wicked Series

Make Music With Me

Snare My Heart

No Treble Allowed

String Me Up

Demented Sons MC Series - Texas

Lock and Load

Styx and Stones

Smoke and Mirrors

Jax and Jokers

Got Your Six (Originally a part of The Remembering Ryan Anthology)

RBMC - Ankeny Iowa

Voodoo

Angel

A Very Venom Christmas

Chains

Haunting Ghost

Charming Phoenix

The Iced Series
Hooking
Tripping
Roughing
Holding
Fighting Love (Coming Soon!)

Heels, Rhymes, & Nursery Crimes
Roses Are Red
Violets Are Blue (Coming Soon!)

Pinched and Cuffed Anthology
The Weight of Honor
The Weight of Blood (by M. Merin—the sister book)

ABOUT THE AUTHOR

Kristine Allen lives in beautiful Central Texas with her adoring husband. They have four brilliant, wacky, and wonderful children. She is surrounded by twenty-six acres, where her five horses, five dogs, and six cats run the place. She's a hockey addict and feeds that addiction with season tickets to the Texas Stars. Kristine realized her dream of becoming a contemporary romance author after years of reading books like they were going out of style and having her own stories running rampant through her head. She works as a night shift nurse, but in stolen moments, taps out ideas and storylines until they culminate in characters and plots that pull her readers in and keep them entranced for hours.

Reviews are the life blood of an indy author. If you enjoyed this story, please consider leaving a review on the sales channel of your choice, bookbub.com, goodreads.com, allauthor.com, or your review platform of choice, to share your experience with other interested readers. Thank you! <3

Follow Kristine on:

Facebook www.facebook.com/kristineallenauthor

Instagram www.instagram.com/_jessica_is_kristine.allen_

Twitter @KAllenAuthor

TikTok: vm.tiktok.com/ZMebdkNpS

All Author www.kristineallen.allauthor.com

BookBub www.bookbub.com/authors/kristine-allen

Goodreads www.goodreads.com/kristineallenauthor

Webpage www.kristineallenauthor.com

Made in United States
North Haven, CT
15 May 2023

36619162R00152